Books by Liz Crowe

Brewing Passion

Tapped
Lightstruck
Conditioned

Conditioned

ISBN # 978-1-78686-187-0

©Copyright Liz Crowe 2017

Cover Art by Posh Gosh ©Copyright 2017

Interior text design by Claire Siemaszkiewicz

Totally Bound Publishing

Brewing Passion

CONDITIONED

LIZ CROWE

Dedication

For Drue Hoffman

Chapter One

Trent stumbled out into the cold winter night air, tugging at his bow tie and shedding his tux jacket at the same time. The scene inside had been a familiar one. One he'd mastered long ago, and claimed to enjoy — to love, even.

But tonight, it had been wrong. All kinds of wrong.

He propped his hands on his knees and sucked in the night air, barely registering how cold it was, only wanting to get away from it — from himself most likely. From the fetish that had driven him for so many years. Driven him to many things — to his first wife, who'd been posing and was now nothing but an expensive thorn in his side, but who'd given him his beloved daughter. To his success in business as he'd been so single-mindedly focused thanks to the release he allowed himself in sex play.

And now to his current sorry, single state as he breached the seminal fortieth birthday, headed straight for forty-one.

It had been a regular night at the exclusive secret club. Nothing new or different had happened. He'd been greeted at the door of the mansion in the suburbs by the usual phalanx of beautiful women dressed in bras, garter belts, stockings, heels and satin masks. He'd had the usual pleasant experience, greeting his fellow Master Dominants in the gathering room over lemon and cucumber-infused water. No alcohol was allowed in the real BDSM clubs and if the guard at the gate smelled it on you, you'd be turned away, regardless of the fact that you'd already paid upwards of ten grand for the pleasure of the evening. There were no refunds.

But something had been off. He'd sensed it — the slightly

sideways sensation he'd had within seconds of walking into the large front room. He'd sensed it in the rarified air. He'd felt it on his neck, the backs of his hands, his face.

As the Doms—five men and two women all dressed to the nines as if they were attending a D.C. charity ball and not about to engage in the sort of kinky sex that some found horrifying—all sat, waiting for the next stage, Trent's leg bounced as if he'd consumed a pot of coffee before showing up. One of the women glanced at it, then up at his face, her elegantly crafted eyebrow raised.

He shot his cuffs, wondering why he wasn't enjoying himself. By this stage, he was usually hard as a rock, eager for a fresh submissive in a mask. He wasn't into hardcore shit, but he knew what he liked and he could usually pick his partner within seconds of seeing her walk into the large room.

Tonight, however, his dick stayed limp and his mind spun. Sweat popped out on his face. *Weird,* he decided, as he sipped some water and wished he had a shot of bourbon. Granted, he had just experienced one of his more stressful weeks. He'd been in a protracted fight with the city of Kalamazoo over his desire to buy and revamp a city block. One of his best bartenders at his most successful pubs had up and quit for no reason, until he'd discovered that the reason had a lot to do with a missing eight-thousand-dollar bank deposit. Plus, he woke with his guts tied in knots every single morning at the thought of facing his biggest challenge—raising his teenaged daughter, alone, with her mother hovering in the background reminding him of her entitlement to his bank account.

Trent sighed and swiped his fingers across his lips, willing himself calm. Reminding himself that this would help. He would coax, and tease, and spank and bite. He'd make the girl come so hard she'd beg him for more. Then, when he came, he would feel better, reset, able to resume his life and start the week off fresh.

But when the women and men were led in, he couldn't

even look at them. If he didn't know better, he'd swear that he had the flu or something equally dire. His palms were sweaty. He could feel damp at the small of his back under the expensive tux shirt and jacket. His leg jittered again. A rush of bile filled his throat at the sight of the women, all dressed in flowing, diaphanous gowns, all staring at the floor, all with heavy leather collars around their necks.

He jumped to his feet, drawing not-so-subtle stares from his fellows. The master of ceremonies, the owner of this particular club that he'd frequented for years, asked a million questions with a single raised eyebrow. Blinking fast, Trent backed away from the subs, who were also peering through their masks, expectant and needy and pulling at him in ways he didn't like.

Throat closing up, he turned and fumbled for the doorknob as sweat dropped into his eyes, blinding him and providing him with the sort of just-out-of-control sensation that he'd banished long ago. The sensations that had driven him as a boy, then a teen, to escape his life and establish complete control over it.

He stumbled through the foyer, past the hostesses who remained silent as he threw himself out into the night, gasping and tugging at his tie.

"Mr. Hettinger," a voice called behind him. "Are you all right?"

He held up a hand, keeping his back to whoever was talking. "I'll be fine," he choked out. "Under the weather. Sorry."

"I'll have them bring your car around," the voice said, as if it were a completely normal occurrence for him to leave his ten-thousand-dollar fee behind, forgoing the many pleasures that were to be provided to him in exchange.

He stood, knees shaking, head pounding as his classic Jeep appeared under the portico. When he climbed behind the wheel, his mind cleared and his heart stopped racing as if turned off by a switch. He took a deep breath, cranked the satellite radio to blasting—his favorite, Nine Inch Nails—

rolled down all the windows and screeched out onto the private road. He floored the gas when he hit I-96, pointed west toward his home in Grand Rapids, smiling when the powerful, rebuilt engine eased the speedometer past eighty-five, then ninety miles an hour in seconds.

The emptiness in his brain allowed him to relax, which in turn led to a distinct rumbling in his stomach. He flipped the turn signal and raced up an exit ramp, heading for his favorite all-night diner.

Kinky, rowdy sex, sometimes performed in front of an audience of like-minded fetishists—or a plate piled high with crisp bacon, a big stack of pancakes and pure maple syrup. He shook his head at his out-of-character choice between the two as he parked, got out, blipped the lock and headed for the brightly lit restaurant. Sometimes a man's needs were simple and he was not one to ignore that fact.

As he shouldered into the warm, coffee and bacon grease-infused space, a sense of peace descended over him, making it clear that he'd made the right choice, at least for tonight. He'd muscled through a D/s session at a club once before when he'd felt rotten. And it had been awful. He'd hurt the girl more than he'd meant to and had sworn off the lifestyle for months afterward. He knew himself well by now and self-congratulated tonight's decision all the way to the diner's long bar.

He leaned forward, eager for coffee and innocuous conversation, untying his bow tie all the way so it dangled from the collar of his once crisp, now slightly wilted white shirt. When he turned the small, cheap, ceramic mug over, indicating his desire for the caffeinated elixir of life and STAT, he felt a cooling breeze against the back of his neck. It was as if someone had opened the door and was holding it that way to allow the steamy heat of the restaurant to dissipate.

He turned, feeling friendly and chatty, to see what was up.

Then he saw her.

Or, rather, the back of her.

She was pouring coffee for one table, laughing and smacking one of the trucker-looking patrons on the shoulder in a friendly, flirty way. Trent's eyes narrowed as he studied her rear view. She was tall and her hips flared out from a small waist in a way that made his palms sweaty again. Her voice was loud enough to be heard over the din of conversation. It was tinged with the sexiest soft accent he'd ever heard.

"Go on, now, you know your wife wouldn't want you flirting with little old me," she was saying to the leering dude. She moved down the booths, dropping checks, picking up empty plates, pouring more coffee. Using that melodious voice that mesmerized him almost as much as the near-perfect roundness of her ass, currently featured in a pair of tight, cheap-looking black pants.

Trent's heartbeat thudded in his ears as he kept staring at her — the Goddess, he now thought of her for some reason. The Latina Goddess who kept laughing and chatting and swinging her hips at the patrons in a way that made fury pepper the edges of his vision.

His.

His Latina Goddess.

She looked over her shoulder at him, as if sensing his inappropriate thoughts about her. Her olive-toned skin was flushed from the heat of the room. Her chocolate-dark eyes met his and narrowed suspiciously. So much so Trent wondered if he'd spoken those words out loud. Then she turned and faced him fully.

Even with a pot of cheap coffee in one hand and two dirty plates in the other, she was the most magnificent creature he had ever laid eyes on. And he'd laid eyes on some serious magnificence. Her breasts were... Trent gulped as he realized he was staring at them...but fuck him sideways, they were huge and high and straining at the buttons of her shirt. His dick surged forward so hard and fast he grunted and turned back to face the counter, his face hot, wincing with the pain of the zipper biting into his flesh.

He slumped over the paper placemat with the map of Michigan on it, staring down, unseeing, unhearing, miserable and yet revived at the same time.

A diner waitress, Hettinger? Seriously? After you paid five figures for the direct attention of the women you left behind?

"Hello," her voice said, filling his head in a way that made him dizzy. "What can I get for you?"

He looked up, directly into her huge, brown eyes, opened his mouth and was completely unable to form coherent words. She tilted her head to one side, which made a lock of her jet-black hair drop from the severe tie-back. "Do I know you from somewhere? I feel like I should..."

He opened and closed his stupid mouth like a fish. "Coffee, please," he managed after a long while. She poured it, then glanced back at him, one glorious hip cocked to one side. He fixed his gaze on the name sewn into the pink shirt that gaped just enough for him to see her cleavage. His dick got harder, if that were possible. He offered her a weak smile.

"Hi, Melody," he said, holding out a hand. "I'm Trent. I don't think we know each other...yet."

Her smile faltered as she took a step back from him, ignoring his outstretched palm. Her face, so prettily flushed already, got even darker and her eyes seemed to flash with the sort of recognition he'd seen before, and understood well.

But no. This is a damn diner on the side of the road in west Michigan, not some overpriced BDSM club. Get a grip on yourself, man.

He swallowed hard, held her gaze in a practiced way, and said, "I'll have a full stack, please, with a side of bacon."

She blinked fast as if unable to process his words, then whirled around and ran through the door to what he presumed was the kitchen.

Dear Lord in heaven, had he been meant to arrive here, at this moment, at this place, to find her?

He sipped his coffee and watched for her to return, hoping

very much that he had been.

Chapter Two

The dream was the same as always.

Shifting shadows. Stale beer mixed with the coconut undertone of sunscreen. Giggles and shuffling and weird voices slowed from normal. That odd split second when I parted ways with my brain and began to simply observe what was being done to me in the name of "partying with the guys".

Guys I had the serious misfortune to call friends, to trust, to think were not base, disgusting animals.

Guys who'd invited me and a few other girls out for an afternoon of water skiing on the lake. Nothing that much out of the ordinary. I'd gone with them before, enjoying the attention, flirting, preening, wearing a skimpy bikini—all the things a girl does when she feels safe amongst a group of friends.

Big mistake, as it turned out.

I yanked myself up and out of the nightmare by the sheer force of my conscious brain. I'd gotten pretty darn good at this little trick over the years. But the smells, sounds and pain—most especially the pain—lingered for an hour or more, driving me to the couch and Netflix at two a.m. for the third night in a row.

Not great for my workday frame of mind. But I'd gotten used to coping and had my methods—four cups of strong coffee, a decent, but not too heavy, breakfast and a super-hot shower. That would get me all the way to about three p.m. when I'd pound a couple of cups of tea in the breakroom, then bend over so my head dangled between my feet. The blood would rush to my sleepy brain and I'd be good to go for the rest of the afternoon.

Luckily, this afternoon was one of the very few I could enjoy with an eye toward going home and not to my second of three jobs — as bartender at a trendy beer bar downtown. Between office grunt work at the beer distributor, tips at the bar during the week, plus the diner on a few weekends a month as a fill-in for the regulars, I may not be considered a fun party-girl but for the first time in my life I had money. And a fair bit of it. All tucked away safely in an interest-bearing savings account.

As I stood, waiting for the afternoon rush of caffeine to take effect, I lifted one foot and rotated my ankle, then put it down and did the same with the other. Thanks to being on my feet almost every single night slinging either overpriced booze or coffee-flavored water, my hips, legs and feet were in a constant state of achiness.

I was a barrel of fun, really. Not that it mattered. I was exhausted, and a date with my pillow, the TV and a pint of ice cream beckoned. Besides, unless they were asking me for more coffee or for the latest sales data for their weekly reports, men were of little use to me.

No. Scratch that.

I was of no use to any man. And I planned to keep it that way.

Head down and work. Make money and put into my savings. Eat enough food to keep the machine going. Take advantage of the opportunity to drink great beer at one of my jobs. Avoid flirting at all costs. Sleep. Rise. Do it again. I was an automaton, according to my friend, Evelyn. But what did she know?

You should open up and tell her why you're such a wet blanket sometime.

Stuff it, I reminded myself. It's nobody's business but mine.

"Hey," a familiar voice punched through my three-p.m. sinking spell. I blinked, forcing myself to smile. "Let's go out tonight, *chica.*"

Evelyn, my work friend — my only friend — flopped onto the fake leather couch in the break room next to me. I glanced at her. She had her long blonde hair up in a messy bun. The sleeves of her work blouse were rolled up to her elbows. Her long, bare legs ended in a pair of sky-high patent leather heels — her "selling shoes" as she liked to call them.

"No thanks," I said. My typical response and she knew it.

She leaned forward and grabbed my hand, startling me a little. "I'm serious, Melody."

"So am I," I said, letting her grip my hand a bit longer before I pulled away from her. Being touched made me nervous, even when it was just a friendly hand-holding thing by a colleague.

"No more excuses," she said, rising to her full, impressive height and towering over me as I sat curled up on the couch with my second cup of hot tea. Her eyes sparkled with something I thought might be mischief. I immediately felt defensive. "It'll be fun. We'll go to Top of the Hops and you can give me a tasting lesson."

I sighed and sipped, forcing myself to be calm. *It's okay. It's Evelyn. She's your friend, remember?*

"Okay, I mean, maybe." I winced when she pumped her fist and held up a hand for me to high-five. Glancing around, worried we were making a total scene, I touched my palm to hers.

"Super! I can drive if you want. I could pick up you up — "

"No, no, I'll meet you there. Seven okay? It's Tuesday so it shouldn't be too crowded."

"Perfect." Evelyn finished the water bottle she'd been holding and tossed it into the garbage then tugged at her skirt and pulled her hair out of its bun. "I'll be all over the west side this afternoon so I may go early and eat something before you get there."

"Try the Portobello burger," I said. "It's really good. They use locally sourced goat cheese."

"Will do." She smiled at me, flapped her fingers at the

other people in the room — all of them men except us — and flounced out, pretending to be unaware of the way they stared at her ass and hips in her short work skirt. When a couple of them let their gaze wander back to me, I shivered and looked down into the remains of my tea, willing them to leave me alone, wishing I were normal, cursing the assholes who'd ruined me for the millionth, zillionth time.

Chapter Three

Most mornings, Trent didn't know which was worse — getting his daughter out of bed for school on time or letting her sleep. Either way it was a pitched battle and one he dreaded like the bubonic plague.

Your choice, pal, he reminded himself firmly — again — as he eased open her bedroom door and slipped inside. She was buried under a mound of duvet and pillows, just a shock of her deep red hair showing. Trent sighed and watched her breathe for a few minutes, relishing the quiet and the time he was allowed to spend loving her so much his chest ached.

It *had* been his choice, being a single dad. And most days he didn't regret it. But as she eased into adolescence he was beginning to worry for his sanity.

He sat on the edge of her bed after making his way through the detritus of dirty clothes, laptop, computer tablet and whatever else lay on the floor. Giving himself an extra few seconds to gaze at the half of her face now exposed since she'd flung the covers off, he could practically feel her perfect infant-self, cuddled into his chest or neck — the only way she would sleep for the first six weeks of her life. Smiling, head locked in on the memory sensations of her in his arms, helpless, his to protect and hold forever, he put a hand on her shoulder.

"Shit," she spat out as she sat up, rubbing her eyes. "Jesus, Dad. You scared me."

Trent sighed and stood, trying not to lurch into pissed off mode at her cursing. It was too early for anger and God knows she'd learned it all from him after all. Why be a hypocrite as long as she knew when not to use such language?

His daughter groaned and flopped onto her back, yanking the covers up over her head. "Five more minutes? Please? Daddy?"

"No, sorry, princess. I gave you an extra ten. Time to make the donuts. Up and at 'em."

"Fuck off," she muttered from underneath the denim-covered duvet.

Trent pulled it back and glared down at her. She matched it, using her mother's beautiful eyes to send him spiraling backward into the sort of memories that were the opposite of sweet. He ground his teeth together, reminding himself that the girl was not her mother. She was her own self—a heady mix of two personalities that had no real business procreating.

"Nope," he said, keeping his voice as neutral as he could manage. "Up. Now." As he headed to her bedroom door and escape, she lobbed her latest volley.

"I hate that school. It's stupid. You should send me to boarding school back east, so I can be challenged…like Mom told you."

Trent rested a hand on the doorjamb and counted to ten before answering. "Taylor, stop baiting me. Get up. Get in the shower. Get dressed. Your breakfast will be ready for you."

"Whatever," came the mumble from behind him.

Deciding that deflection made up the better part of valor this day, Trent walked out into the hall, down the steps and into the kitchen, leaving her to her anger for a while longer.

By the time Taylor finally emerged he was fastening on his watch and had cleared the tall granite eating counter of all dishes. She glared at him from under her bangs. "Great. Starving me now?"

"Yep. That's me. Dad the torturer king. Here." He tossed her a granola bar. She caught it and shoved it into her backpack along with the lunch he'd already packed for her.

"Get your ass in here on time and you get a hot breakfast. You've known this rule for how long?"

She scowled at him, setting him back for a split second at her increasingly eerie resemblance to her gorgeous bitch of a mother. He smiled at her, determined not to touch a match to the simmering pile of potential confrontation. He had a long day ahead and needed to focus.

"Ready?" he asked, sliding open the metal door of the loft to the hall.

She shouldered her pack and stomped toward the elevator. Trent bit his tongue hard against the urge to mention the ripped tights and the short skirt. She knew the dress code — had violated it enough times to be on semi-permanent probation over it. The row of shiny earrings in the delicate cartilage of each of her ears caught his gaze but he bit down harder. He'd lost that battle in a massive compromise — she could pierce whatever she wanted as long as it wasn't her nipples or genitals and he'd not protest, as long as her fair, perfect skin remained ink-free.

So far, so good on that.

So far as he knew, of course.

Shoving down the creeping anxiety that threatened to overwhelm him, he hit the button and the elevator doors slid open. Taylor flounced into the lift, her eyes on her phone. There were times when he wanted to turn back the clock and be the dad chasing the toddler around, getting up every four hours with the newborn, playing his eighth consecutive game of CandyLand — anything but this. It was as if she'd turned sixteen and a switch was flipped whereby he was relegated to the realm of the barely tolerable. And this from the little girl who'd been his shadow, going with him to construction sites, the office, the hardware store — barely able to let him out of her sight.

When she flopped into the passenger's seat of the Jeep, Trent knew she was itching for a fight. But he didn't have the energy for it this morning. He let her sulk on the drive to her high school, blew her a kiss as she got out and forced himself to smile when she flipped him off before flouncing down the sidewalk to the delight of way too many punk-asshole boys.

As he waited impatiently for the traffic to move around the circle and back out to the main road, he indulged in his usual form of self-torture — recalling his precious little girl once she'd grown out of her super-colicky baby stage and had latched on to him as if her life depended on it. She'd been a hardcore daddy's girl from the get-go. And he'd adored being her hero, father, champion, everything she needed in the entire universe. He'd never felt more alive than he had then.

But no need to let thoughts of his pretty, precocious, more than a little spoiled, auburn-haired waif of a daughter — replete in her pink tutus and princess crowns and clutching as many tiny stuffed animals as she could carry — spill over into memories of how much he hadn't wanted to have her in the first place. Not if it had meant tying himself to her mother, Sheila, the ex-Mrs. Hettinger.

But he had. Because he was the sort of guy who always did the right thing.

The light beep of a horn behind him dragged him back to the present, and to the day ahead. He waved by way of apology and sped out into the street, joining the line of traffic heading away from the school.

* * * *

"Yo, Brad, you here? How's it hanging?"

"Low and heavy, or so the wife tells me," he called back. "You ready for this wild-ass day, pard?"

"That's a double hell to the yeah."

Trent smiled at the tall, bearded man who was stacking boxes of liquor bottles in the tiny cramped office space behind his original store. When he'd decided to make the leap from mere employee to owning retail, he'd only hesitated for a second. Thanks to the success of this, his first big liquor store, he'd been keeping an eye on a few of the better locations for a while and had also latched on to the looming craft beer boom in the nineties. When the opportunity had come to buy out the old guy retiring and heading south who'd owned The Wine Cellar for the last thirty years, he'd jumped.

That had been almost fifteen years ago now, he mused, flipping open his laptop and pondering the myriad fires to be extinguished in his mini-empire today. Running a hand across the smoothness of his scalp, he allowed the love of his job — of controlling his own destiny on a day-to-day basis — to muffle the vague sense of worry and frustration over Taylor.

When the email he'd been dreading hit his inbox, he sighed, opened it and started plotting how he might salvage his purchase of an abandoned city block in Kalamazoo. He had hoped to open a coffee bar there — something new for him, but he had an expert coffee guy ready to jump in and run it, plus leads on at least three other high-profile potential tenants. The damn city wouldn't allow it for some reason, and he figured it probably had something to do with the fact of his own success. He was victim of it, in some sense. There were too many small-minded eggheads on the city council who simply didn't want him to expand.

Small-minded fuckers.

He leaned back in his creaky chair — a leftover from when the old guy still owned the place since Trent knew what to throw away and what to keep. With a glance at the large whiteboard he'd installed during his first week of ownership, he studied the last month's-worth of sales reports. He now owned two large, thriving liquor stores, one of which was among the first to feature craft beer on its shelves. Both stores were in Grand Rapids, anchoring it on east and west sides. He also was part owner of a successful farm-to-table restaurant, a somewhat dive-y beer and burger joint that he was angling to buy out in the next year, and had recently been approached by a restaurant ownership group about a new, exciting project downtown.

But now, he wanted this goddamned coffee bar and the mother fucking empty city block.

"You're too single-minded," Sheila's bitch-voice popped into his brain. *"You get focused on one thing and won't let go of it until it goes your way."*

"Yeah," he said to her, relegating her back to the dark recesses of his brain. "Which is probably why I've got a cool two million in the bank, bitch. And that's just my walkin' around money."

With a lunge forward, he started typing out his reply to the council's rejection of his city block project. Two hours later, satisfied that his response was both obsequious in deference to their collective egos, but at the same time firm in his resolve that the damn block should be his to revive, he rubbed his eyes and looked up from the screen. Someone was calling his name.

"Trent? Yo, dude, you need to take this call."

Hank, the bearded, long-time manager of his flagship store, was peering around the office door, holding the store's cordless phone in one hand. On reflex, he stuck his hand into his inner jacket pocket and pulled out his phone. Ten missed calls. All from Grand Rapids High.

Shit.

Fuck.

Hell.

He held out his hand. With a sympathetic look, Hank handed it over then shut the door behind him. Trent took a breath, then put the receiver to his ear.

"Hello. This is Taylor Hettinger's father," he said, laying his head down on the desk in front of him.

Chapter Four

When the text message hit my phone, I winced. I'd assumed—hoped, really—that Evelyn would forget about her invite out from earlier in the day. I was standing at my car, clutching the phone and trying to find an excuse, when the thing actually rang. I put it to my ear.

"Don't you dare flake out on me tonight, *chica*," Evelyn blurted out before I could even say hello.

"I…was… I mean…"

"I know you're trying to concoct a reason to go home. But I'm telling you, don't do it. Come out with me. Remember how much fun we had last month? At that goofy art show with the naked dudes and the cheap wine?"

"*Si*," I said with a sigh as I unlocked the car. "I remember."

"So, let's have another fun girls' night. Top of the Hops. I'm headed there now."

"I thought you'd already be there by now."

"Yeah, I got waylaid at a few places. But this way we can eat something together. See you there!" She hung up before I could answer.

Evelyn Benedict was a good friend and I didn't want to disappoint her. I knew she was between guys at the moment, and bored, and she was fun to hang out with.

So, go, chiquita. *Why wouldn't you?*

Because, I argued with myself even as I put on some fresh lip gloss and tugged the ponytail holder from my hair, letting it cascade past my shoulders. *Because I don't go out. It's just not what I do. Not anymore.*

I kept up the inner back-and-forth as I pulled out of the parking lot and into the late evening traffic. By the time I made it downtown, it was a solid thirty-five minutes later and I'd broken out in a light, panicky sweat. As I held on to the steering wheel in the tightest of all possible death-grips, I forced myself to take deep breaths and remember that this wasn't a party. It was just a bar. It was nothing new. My friend was inside waiting on me to eat, drink too many beers and have to ride-share home.

No biggie.

But as I put my hand on the car door handle, a wave of nausea hit me, bringing with it the smell of salt water and sunscreen, the sound of masculine laughter, the dry, excruciatingly painful rasp of sand rubbing against my bare skin. A tiny noise emerged from my throat—something between a whimper and a moan. I put my hand back on the steering wheel and stared through the front windshield.

A rap on the window near my ear made me yelp in surprise. I met Evelyn's bright eyes and big smile on the other side of the driver's side door. I opened the door and dragged out my purse, praying I wouldn't fall over onto the asphalt, wishing I had more strength to handle something as innocuous as walking into the front of a crowded bar as opposed to behind it.

"Hey, I thought that was you," Evelyn said, stepping back to give me room to emerge from my car. "Let's go. I'm famished."

As I pep-talked myself, I watched her head for the door, her long blonde hair swaying, her perfectly clad body drawing all sorts of attention. I gulped, shouldered my purse and followed her, head down, determined not to meet any strange man's gaze.

The front door made a funny tinkling sound when it opened, which reminded me that I had never entered the bar using this door. Even for my interview I'd been instructed to use the side door and now, of course, I came in the back entrance for my thrice-a-week shifts.

I knew damn good and well I pulled on a different persona when I entered this building. One that was confident, sexy, flirty and irascible. Using my semi-native Spanish willy-nilly, showing off, cussing people out in a language they didn't understand but that sounded as sexy as hell. I made killer tips when I bartended as a result but it was a persona, something I put on like a pair of expensive and very uncomfortable high heels. When I snuck out the back at two or sometimes three in the morning after sharing a beer and clean-up with the wait staff I'd step out of the sexy shoes and resume my clumpy, clog-like life.

Melody Rodriguez—the girl no one ever noticed, if they weren't taking advantage of her, that is.

That realization hit me between the eyes like a lightning bolt. I hesitated as the over-cooled indoor air rushed past me, catching up with the hot summer evening. The bar looked like a different place from this perspective. A chill ran down my spine. My throat closed up. Tears burned the backs of my eyes. The only sound as I stood in the middle of a semi-busy bar was that of my pounding heartbeat in my ears.

Evelyn turned and motioned for me. "I found a table," she hollered.

At that moment, my ears seemed to open up, allowing a rush of noise that knocked me for a loop. Raucous laughter, clinking glasses, blasting music—it all hit my eardrums with the force of a thunderclap.

Evelyn was already seated, talking with people at a nearby table and swiping the surface clean with a napkin. She was so easy-going—nothing ever fazed her. I was jealous of her on plenty of levels, but more grateful that she kept talking to me, kept trying to get me to go out with her. I jammed a smile on my face. But it must've looked more like a grimace since Evelyn did a double take when she glanced at me.

"Come on, sit," she demanded, patting the worn-down seat of the chair next to her. "I can't wait for you to give me a tasting lesson. What'll it be today?" She squinted up at the beer board. "I know—let's do sours."

"No," I said, hanging my purse on the back of the chair

and taking a seat. "The ones we're pouring now are garbage. Let's compare the IPAs. God knows there are enough of them."

She grinned and leaned closer to me. "I knew you'd get into the spirit."

I sighed, opened my mouth to reply but before I could, I met the gaze of the man from the diner.

I got that stupid, clichéd pinpoint narrowing sensation again—like I'd gotten the previous weekend when he'd been so...so...what? Hot as shit in his rumpled tux shirt, tie and trousers? *Mi Dios*, he had lips to die for and eyes that were somewhere between blue and green and utterly beautiful, that's what. His tan skin was only marred by a thin line of paleness at each temple—from sunglasses, I knew. He was bald but something about it made him even sexier. He owned it, the way very few men might.

I swallowed past the rising panic in my throat but could not stop staring at him. He was in a blue dress shirt today, with dark trousers. His eyes narrowed, then shifted slightly to my left.

"Oh shit, it's Trent," Evelyn whisper-shouted in my ear, breaking into the porn loop that starred the sexy bald man that had been running through my brain.

"Who?" I broke our stare and focused down on my tightly clenched hands. "I mean...what?"

The bar noise ramped up again, filling my head, deafening me, reminding me that I did not belong on this side of the bar.

"You know, the guy I've gone out with a few times. I told you." Evelyn bumped my shoulder.

"Oh, right," I said, not recalling anything she'd said about the man that I could sense burning a hole in me with his gaze.

Wow. I guess I did need to get out more. The clichés were coming hard and fast now.

I cleared my throat and stood so fast my chair fell over backward behind me, making a gunshot-loud crack of noise. As I reached down to grab it, I found it already being set up for me. By him, of course. I shivered and moved away from the table.

"Evelyn," he said, his voice a deep, musically masculine timbre. "So great to see you."

She beamed up at him. And who would blame her? If anything, the man was even hotter when not in a crumpled white shirt and dangling bow tie. I kept my gaze fixed on her but my hearing went all buzzy. I watched her lips move, saw her flick her hair, lean forward, then backward — doing her mating dance.

"I'll get us some drinks," I blurted out, making them both stare at me as if startled I was still nearby. The beautiful man's eyes seemed to flicker past me, then settle back on my friend — the beautiful, sexy Evelyn. And thank God for that.

I ran for the bar and leaned on it, catching my breath.

"*Hola, chica,*" a familiar voice called out. I raised my aching head, willing myself home, away from this awful scene.

"*Hola,*" I said, raising a finger to one of my fellow bartenders. "A flight of IPAs, *por favor.*" I glanced back at the table. The painfully *guapo anglo* had taken my seat, I noticed, and was practically salivating all over Evelyn. No big surprise there. But I was surprised by the rush of jealousy that turned my entire body into a million tiny nerve endings, each of them screaming that I should leave. Now. If not sooner.

The flight of beers materialized in front of me. "Add the chocolate stout, on nitro," I said, not even knowing why. "I'll be back for it."

I carried the flight to the table, set it down, let them keep ignoring me then went back for the deep brown brew with the creamy bubbles flowing through it. "This one's for you," I said, more boldly than I felt, as I set it in front of Mr. *Guapo*.

He grinned up at me, his teeth bright, his eyes shining. Evelyn must have agreed to go out with him. Using this manufactured fact as my shield, I sat across from him. He sipped the beer, smacked his distressingly full lips then downed half of it. Evelyn seemed a bit uptight but turned to me and declared herself ready for our beer lesson.

The next forty minutes I spent walking her through the various taste profiles of each ale, giving her pointers on how to pinpoint certain hops used, how one of them was woefully out of balance with way too many hops versus malt and how one of them tasted like buttered popcorn—which meant it was spoiled.

The entire time, Mr. Hot Stuff sat, watching and listening. He finished the stout I'd brought and signaled the waiter for another. As I was getting up to complain about the spoiled beer—hoping it wasn't the beer supply lines running from the kegs in the basement to the taps above—I lost my footing at the same moment I realized I hadn't eaten much all day. As I was preparing myself for the ultimate embarrassment—a face-plant on the floor—a hand wrapped around my arm and kept me on my feet.

"Thanks," I muttered, jerking myself out of his grip and heading for the bar—tipsy, yes. And drunk with lust for reasons that I would never, ever be able to explain.

I'd sworn off men for good. What about *this* guy was any different from any other earnest effort on the part of other men in the years since I'd made that vow?

"The double IPA has diacetyl," I said to the manager, using the term for the chemical created that caused the off-flavor I'd pointed out to Evelyn.

"No, it doesn't," he said, not looking at me.

"Try it," I insisted. "It's like drinking a box of caramel corn."

He sighed, poured a small glass, sniffed it then drank. His expression was all I needed for vindication.

"Pull that keg," he barked at one of the bar backs. "What is this shit anyway?" He peered at our cheat sheet next to the long line of taps. "Fitzgerald? Wow. That's surprising. They're always good."

"We rep them," I said, reaching over and pouring myself a glass of water from the beverage wand. "I'll check and see who has the account and let him know." Rumors of bad batches had been flying around about Fitzgerald a lot lately. I turned, putting the cool glass to my flaming hot face. When I pressed it to my exposed upper chest, seeking relief, the handsome man who'd made his way into my life twice in the last two weeks was staring right at me. His odd-shaded eyes were wide, as if shocked or horrified by what I was doing. He leaned back and finished his beer.

As he rose, I worried he was going to come over and say something to me. Instead, and to my immediate, shocked, fury, he picked up Evelyn's hand, kissed it, then leaned over and kissed her lips, lingering a bit too long for public consumption.

When he broke from her, he stared straight at me, as if to say "watch me work".

I whirled away from him, furious at myself for caring, horrified at myself for caring so much. When I checked again, he was gone.

I made my way to the table, my pulse racing, my heartbeat whamming in my ears. Evelyn was sipping one of the remaining IPAs and flicking through her phone messages. Her face was flushed. And why wouldn't it be?

I dropped into my chair — the one he'd commandeered — and slammed one of the other IPAs, barely tasting it. "I should go home," I said, reaching for my purse.

"No, please don't," Evelyn said, putting her hand on my arm. "I need to talk to somebody."

I sighed and nodded, motioning for the roaming waiter. "I need something stronger," I said. "Patrón," I told the roaming waiter kid whose name I'd forgotten. "Two glasses. Two fresh lime wedges. Salt."

His grin widened. I had just ordered twenty-four dollars'-worth of shots, after all.

"Wow," Evelyn said, leaning back and pulling her long blonde hair up in a ponytail. "Big spender."

"Not really. I get a discount. And I need…"

"I know. Something stronger." She leaned forward on her elbows, her gaze sharp. I felt myself tense. "You are so mysterious," she said, tapping her red-painted fingernail on the table. "Maybe if I get you sloshed on expensive hooch…"

"My lips will remain sealed, I assure you," I said, finishing the last IPA dregs and sensing the alcohol begin to work its magic. This brought with it a surge of panic, almost like nausea, up my spine and into the back of my throat. But I forced myself to be calm. I was with Evelyn. No one would hurt me.

"I can't go out with him anymore," she said, staring morosely at her phone.

"Oh? Who?" I knew who. And she knew I knew. She shot me an arch look. "What?"

"I can't go out with Trent anymore." She pointed toward a table where Sir Hot Stuff was holding court, it would seem, with a bunch of be-suited business types. I put a hand to my throat, unable to stop myself. His rear view was lovelier than I'd imagined. He was tall—probably six foot four or even five—with a classic V-shaped body made up of wide shoulders tapering to a trim waist. His ass—I felt myself flush hot even thinking the word—was firm-looking under the well-tailored dress slacks.

As I studied him, I marveled that a man with no hair at all would be so hot. As if sensing my gaze, he ran a large hand around the back of his scalp, then down to his neck. I heard his deep voice booming across the noisy interior but couldn't make out the words.

Evelyn cleared her throat. I flinched. She had one eyebrow raised at me, all-knowing, it would seem. Our drinks arrived, saving me for the time being. We clinked, touched our tongues to the salt on our hands and drank, chasing it quickly afterward with the fresh lime juice.

The table next to ours—full of men whom I didn't even see, now that he, Trent, had imprinted on my retinas—

cheered, and offered to buy us another round.

"Sure thing," Evelyn said, motioning for the waiter. "Wait'll they get the bill," she muttered out of the side of her mouth to me.

"Why can't you go out with him anymore? I blurted, knowing the booze had loosened me up. "Surely he knows how to...um...show you a good time?"

Evelyn giggled and rolled her eyes. "Oh, yes. He does. He's into some seriously kinky stuff, though. It was fun but I'm not sure it's my scene."

My face got hot again. I glanced over Evelyn's shoulder and sure enough, there he was, sipping his beer and studying me like some germ under a microscope. We took our second tequila shots. And our third.

"Baggage," Evelyn said, her voice only a little slurred. "Man's got waaaay too much baggage."

"What do you mean?" I bit down on the lime wedge, needing the tartness between my teeth for something that would keep me from ogling Trent's backside. He'd been moving around the table, engaging each person at it in some form of personal conversation for the last hour. He was fun to watch.

I made myself stop watching. It would do me no good.

"You know!" Evelyn smacked her palm on the table to get my attention. She pointed at me, but her finger wavered in my vision. I blinked, smacked her hand away, opened my mouth to say something useful and hiccupped so loudly the table of guys next to us all turned. Evelyn burst into giggles, flopping back in her seat, her legs splayed out in front of her.

I sensed the gazes of every man next door shoot right to her thighs. The hairs on the back of my neck tingled as I leaned over and shoved her knees back together. "I'm sure I don't know." My hiccups were making me lightheaded. I tried to drink water, hold my breath, everything. But nothing helped.

Evelyn stood, gripping the back of her chair and winked

at me. "I've gotta pee," she said. A couple of the guys elbowed each other.

"I'll go with you," I declared, glaring at the men who had the decency to look sheepish before turning back to their drinks.

We wobbled our way to the bathroom. I hopped up onto the counter next to the sink and waited while Evelyn did her business. When she emerged, tucking her shirt into her skirt, her eyes were swimming with tears.

I jumped down and helped her, since the shirt was all twisted up, even though I was easily as sloshed as she was. "Oh shit," she spat out before washing her hands, making a slow, drunken show of inspecting her face then her hair before turning to glare at me.

"He's got a kid — a teenager."

I blinked trying to decide if I should pee or just get my drunk ass home somehow. "Who?"

"Trent, you little bitch," she said, giggling again. She leaned into my ear. "He's hot as holy hell. No lie." She waved a hand in front of her face.

"I'm sure," I said, deciding at that moment that getting my drunk ass home should be job one.

"Teach me a swear word," she said. "A good one."

I sighed and realized that my hiccups had stopped. "*Me cago en todo lo que se menea!*" I washed my hands for lack of anything better to do as she tried it out a few times.

"What does it mean?"

"I shit on everything that moves," I said, leaning back and observing as she stood, slumped against the bathroom wall, devastating even in her drunkenness.

"More," she insisted as we headed back out into the ever-louder bar.

"*Hijo de puta,*" I said. "Son of a bitch."

"Ooo, that's a good one. I'm gonna try it out right now." She stomped over to our empty table.

"Nope," I said, grabbing her elbow and slowing her down. "Not today."

"Aw, you're no fun at all." She slumped into me. "I feel like such a bitch. A...*puta*."

"You're not. We should eat something, maybe."

"Yeah. I want a cheeseburger. Fuck diets."

"Agreed." We sat, giggling and sipping water, then ordered our food and more water.

"So, a teenaged daughter, eh?" I couldn't believe I was asking. It was the tequila talking.

"Yep," she said with a heavy sigh. She leaned on her elbow and watched Trent as his party seemed to be wrapping up. He laughed, patted guys' backs and shoulders and guided them all to the door. "God damn I'm an idiot. We had some good times. But something didn't really click. But you know, sometimes you just know, you know?"

"I know," I said, solemnly. Which sent us both back into paroxysms of giggles.

I'm embarrassed to admit that I barely remembered eating, even though I could see a fully decimated plate boasting a limp piece of lettuce and a few fries in front of me. My head was pounding and not in a good way. My gut roiled. Evelyn's eyes were glassy as she sipped a beer. I blinked at my own beer, wondering when the hell we'd ordered them.

Our Casanovas at the next table had moved closer. One of them had an arm draped over Evelyn's shoulders and was brazenly leering down her shirt. I made myself snap to, set the beer down and drank a whole glass of water, hoping it would counteract the alcohol and knowing it was far too late at this juncture in the festivities.

I smacked at the man's hand that dangled like a teenager's over Evelyn's left breast. She blew out a puff of air, stood up fast and ran for the bathroom. We all watched, my brain accepting what was happening even as my body acted of its own accord. I stood, wavering badly, and stomped after her. I'd barely made it to the women's room door when a hand gripped my shoulder and spun me around.

"Come on, *mamacita*," some asshole was saying, his lips

too close to my face. "You owe me at least one kiss. Those were expensive fucking tequila shots."

"Get off me," I yelped, struggling as I was tossed straight back into the void—the place where I'd drunk too much, trying to impress a bunch of girls who'd never be my friends no matter what.

And again, not that long ago, at the hands of a man I'd trusted.

"No!" I kneed somebody's balls. Stepped on someone else's foot. Shoved the heel of my hand into some other somebody's chin. Curses filled my head. The smell of stale beer, sand and sea water filled my nose. Someone shoved me against a wall and held my wrists. We must have somehow made our way into the men's room because the air stank even stronger of piss.

When I sensed someone's tongue in my mouth, I bit down as hard as I could. The pain that exploded in my head right after that centered on my nose.

At that odd, painful moment, everything stopped. I slid to the floor, sobbing, dizzy, sick.

Fulfilling your destiny, eh, Melody? Showing off, getting drunk and getting what you deserve. Again.

I tried to focus on the action around me but all I heard were loud grunts, more cursing and the meaty thud of fists against flesh. Finally, someone took me by the arms and helped me up, even as I struggled against him.

I knew it was him. That he'd seen me at my worst already.

"Let me go," I demanded, turning to spit blood into the dirty men's room sink. He stood behind me, his presence soothing and irritating at the same time. I rinsed my mouth a few times, before hazarding a glance at my face. "Oh my god. I'm… Shit."

Trent took me by the elbow. "Let's grab Evelyn and get you to the ER. You're gonna need to get your nose reset."

My eyes stung with tears as I let him lead me out. Our asshole table buddies were long gone. Evelyn was sitting at the bar, nursing a soda until she saw us and ran toward me, making noises I couldn't hear.

Trent's strong arm was around me. I leaned into him and let myself enjoy the moment. But right after I smelled the stale beer, the ocean, the moldy interior of the shed where they left me once they were done, everything went dark.

Chapter Five

Trent sat in the uncomfortable chair next to the bed, watching her sleep. He'd been sitting there for two hours before he remembered to move. Which made for more than a little pain, considering he was no spring chicken.

With a groan, he stood slowly, rolled his shoulders, popped his neck first one way then the other and bent over to make sure he could still touch his toes.

"Being forty sucks," he muttered to himself as he walked around, waiting for his legs to stop tingling while his circulation got back to normal.

On the bed behind him, Melody sucked in a breath. He turned, heart in his throat. Her eyes were open wide, glaring at the ceiling. He wasn't sure if she was fully awake and didn't want to startle her so he held back. At least that's what he told himself. He had another reason for it. And it had everything to do with the terrifying, overwhelming urge he had to slide in beside her and hold her tight until she knew she was safe.

He shook his head.

Stop it, Hettinger. Not every woman needs a Big Strong Hero. This woman seems pretty fucking strong.

Some asshole had broken her nose and she still managed to almost blind one of them with her thumb and render another one incapacitated with a hard knee to the balls. By the time he'd figured out what was going on and kicked open the men's room door, two of her attackers had been yelping and either hopping around or curled up on the dirty floor. Only one of the three jerks still had his hands on her.

But that had been enough for him.

That sorry son-of-a-bitch would be spending a good long time in the hospital.

"Hey," a voice called from the half-open door. "Can I come in?"

Trent backed away from the bed, his throat closed up. The whole thing had been a buzz—from the second he'd clapped eyes on her, through the awkward beer lesson, to the moment he realized that she was staring at him as much as he had been her. Determined to monitor their booze intake, he'd stretched out his super boring meeting with the town eggheads, so he had an excuse to stick around. Just in case.

Just in case anything went wrong.

Sue me. I'm a hero. I wanted to make sure she got out of there okay and she almost didn't so shut up.

Evelyn eased into the dim room. "Melody? Honey? You awake?" She was clutching a bouquet of tulips and a couple of milkshakes. "I brought sustenance."

A sob erupted from the bed, sending a shard of ice through Trent's heart. But he held back.

Evelyn ran to the bed. "What is it? Do you need some pain medicine? We can get you the good stuff in here."

Trent backed up more until he felt the wall behind him, studying the blonde woman beside the hospital bed. Evelyn Benedict was drop dead gorgeous. There was no arguing that point. She had a gorgeous, hourglass figure which she always emphasized with great clothes. Her willingness to highlight her height by wearing heels had turned him on no end. Well, okay, that and her tits. She had tits that would make a grown man cry.

What? I said I was a hero, not a saint.

They'd had a couple of vanilla dates which had been nice. She had a sharp, self-deprecating sense of humor and a healthy, realistic appetite. Women who ordered a salad and ate three bites of lettuce before declaring themselves "stuffed" made him nuts.

He'd know. He'd been married to one.

They'd been set up by a mutual friend, a manager at a brewery who knew them both. The dinner party had included six other couples so it hadn't been totally awkward. He'd liked her from the start and it had been mutual. But he'd been reluctant to draw her into anything more than a third date, which had ended nicely.

He'd avoided her for almost a month after that and to her credit, she had taken the hint. After spending a long weekend at a retreat with fellow business owners that had involved periods of quiet meditation, hours of exercise and intense workshops about all aspects of running their perspective companies, he'd come home refreshed and ready.

She'd agreed to accompany him to one party "just to observe". That had ended even more nicely but, again, in a fairly vanilla fashion. The next weekend he'd taken a chance and taken her out of town, to one of the Georgia barrier islands and an exclusive club he'd found through a friend back in Ann Arbor. "Full immersion," she'd claimed to want. "Nothing halfway."

And it had been all of that, and some more. A shiver shot down his spine at the memory of her, of them, that long, erotic weekend. But the sense that she'd been acting the part, humoring him, had lingered after that and since then, they'd cooled it. And he'd not really missed her. Which was a good sign he'd made the right call.

He watched as she hovered over Melody, long, honey-blonde hair hiding most of her near-perfect profile. Evelyn was probably the closest he'd come to having a girlfriend since his disaster of a marriage. And it hadn't been right. They'd both known it.

And now...

"Hurts," Melody whispered from the bed. "I need some water."

He grabbed a cup and straw that he'd been guarding like a mama lion and handed it to Evelyn. She took it without looking at him and held it to Melody's dry lips. Trent licked his lips on reflex, believing that he could feel her pain radiating through his own sinuses. He'd had two broken noses in his day. It was a function of playing sports in high school. They hurt like hell but did heal pretty fast.

But now…

Now. He honestly believed he could feel every twinge she felt.

That realization made him stumble back, heart racing. He'd felt this way before—but that had turned out to be a fraud and had landed him with huge alimony payments and misery. He wouldn't go here again. He didn't trust himself or his instincts anymore.

He needed to get the hell out of here.

"Trent?" Evelyn stood, set the cup on the rolling table and patted Melody's arm.

"I'll…uh…go now. Since you're here."

"Wait."

But he was halfway down the rubbery-smelling hallway, in the elevator, his legs shaking, into his Jeep and racing home before he allowed himself to breathe normally. Which was a relief.

Or was it?

* * * *

"What the fuck, man?"

He winced and held the phone away from his ear as he struggled up from sleep. Glancing around, confused for a hot second, he realized he'd only made it as far as the couch before passing out cold from depleted adrenaline and his own healthy helping of beer the night before. "Good morning to you too, Glory."

"Fuck you. What the hell do you mean, running out of her room like that?"

"I'm… I…" He set his feet on the floor, trying to get his bearings and defend what was in essence, indefensible.

"I'm sorry. Is she all right?"

"She's all right. Mortified, embarrassed, all the shit that you could have set her straight on, you massive asshat."

Trent felt his ears get hot, a clear precursor to anger. But he took a breath, got up and headed for the kitchen and a glass of water, allowing himself a few seconds to respond. And for Evelyn to calm down.

"Sorry," she said. "But Jesus, Trent. You ran out like your nuts were on fire. She was pretty upset."

He drank two full glasses of water before he felt like he had the wherewithal to answer. This had a tinge of surrealism to it anyway. As recently as the night before, he'd asked Evelyn out again, right in front of Melody. For reasons that had more to do with immaturity, he knew, than anything else. Unfair to both women.

Asshat, indeed.

"Listen, Evelyn, I..."

An uncomfortable beat of silence took on a life of its own.

"What?" She exhaled loudly. "Trent, you and I... We aren't going to work. You know it as well as I do. I like you. You're...fun and sexy and..."

He grinned and leaned back against his sink. "Go on."

"No, jerk. You know what I mean."

"Yes, I do. You're not too bad yourself. But I agree. We're better off as friends."

"Right. So...about Melody."

"What about her?"

"Dear Lord, you are seriously saying that to me?"

"I am." He ran a shaking hand down his face. "I have... It's weird, Evelyn. I don't know how to explain it. She sort of...scares me."

"That's no excuse."

Fury flared in his brain. He rolled his neck, wincing at the stiffness from sleeping on the couch. "Tell you what, I'll —"

"*You'll* go pick her up at two today and take her home, that's what."

"I'm busy," he blustered.

"Get un-busy. You can manage it, I'll bet."

He heard Taylor wander into the living room. His fury flared hot again.

Women. His life was choked with them and they would, without a doubt, kill him.

"Fine. I'll take her home. Now if you'll excuse me, I—"

But he was talking to a dead phone. Evelyn had already hung up.

Chapter Six

I sat, staring out of the window of Trent's Jeep, nose aching, heart pounding, mouth dry. "I don't know why you're doing this," I repeated for the second, or maybe the fifth, time. "I could have gotten a ride home."

He downshifted so violently, the whole vehicle shook. "It's fine," he said, not even glancing at me. "I wanted to."

"Okay." I looked out of the windshield, not soothed by any of this. Damn Evelyn. Woman was too nosy for her own good. "Turn here," I said, pointing to the faux pretentious sign indicating my apartment complex. He turned so fast I had to grip the armrest to keep from sliding into his lap.

"Sorry," he muttered. "Which way now?"

I stared at him, confused and rattled by his seeming curtness. I pointed left, then directed him through the rat's maze of buildings until we reached mine. A white aluminum-sided, three-story affair, with six units flanking an outdoor staircase. I had the cheap unit—the studio on the basement level. It did walk out to a small, goose-infested pond. But between the goose-shit and their infernal honking, I never opened the sliding glass door much wider than a few inches.

He parked and sat, his fingers white-knuckled around the steering wheel. I sighed. I was obviously not someone he wanted to be around. No matter the superhero move he'd pulled with my attacker in the men's room.

"So, thanks. For everything." I wrenched open the door and climbed out, gave him a non-committal wave without looking and turned toward the building. My nose ached. My head was weird and echo-y in a way that made me nervous. I didn't want to be alone. But I'd weathered worse than this. I'd be fine.

As I was heading down the stairs toward my door, my face jangling in pain with every step, I couldn't hold back self-pitying tears. I sucked in a snotty breath, and tried to see where to stick the key through my weepy vision. The damn things fell out of my hands with a loud clank on the metal threshold. "Fucking fuck," I muttered, reaching for them.

I saw a set of shoes — box-toed, brown, dressy — near the keys. My skin tingled. I set my jaw. I didn't need this right now. I didn't want it — ever.

His hand covered mine so I let go of the keys. He stuck the right one straight into the lock without even trying. The door swung open. We stood, staring into the depths of my place — a place I'd innocently left Wednesday morning for work, not knowing anything. Much less that the incredible man standing close enough to me that I believed I could sense the heat of his skin would be here, making me weak and not from pain, either.

"Well," I said, my voice all nasally and weird. "Thanks. Again."

He stood there, his jaw clenched so hard I could hear his teeth grinding. Before I could stop myself, my hand lifted and my fingers grazed his dark stubble. He closed his eyes and took a step back.

"Sorry," I said, unable to take my eyes off him. I wanted to touch him. My fingers itched — they burned — to feel his skin. My legs got wobbly again. I took the step over the threshold, leaving him standing there, looking miserable. I shut the door halfway, using it as a shield between us. He put a hand on it, pressing against it. I pushed back, feeling defensive all of a sudden. This was my space. I didn't want him in it.

I did. But that was beside the current point.

I didn't trust myself around him. The last thing I needed was this kind of bizarre neediness.

"Can I come in?" he asked, his voice rough.

"Sure," I said, opening it all the way.

Nice one, chica. *Way to be strong.*

He stepped inside, instantly overwhelming my small space. I turned into the kitchen area, flipping on the kettle for something to do. He stood, hands in his pockets, watching me as I busy-worked for a few seconds. I mixed the hot water with my mama's spiced tea mix, stirred the two cups and handed him one. He smiled and sniffed it.

"Yum."

"Family recipe."

We sipped. Silence descended like a heavy blanket. I sighed and put my cup down.

"How's the nose?" he asked, leaning against the tall counter that separated the kitchen from the living room.

"Painful," I admitted. Exhaustion washed over me, making me sway on my feet.

He grabbed my arm. "Come on. Let's get you set up somewhere horizontal."

"I'm not usually this much of a wimp," I insisted, letting him lead me to the couch. "I swear it."

"I'm sure." He grabbed pillows and propped them all at one end, sat me down and gave me a tiny shove so I flopped back. "There. Consider yourself nurtured." He grinned at me. I felt something unclench in my chest. I stretched my arms up over my head and my feet out behind him. He grabbed the blanket over the back of the couch and tossed it down over me. "See. This is me, Mr. Sensitive."

I pulled the blanket up around me. The remnants of the painkillers were wearing off. The soft edges of the pain in my face were taking on a bite, making me squint in the light. "Would you mind grabbing the pills in my purse? And a glass of water?"

He gave my leg a quick pat, sending all my nerve endings down happy lane. I pulled the blanket up higher, watching as he dug through my bag, then poured a glass of water. "One or two?"

"Just one, thanks."

He crouched down beside the couch and handed me the pill, then the water. I swallowed it and dropped back, half asleep already. He must have grabbed the glass. Sighing, I stretched again, loving the sensation of being in my own space. And yes, the fact of Trent's presence. That he'd come to get me, driven me home, unlocked my door when I was too weepy to deal. And he'd just brought me a pain pill.

My brain was shutting down. But I reached out anyway. His warm hand closed around mine. "I'm right here," he said. "I'll stay, if you want me to."

I nodded, rolling onto my side. His dark, handsome face was the last thing I saw before falling into a deep, drug-induced sleep.

* * * *

I woke with a start, dragging myself up from a deep hole filled with old beer smells, the ocean, moldy buildings and pain. I sat up too fast, slamming straight into a wall of actual pain. "Holy shit," I said, touching the bandages on my nose. The room was dark — too dark.

I sat and wrapped the blanket around myself, trying to shake the cobwebs. The doorknob rattled, making me jump up, heart in my throat. Trent appeared holding a greasy bag that smelled amazing. "You scared me," I said, running a hand through my hair and my tongue over my fuzzy teeth. "I need a shower."

He put the bag on the tall counter and took a few steps toward me. I held up a hand, unable to stop the giggle. "I'm good, thanks. I think I can manage it."

"Right. I'll get the food out."

"Yes. Good plan." I smiled at him. He took another step closer. I put up both hands. "Nope. I reek from head to toe. Go there." I pointed to the kitchen. "Be useful."

"I'm pretty damn useful," he said, running both hands down his chest. I tried not to gulp, settling my face in a firm expression.

"Yeah? Prove it." I headed for the back of the apartment where my small bedroom space adjoined the bathroom. One hot shower and a careful tooth brushing session later, I emerged, feeling slightly better — if woozy from the pills. I had to wean myself off, step down to some regular old ibuprofen. I could hear music — something that sounded a lot like the Beatles — and smelled the sharp edge of takeout Indian food.

Perfect.

I grabbed a pair of yoga pants and a long, shapeless sweatshirt, dragging it down over my sports bra. On the way down, I managed to whap my own nose, which forced me to sit before I fell down from the dizzying pain. "Fuck, that hurts."

"Yeah, I can imagine," Trent said. Startled, I stood, tugging the ragged edges of the sweatshirt down to cover my crotch. His eyes gleamed in the gloom in the back of the apartment. "Hungry?" He held out his elbow.

"I was," I said, ignoring his arm and heading toward the good smells and happy noises. "Then I smacked my own nose."

He circled around me and headed into the kitchen, then turned to me, brandishing two full plates of food. "Your feast, madam."

"*Gracias, guapo.*"

"Huh. Yes, I am quite handsome, now that you mention it." He tilted his head, studying me again. "You surprised I understood you?"

"Nope. I've decided that nothing about you will surprise me." I set my plate on the counter and dragged one of the two tall chairs that I'd found at a cheap furniture store. They were still too short — the damn surface was so unnaturally high. Trent set his plate down next to mine. I picked up my fork, but my hand shook so much I dropped it and clenched my fingers together in my lap.

"In pain?" Trent was reaching for the small packet of pills

I'd gotten from the hospital pharmacy. I shook my head and pointed to a cabinet behind him. He opened them until he located the small cache of over-the-counter pills and grabbed the bottle of ibuprofen. I nodded and caught the bottle when he tossed it to me, popped a couple of them into my mouth and drank the water.

I took a tiny bite of the biryani—my favorite Indian dish and how the hell did he know that? He sat next to me and dug into his food. When he ripped the naan in half and handed me some, I nodded but stayed silent. The food was so good, I couldn't imagine taking the time to speak. The Beatles made up our background. All we lacked was the cheap Chianti bottle with a waxy candle.

Finally, I leaned back, patting my overfull stomach. He mirrored me with a groan of satisfaction that made me tingle in areas of my body that hadn't tingled in over a decade. My phone buzzed its way across the counter, relieving me of the burden to speak. Trent reached over and snagged the thing, glancing at it before handing it to me. I frowned at him, but in truth, I loved how comfortable he was in my space.

Oh, Melody, you are fucked. Royally.

"Hey, Evelyn," I said. "What's up?"

"Just checking on you, *chica*. How're things?"

"Pretty sore." I touched the bandage over my busted nose. "I took a nap."

Trent got up and took the plates and forks to the sink, rinsed them and stuck them in the dishwasher. It was too much. How could this guy be real? I got up and headed to the couch, tossing the blanket around my shoulders on the way there.

"And…"

I rolled my eyes and sat, curling my legs up under me. "What?"

"God damn it, woman, don't make me say it."

"He's here," I whispered, as Trent whistled his way through putting the leftovers in the fridge before he started poking around in my cabinets.

"Sweet!" Evelyn's voice was high, like a teenager's.

"Stop," I said, my face flushed hot. "It's nothing. He just brought me home."

"Yeah, five hours ago."

"Evelyn… I'm not… He's… I can't."

"Never say never, sweetie. Enjoy."

I answered her, but the phone was dead. I stared down at the device, then tossed it on the Ikea special coffee table. Trent sat and stuck his sock feet on the same table. "Evelyn?"

I nodded. "She hung up on me."

"She's good at that." He handed me a glass of wine and held his up. We clinked and sipped. He was sitting within a foot of me, so close. But yet…

I shifted, putting more air between us. "You guys are…"

He shot me an arch look. "We went out a few times. Decided we're better as friends."

"Ah. Okay." I sipped more, frozen with terror and uneasy anticipation.

"Do you have decent cable?" He grabbed my remote and flicked on the small flat screen television.

"Actually, I don't have cable at all." I tossed him the smaller remote. "It's all streaming. All the time."

"So, how do you watch football?"

"Easy." I held out a hand. He put the small remote in it and I flipped directly to the Spanish language soccer channels. "There you go, *guapo*."

"There you go again. Reminding me how handsome I am." He glanced at the screen. "No, no, no. Not that. *Real* football." He glanced at his watch. "Michigan's playing."

I grinned and settled back, putting the remote on my lap. "I only watch the beautiful game."

He frowned at my screen, then stuck his socked feet up on the table once more. "I hate this game."

"Well, then you're going to have to leave and never return."

47

He sighed, sipped his wine then smiled at me. I melted even more. But for the next hour we sat and watched soccer—or more like I explained soccer to him and he lapped up it up like a thirsty dog. When the game was over with an unsurprising Real Madrid win, he stood and stretched, giving me a mouth-watering rear view. I averted my eyes and fiddled with the remote.

Maybe he'd try to kiss me now.

But he didn't.

He brought me a glass of water, another ibuprofen, patted my head and left. Just like that.

I ran for my phone, hitting speed dial back to Evelyn. "He left," I said, by way of response when she answered.

"And?"

"And nothing. We ate. He brought me Indian food. I made him watch a soccer game while he obsessively checked his phone for the Michigan football game score. Then he just… walked out the door."

"Just like that?"

"Just like that."

"Oh shit, girl, I think he loves you."

"Don't be ridiculous." But I was tingling all over again. And I liked it.

"Call him," she insisted. "Call him right now."

"No," I said, toying with the edges of the blanket. "You're *loco*."

"I am not. I'm an expert."

"I am not calling him. That's his job."

"Oh Lord have mercy. Join us in the twenty-first century, already."

"I'm here with you, *chica*. But I still think he should call me. Period."

"Fine. Be that way. Want to do something this weekend?"

I curled my legs under me, as reality hit me hard. I had two long shifts at the diner and that was after a closing shift at the bar tomorrow. "Crap."

"What?"

"Can't. Gotta work."

"The bar?"

"Yeah. And I also work at a diner. Marlo's. Out on Field Road. I fill in when they need it and one of their servers is out on maternity leave."

"Oh. I didn't know."

"Yeah, well, now you do."

"Melody, you can't pull a bar shift and one at the diner. You're injured."

"Two at the diner, actually. I gotta go, Evelyn. Thanks for calling."

This time, it was my turn to hang up on her.

Chapter Seven

"Dad, you're being an asshole again."

Trent raised his eyes from the paperwork in front of him, honestly befuddled by her comment. "Huh?" He sipped coffee that had gone cold, then got up to pour some fresh out of the pot. "What the hell happened to all the coffee?" he asked as he rattled the empty stainless steel carafe.

"You drank it," Taylor said.

He turned around to stare at her. She was dressed in jeans with more holes than fabric, and one of his old, threadbare U of M sweatshirts. Her rich, auburn hair—her mother's legacy—was yanked back in a tight ponytail. She was nibbling on a piece of bacon. His gaze was drawn to her fingernails—pitch black. And her nose, which she was trying to cover with one hand.

"What the fuck," he yelled across the large kitchen at her, "is in your goddamned face, young lady?"

"Oh this?" She touched the jewel that looked like a diamond, now nestled in the left side of her perfect nose. "It's a piercing." Her expression made the unspoken word "duh!" echo around in his head. "What?"

Trent gripped the handle of the empty coffee carafe even tighter as he glared at her. "How... You're not eighteen... I mean..."

"Mom signed for me. Yesterday. When you were 'too busy to talk to me'." She hooked her fingers around the last phrase, simultaneously rolling her eyes. Reminding him of how she'd morph into a toddler whenever he'd tell her he was out, which he usually let imply that he was 'with a woman'. But this was beyond the pale.

He turned back to the sink, filled the carafe again and counted to a hundred, then two hundred and fifty as he ground the coffee beans, poured them into the filter and turned on the machine. This was just Taylor trying to control him again and he knew it. Reacting—even if he wanted to—was useless.

"So, what are you doing today? he said, his voice low and tight which was the only indication of the precarious grip he had on his temper.

"Oh..." She waved a hand around. "I'm going to work out first, then I thought I'd take a nap." She met his gaze, her green eyes jolting him hard, like they always did. They were, of course, the very eyes that, in the face of her mother, had grabbed him by the nuts first, then the brain. He shook his head to clear it. *Taylor is not Sheila,* he said in his head for the zillionth time. *Taylor is Taylor. Don't project.*

"Right, so here's what I say you're going to do, since this is not meant to be a vacation, but a suspension." He grabbed his cup of cold coffee and sipped it, to keep his anger at bay. "First, you'll clean your room—including washing your sheets and all the laundry on the floor. Bring all the dishes piled up on the bedside table here, and put them in the dishwasher. Then you clean that bathroom of yours—floor to ceiling."

"But, Dad," she said, pouting just enough to infuriate him all over again. "Winnie can clean it, can't she? I'll let her in this time."

"Winnie has been told to never set foot in your room. Your words if I recall correctly. And I agree. She shouldn't ever go in there. Which means you clean it. And if you don't, you lose a month of allowance." The coffee maker dinged, indicating he could pour off a cup while the rest of the pot brewed. Once he had reinforced the caffeine, he turned back to her, his precious gem of a baby girl, who at this moment resembled something more like a pissed-off, red-headed harpy.

Which was something he was also very familiar with,

considering.

He sat, and picked up the reports full of requirements for the city block renovation that he'd gotten the night before from city council. They were, in a word, ridiculous. But he was determined to make this work. He'd made up his mind about that section of town and he wanted to be one of the first to draw jobs and residents to it. And when he made up his mind about something he was rarely deterred, even by stuffy, short-sighted bureaucrats.

The heavy sigh coming from across the table reminded him that she was still here, at home, not at school, because she'd gotten caught smoking pot in the men's room with some punk boy. He set the papers down and focused on her fully. "You know you're damn lucky you didn't get expelled, right? I mean, thank God you're a four-oh student and all."

"Yeah, so?" She dragged her fingertip through a puddle of pancake syrup and put it to her lips. Something that made him crazy, as she damn well knew. He forced a smile onto his face.

"So, I suggest you get to work. After you clean your room and bathroom, I'll take a look, and then you can get on the laundry. After that, I've arranged for you to work as a busser downtown. You're expected at…" He made a show of checking his watch. "Four-thirty. Wear comfortable shoes and black jeans without holes in them. They'll issue you a company T-shirt."

Taylor lurched forward, knocking over her empty orange juice glass. Trent caught it before it hit the hardwood, set it beside her plate and smiled wider.

"A busser? Downtown? You don't mean at GrandBrew, do you? That place is a dump."

"You mean, that's a place where your friends might be having dinner with their families and see you, actually working? Yes, that's the place." He picked up the reports again and sipped his coffee. "I have work to do, Tay. And so do you."

"How much?" she demanded, poking her black-lacquered fingernail over the top of the papers he was studying.

"How much what?" He sipped, willing her to ask so he could break a bit of reality news to her.

"For the work? You know? Minimum wage or what?"

"For starters, my love, bussers and wait staff don't make minimum wage. At my restaurants they make a hell of a lot closer to it than most places but they also make great tips, if they give great service. Typically, the wait staff tips out to the bussers to flesh out their wages." Taylor's green eyes flickered. Trent smiled at her, even as he cursed himself — and Sheila — for coddling the kid this late into her life. "However, your tips will be set aside for me to put in your college fund. Along with your paycheck, such as it will be."

"But...Da — ad!" She dragged out the short word for so long he winced. "You can afford to send me anywhere. Mom told me so." She was in full pout mode now. Hunched down in her chair, arms crossed, lower lip stuck out so far he wanted to snatch it right off her face.

No, Hettinger. You own this shit. You made her into this. Now turn it around before it's too late.

He put the papers down and took her hands. She relaxed, thinking he was going to cave again, no doubt. "Even though that may be the case, I've decided it's time for a Taylor reality check. This last little stunt at school, which forced me to spend half a day with the principal and the superintendent convincing them to let you stay after a two-week suspension, was the last time I'm bailing you out. So, in order for you to get a grip on what real people do, as opposed to what we do, here in our little rich-person's bubble, you are going to put your ass to work. Once you start school again, you'll keep working, after school and on weekends. Got me?"

Her big green eyes filled with tears. Trent steeled himself, not breaking their stare. She yanked her hand out of his. "What about my piano lessons? You think Mom's going to let me just stop doing those things? I'm pretty good, you know. And you already told me you'd get me a guitar so I could start learning that."

"I do know, honey. And I'm proud at the effort you make on both of those things. However, I've decided that you should pick one of them and focus on it, so you can fit your work schedule around it." He picked up his papers, wishing this scene finished but knowing it for something that would resonate far into his immediate future.

"You are such...such...an *asshole!*" His precious daughter's shriek filled the open loft-space they inhabited. But Trent was determined to right this course. He was not going to unleash his child into the world as some kind of pampered elitist.

"Yes, well, be that as it may, you and I will also be spending two hours every Sunday afternoon making and serving meals at St. Francis."

"Serving...meals? To whom?" She was standing now, glaring at him.

He rose slowly, towering over her, using the full power of his alpha personality. While part of him experienced a thrill of pride that she didn't back down an inch, the bigger part of him realized that he'd failed her. He'd failed to teach her respect. "Taylor Elizabeth Hettinger, you will turn around from me right now and go to your room. I don't want to hear your voice for a solid two hours but I fully expect to hear sounds of serious cleaning."

She opened her mouth. He held up a hand. Her gaze flickered away from his, thank God.

"This shit stops now, Taylor. Have I made myself clear?"

She nodded, biting her lower lip. He sucked in a breath, mentally sitting on his hands to keep from hugging her.

Time for tough love, Hettinger, my man. It's that, or create another Sheila.

"I can't hear you."

"Yes."

He glared at her when she glanced up at him.

"Yes, sir."

"Go clean. Watch the clock. You get docked if you're late for work."

"But..."

He held up a hand. "Nope. Too late for all that. Go, now, before I lose it. I'm not kidding."

She blinked fast, turned and headed for her room.

"If you slam the door, Taylor, that's a second month of no allowance."

Her door clicked shut. He exhaled and fell into the seat behind him, swiping a hand down his sweaty face. He was exhausted, and it was only nine a.m. He picked up his reports and lost himself in them, making to-do lists, assigning budgets and feeling like he had control over something in his life.

At noon, Taylor emerged, followed by a waft of bleach. She carried a towering basket of laundry past him and into the wash room off the kitchen. He heard the washer start, then looked up to say something supportive to her. But she breezed by him without a word. He got up and made a couple of sandwiches and poured them both a glass of almond milk.

He knocked on her door. "Tay? Are you hungry?"

"No," she said, but it wasn't confrontational. It was flat, devoid of affect.

He shrugged. "I'll put your sandwich in the fridge, in case you change your mind. I have to head to Kalamazoo for the afternoon. I'm putting my transit card on the table. You can use it to get to work."

"Whatever," she declared.

"Exactly," he said. He ate his sandwich, drank his milk, finalized his lists and grabbed a shower. As he emerged and wrapped the towel around his waist, he took a moment to study himself in the mirror. Running a hand across his bald pate, he noted fresh lines on the sides of his eyes. *Thanks, Taylor*.

The memory of Melody the night before popped into his brain, making him curse under his breath. He'd been so absorbed with work and teenager bullshit this morning he'd been able to forget her. But of course, he couldn't do that forever.

He let his hand drop to his chest, then to his set of hard-won flat abs, and lower, where his dick was doing an impressive tent pole imitation under the towel.

No. Keep control. It's all you have in the face of the terrifying, undeniable attraction you have to her. Jacking off while thinking about her is not the answer, dude. Not at all.

He sighed, brushed his teeth, waited until his erection softened then pulled on jeans and a crisply pressed white shirt.

Think about work. Think about Taylor. Think about your golf game. Anything but her.

He rolled up his sleeves and slipped on his heavy watch. He took a moment to study his wedding ring that he kept on a chain he'd given Sheila once—her supposed collar—hanging from the side of the dresser mirror. He touched it, as he always did, by way of a reminder of his biggest mistake. To remind him of Sheila. And of his initial, gut-deep reaction to her. Not that different from the feelings pinging around in his chest right now regarding the beautiful Latina Goddess, Melody Rodriquez.

Never again, remember?

He stomped out into the hall then into the large open living space. He'd forgone the suburban life in purpose, choosing a downtown Grand Rapids loft over the four-bedroom McMansion in the 'burbs. Today, he'd taken steps today to guide his daughter—the one human in the world he was one hundred percent responsible for besides himself—even further away from that path of entitlement. He'd done a lot in a few hours.

Don't think about Melody—or her deep brown eyes, her thick, ebony hair, or her full lips, perfectly rounded ass, her legs...

"Stop," he said out loud. "Stop it now."

"Dad?"

He turned, heart in his throat, brain spinning with the

sort of confusion that he despised. Taylor stood there in her holey jeans and Michigan sweatshirt—a school he'd worked his ass off to afford between scholarships, grants and part-time jobs—her eyes wide with concern. He blew out a breath and smiled to reassure her.

"Sorry. Just pre-thinking my way into a meeting."

"The eggheads?"

"Yeah, honey, the eggheads."

"Okay, so…" She touched the piercing in her nose. Trent bit the inside of his cheek to keep from reacting. "I just talked to Mom."

He crossed his arms, ready to deflect anything Sheila had said to enable Taylor to avoid his come-to-Jesus two-week plan for their daughter. "She said…um…that you were right."

Trent frowned, suspicious. "Well, that's a first. We're all on the same page, then."

"Yeah. She…uh, wants to talk to you."

Trent sighed, seeing that familiar, eager hopefulness in Taylor's eyes. She never would give up on her parents getting back together. He put a hand on her shoulder. "I'll call her later, honey, all right?"

She nodded and slumped into him. He hugged her tight, kissed the top of her head and let her go, giving her a tiny push. "Get a shower. You have some essays to write, according to your principal. You can knock those out before you go to work."

She nodded. *Order*, Trent thought. *Imposing order was the only way to get through life.* Filling the minutes and hours with tasks. He'd done it, and it had worked out pretty well. For most of his life, it had been all he had to cling to—imposing his own, strict order on the extreme chaos all around him.

"Catch you later, Daddio," she called out.

Suspicious all over again, he shot her a quick salute then grabbed his briefcase. He had forty-eight hours to respond to the eggheads' demands. The clock was ticking. He hit the interstate, his brain ticking away on the budgets and to-do lists, mentally assigning his staff to various tasks. When his phone buzzed with a text, he startled, realizing that he'd barely even been paying attention to the road, he'd been so deeply immersed in the project. He looked at the phone screen, noting with dismay that it was from her, from Melody.

Hey Guapo. There's a good football game on tomorrow afternoon. Want to come over?

Grinning like an idiot, he spoke into the phone, waiting for the text to populate. "For the hundredth time, I know I'm handsome. And Michigan is off this week so I don't know what football you could possibly mean."

Real football. Not that sissy game with all the padding and helmets. It's on at 1. I'll make lunch.

Don't do it, Trent. Don't go to her place again. If you do, you're doomed.
"Sure," he said into the phone with a mental wince. "I'll be there. As long as you keep calling me handsome."

Her reply was a winky face and a thumbs-up. He stared at them as he waited at a traffic light until the beep of a horn behind him brought him out of his trance.

Chapter Eight

The morning shift at the diner dragged slower than a snail trail but when my boss gave me the high sign at eleven forty-five, I shed my apron, reported and pocketed my tips and jumped in the car, heart trip-hammering with anxiety and anticipation.

A date. I have an honest-to-God date. And I initiated it.

Shivering in the heat, I parked my car and jumped out, determined to put the final, perfect touches on the meal we'd share while watching *La Liga* — two of my favorite things. Now all wrapped up in the possibility of a third favorite thing — the delicious possibility of Trent Hettinger.

I ran into the kitchen, checking the pork roast covered in spices and oil I'd put into the slow cooker at four that morning, before my diner shift. I'd spent the hour before that chopping onions, mixing up homemade salsa and soaking the beans for the soup I'd planned as a side dish. This after four restless hours of sleep, after a long day at the office and a quick shift behind the bar. The manager had cut me early due to slow business and my somewhat less-than-ideal visage.

"No offense, *chica*. You know I think you're beautiful and I'd take you out to dinner in a minute if you'd let me." His sad eyes had sagged even more. "But you're scaring the locals, you know? You look like you were in a damn cage fight."

"I know. I'm sorry. I'll go."

"There's a girl," the old-school guy had said, ever the pseudo-gentlemen.

"I'm hardly a girl, Bob," I'd reminded him, not insulted in

59

the slightest. Some people would never change and were, essentially, harmless. The key was to know who's a true misogynist and who's too old to understand that what they say to women is wrong.

I'd tried to sleep, and had managed some but had jumped up ten minutes before the alarm to prep the food. Hoping that the diner manager wouldn't feel the same way about me and cut me — not earning money during a time I was used to earning, it made me twitchy — I'd slathered as much makeup over my nose and under my eyes as I could. And luckily, one of the other servers had called in sick, so they had to let me stay.

I'd fended off plenty of growly regulars making threats about "the asshole who did that to you, sweetheart. Just give me his name. I'll find him". Floating around on a bubble of anticipation over having Trent in my space again, I'd waved them off, poured the coffee, slung the breakfasts, and now was home, chewing on my lip and wondering if he'd like the meal I'd prepared.

Too bad if he doesn't. Right?

Right.

I took a quick shower, taking special care to wash the diner smell out of my hair. While I was shaving my legs, I noted that I had neglected my usual bikini wax regimen. When you don't pay a lot of attention to yourself down there, it's something that gets left behind in the daily rush to make a living and not make waves, or be noticed by too many people. I stood under the cooling, weak stream of water, pondering the general state of unkempt fuzziness.

I made a few swipes at it around the edges, wondering why in the hell I was even bothering. I had no intention of letting *El Guapo* near my furry girl bits today, if ever.

Liar, liar, fuzzy pants on fire. At least tell the truth to your own sorry self.

I climbed out, shivering as the water had gone totally cold by the time I'd made a dent in the fur barrier. Even as I cursed myself while doing it, I found my manicure scissors and did a bit of extremely careful clipping at the longest pieces, making a mental appointment at the waxer Evelyn had told me about. "He uses the hard wax. You barely feel it."

"He?" I'd reared away from her, honestly horrified at the thought of a man waxing anywhere below my belly button.

"Yep." She'd patted my hand. "He's a true artist."

Fine, I thought, as I flushed the pubes down the toilet. *I'll visit the man and let him clean up the chaos down there. Maybe. Depending.*

I slathered on my favorite lotion, leaving a mild, fresh floral scent on my skin. I never wore cologne—couldn't stand it actually. But I did like to smell clean. After pondering the clothing options for so long I got mad at myself for acting stupid, I grabbed a pair of dark blue jeans and my lucky Real Madrid jersey. A few waves with the blow dryer and enough makeup so my beat-up face wasn't too scary—he'd seen me at my worst after all—and I declared myself primped.

When I checked the time, the rush of anxiety over this whole, misguided thing almost knocked me into the wall. But I had food to prep so I let that steady me for the next half hour.

Limes—cut.

Onions—diced.

Cilantro—ditto.

Meat—perfectly spiced and shredded.

Tortillas—waiting in the oven to be warmed.

Soup—simmering.

I pondered the beer options I'd purchased, decided it would have to do and sat down to wait.

One p.m. came and went, as did one-fifteen. When the numbers on my phone approached one-thirty, the doorbell rang, making me jump up and run to the door, pulse racing so fast I felt faint. "You're late," I called through the door. "I hate it when people are late."

"I have a note. I swear it. Please let me in."

"I don't know…." I leaned against the door, willing my heartbeat to slow.

"Have you ever had to ride herd on a teenager?"

I frowned and peeked through the peephole. Until that minute, I'd forgotten Evelyn's drunken complaint about Trent's baggage. "No, can't say that I have." I unhooked the lock and opened the door, keeping it half closed so I could determine his mood. He sounded not so great, to be honest. My innate need to help was lurching well ahead of my compulsion to keep him at a safe arm's length.

As usual, he looked devastating. Today his no doubt perfect bod was clad in dark jeans and a plain black T-shirt. Nothing more was needed to highlight the width of his shoulders, the firm terrain of his torso, the bulky strength in his upper arms. "I'm sorry. Come in." I opened the door all the way and stepped back. He brushed my cheek with his lips, which made me sway on my feet a second, before putting a bottle of Patrón on the counter, alongside a riotous bouquet of summer flowers.

"Pretty," I said, picking them up and reaching for the single vase I owned. "Thank you."

As I arranged them, he stood, tapping his fingertips on the Formica, his stress and anger coming off him in near-visible waves. "There," I said, putting the vase next to the expensive bottle of hooch. "I'll handle this too." I put it in the freezer, for later. Maybe. "Hungry?" I gestured at the spread I'd made.

He glanced at it, then at me, then he turned away and stuffed his fingers into his jeans pockets. Confused, and getting a tad concerned, I stepped out from behind the counter and put my hand on his arm. He flinched, then sighed. "I'm sorry, Melody. I…I may not be the best company today."

"Well, you have to at least eat. I've been up since four a.m. making this, so it would be completely rude not to." I turned him gently and tugged him into the small kitchen space, put a plate in his hand and plunked a tortilla on it. He eyed the buffet and his smile appeared, warming my heart. "Go on. There's the meat." I pointed to the slow cooker.

I made myself turn away from him so I wouldn't get caught drooling or with my stupid tongue hanging out as he did such an innocuous thing as making a couple of tacos.

"Hey, where's the cheese?" He dropped a dollop of guacamole on top of the salsa he'd put on the meat and onions.

"No cheese. These are authentic, *Guapo*. Only Anglos think an overpriced, overstuffed burrito from a fake fast-food place is how you're supposed to eat these things."

He rolled his eyes, then stuck his finger in the guac before putting it in his mouth. I watched, mesmerized by his full, perfect, lips. "Damn, this is good."

"I know that." I smacked his arm, embarrassed by my need to touch him. "Go sit. I'll bring the soup. What beer do you want?"

"Something like a pilsner if you have it."

"Of course." I ladled up two small bowls of black bean soup, sprinkled cilantro and squeezed lime juice over each. I set them on the table in front of him then grabbed two local pilsners from the fridge and poured them into pint glasses.

"Cheers," I said, handing him one and holding my glass out. My heartbeat had calmed a little, as I'd distracted myself with making him happy or at least less worked-up over whatever was going on with his kid.

His smile widened, as if he'd only just now realized what was going on. "Cheers," he said, touching his glass to mine.

We drank. I sat, leaving plenty of air between us.

I took a few spoonfuls of my soup, watching him tear into the tacos like a hungry lion. Which made me happy. And, perversely, horny—a sensation I'd avoided, shut down, cut off or otherwise ignored for the better part of fifteen years.

A shiver shot down my spine, nestling in the small of my back and making me shift in my seat.

He grabbed the remote and handed it to me between bites.

"Well? I thought I was getting subjected to that horrible game."

I took the remote, stuck my tongue out at him and clicked on the telly. The match flickered on after a few seconds.

"Ah, right," he said, sipping his beer, then tucking into the soup. "The pretty boys game."

"Damn straight," I said, taking a bite of my own *carnitas* creation. Pretty damn good if I say so myself. "These men are fine."

"*Guapo?*" He raised a dark eyebrow at me, which intensified the heat gathering in areas of my body I'd forgotten I even had.

"No. They're too *prima donna* to be truly *guapo.*"

"Good. I like that word being reserved for me." He stood. "I need another one of those amazing tacos. And you're right. I hardly miss the cheese."

"Of course I'm right." I winked at him, then felt my face flush so hot I put my hand to my cheek.

We sat in companionable silence, regarding the game and eating for a while. As we leaned back, our feet up on the table, finishing our second beers, the match got more intense. At one point I leapt up and started cursing a stream of Spanish at the official.

"Calm down, already. What happened?" Trent asked, amusement on his face.

"That *hijo de puta* claimed offsides and called back that goal! Are you blind? *Mierda!*"

I flopped back onto the couch, this time so close our thighs brushed together when I propped my feet back on the table.

"Offsides, eh?" Trent put his glass to his lips and eyed me over the rim. "I have no idea what that means, at least in this game."

I shoved our plates aside, grabbed the salt and pepper shakers and the empty beer bottles and attempted to explain it. After ten utterly frustrating minutes, I gave up and threw my napkin at his face after he asked one more stupid question. "*Mierda! El burro sabe mas que te!*"

He leaned back in mock horror. "Did you just call me a burro? Is that like an ass?"

I dissolved into giggles at the look on his face. "*¡Mira qué cabrón!* There, I just called you a smartass."

"Neat," he said, grinning widely. We stared at each other for a few seconds too long, then both turned to the match.

"For the record, I did say a burro was smarter than you."

"Ah, of course," he said, getting up and stretching right in front of me. I swallowed hard and made myself not look at his ass. When he turned around again, his face had gone pensive. "Your poor, beautiful face," he said, out of the clear blue. "It's all I can do to look at you and not run out of here and kill that motherfucker."

I blinked fast, covered by grabbing my beer and totally missed my mouth. A dollop of the brew landed right on my best Real jersey. I stared down at it in horror. Trent chuckled. I glared up at him, daring him to say anything. He tried to stop laughing, but that made it worse. By the time I'd gotten up for a towel and maybe a shot of that tequila, he was practically rolling around on the floor in hysterics.

"Are you quite finished?" I asked, brushing at the stain, my face so hot I could have warmed a whole house in the middle of winter. I'd kept my back to him, the tall counter between us. Mortification was making my vision blur. Or was that tears? Shit, I'd never get this right. I was ruined. Ruined for relationships with real men, anyway. I whirled around to tell him to take his funny bone and get the fuck out of my apartment.

"I think…oh…"

He was there, in front of me, too close for it to be in any way considered casual. His broad, black-cotton-covered chest filled my vision. His scent—a clean, fresh, outdoorsy odor—filled my nose. His voice—deep and musical—filled my soul.

"Melody," he said, as he took my hands in his and brought them to his lips. *Mi Dios*, those lips! He kissed each one of my knuckles softly, keeping his eyes on mine. Then he turned my hands over and pressed his lips to first one, then the other of my palms.

"Trent," I whispered, my mind awash with images and sensations, all of them good for a change.

"Sh," he whispered, placing my hands on his shoulders, then sliding his hands around to the small of my back. "Sh, no talking." His smile lit up my entire universe — corny, but true and I'm not ashamed to admit it. "I have wanted to kiss you since I saw you across that diner."

"When… Oh, right," I said, my voice breaking at the end like a silly virginal teenager's.

Surely he won't want me, when he finds out I'm spoiled goods. Surely he won't…Surely he has got to be the best kisser in the entire known universe.

I sighed and melded my body against his as he slanted those amazing lips over mine, caressing, teasing, licking my lips with his tongue then breaching to explore the inside of my mouth.

I honestly felt as if I were on a cloud, up in the air, weightless, brainless to be certain. But no matter. I was being kissed by a god among men. And although I was sure it wouldn't last I was determined to enjoy it.

He broke our contact, and his hands moved up my back and into my hair, tangling there, until one hand cradled my cheek and other remained wrapped up behind my head. "This is okay?"

"Yes," I breathed, nodding. "It's…very nice."

His grin turned slightly wicked. "Just nice? I need to up my game."

He pressed me back against the counter and dove in again, owning me with those lips, that tongue, his hands, which remained innocent but at the same time drove me wild with lust. He tugged my hair, forcing my head back as his lips found my jaw, then my neck, then my shoulder. I could hear my heartbeat in my ears. Sensed my breathing getting raspy as he licked and nibbled and teased his way around to the other side of my neck, ending with a quick bite on my earlobe.

"*Mi Dios*," I muttered again. I could sense my nipples — for the first time in my life I could say this — straining against the inside of my bra. I was warm all over and a serious melty sensation was forming low in my stomach. "Ah, *guapo*, don't stop." I wrapped my arms around his neck, trailing my fingertips along the bare skin of his scalp. I saw the goosebumps raise there, and felt him shudder as his lips found mine once more. He groaned into my mouth as our tongues met, and clashed, our teeth clicking together in an unpracticed, amateur way. He broke from me, his breathing coming in ragged gasps, like mine.

"You taste like chocolate and cinnamon," he whispered in my ear. "I love it."

I sighed and the melty sensation traveled in a southerly direction, making me want to spread my legs, to feel his touch there. An alarm clanged in my head, replacing the woozy, lusty, fogginess. I fought it. God help me I did, but all of a sudden all I smelled was old beer, saltiness, mildew and rot. Gagging, I pushed Trent away, hand over my mouth. He stood there, his hands out as if he were still holding me close.

Tears clouded my eyes as I shoved past him, running for the bathroom, desiring nothing but escape. And hating myself the whole time for being such a complete loser. As I rounded the corner of my bed and was about to slam the bathroom door behind me, a hand shot out, denying me.

"Melody, what the hell? Did I hurt you?"

Hand still clapped over my mouth, I shook my head, backing myself into the corner. He loomed over me, but instead of being afraid, I felt soothed. My hair flew as I kept shaking my head, speechless with embarrassment. I took a breath as he moved my hand away from my mouth.

"Come on," he said, his musical, perfect voice filling me again, making me feel safe. "Let's go sit. That went too fast. I thought so too."

"No…I mean. Yes. *Dios*. I'm such a loser."

"Hardly," he said, kissing my hand, then tucking it into his elbow. "Let's put a dent in that tequila, *mamacita*." He waggled his dark eyebrows at me.

"Don't call me that. It's demeaning." I leaned into his shoulder, sucking in greedy breaths of him, forcing out the old, scary, nasty odors that had haunted me for years.

"What should I call you then?" He guided me to the couch, eased me down, pressed a soft kiss to my forehead then headed back to the kitchen. "What's the best word to go with what you call me?" He grabbed the limes and found some small glasses.

"I don't know. *Bella*? It means beauty." I touched my nose. "I'm hardly that anymore."

"Okay, that'll do for now. I'll figure out something better later."

"You could also go with *angelita*. Or even *querida*."

"I like those. But I like how you say them more."

He popped the cork on the expensive bottle, poured a couple of hits and handed me a lime wedge. "Bottoms up," he said, his eyes bright. I held up my glass.

"'*¡Salud!*' you mean."

"Yeah, that." He grabbed my hand, licked the soft spot between my thumb and forefinger, sprinkled salt there, then licked it again, took a drink and squeezed the lime into his mouth. "Your turn," he said, holding out his hand.

I took it, touched my tongue to his skin, closing my eyes at the sensation. I salted it, licked it, drank and squeezed the lime. The booze suffused my entire body. Or, more likely, the fact that I had tasted the skin of his hand and it was like nectar. I leaned away from him, smiling, trying not to feel self-conscious about my busted-up face.

"I'm sorry," I finally said. "I didn't mean to make such a…such a fuss, before."

His arm had been draped across the back of the couch, so he reached out a finger and touched my cheek, tucked my hair behind my ear, and sighed. "I didn't want to rush, so

I don't mind taking it slow. That's new to me, to be honest with you. I'm game."

I looked down at my lap. "It's not that, exactly."

He tilted my chin up so I had to meet his eyes. "Then tell me what, exactly, that it is." His voice had dropped lower, taken on an odd sort of edge. It made me sit up straighter, and sent a shot of something equally odd through my nervous system. Courage? Maybe.

"I was raped when I was eighteen. Gang raped. By a bunch of boys I thought were my friends. After I got drunk with a bunch of girls I thought liked me but who set me up for the whole thing."

Trent leaned away from me, crossing his arms. His jaw clenched in that way I'd noticed before.

"I was…well, it was bad. I was passed out at the end. I have no idea how…" My throat clicked with anxiety. "How many of them…did it to me. My mother found me. She took me home, put me to bed and made me promise I wouldn't ever tell anyone what had happened. I hid in my house for weeks, waiting for the bruises and shit to heal." I touched my nose. "I've had one of these before too." Taking a deep breath, bolstered by him somehow, I plowed onward. "That was the summer before college, so luckily I never had to see them again. I went to Grand Valley," I said, naming the small university here in town. "On academic scholarship. Got my degree in business." I bit my lip and looked away.

His silence in the face of my confession spoke volumes. I stood and headed for the kitchen. "You don't want any of this. I'm a mess. You have your own issues. What with the teenager and all." I started putting the food away, blinded by tears. Always with the stupid tears.

Warm hands on my shoulders made me shiver and lean back, finding him there, his strong, comforting form. He wrapped his arms around me and held me, how long I couldn't even say it felt so amazing to be treasured this way.

"What happened after college?" he asked, still holding me tight from behind.

"I got a job. A pretty good one, considering. At a bank, in mergers and acquisitions. I had to buy a whole new wardrobe." I sighed and closed my eyes, unwilling to revisit this, but knowing full well I had to. Trent stayed silent, letting me proceed at my own pace. "I'd been there three years. Was in line for a promotion to manager. I loved it—every power-suited, high-heeled, salad-for-lunch moment of it." I let myself slump into him more, unsure if I could finish.

I felt his lips on my hair. His arms tightened. "Go on, Melody. You can trust me."

I took a shuddery breath.

Trust. What a concept.

I put my hands on the counter, pressing down as if holding myself up. "My b-b-b-boss called me into his office, told me we had an offsite, where we'd talk about how things were going to change around the office. I believed him, of course. I'm stupid that way."

"You're not stupid."

"Whatever. So, like a dummy, I agreed to meet him, thinking it would be a bunch of us, you know, for a legit offsite. But all I saw was him, sitting at a table in the hotel bar. I sat, let him buy me a drink. Then two drinks. He… uh…oh God, Trent. I can't."

"I want it all, Melody. Give it to me. Share it. It will help." His lips were at my ear. "I promise."

I froze. I smelled him—his overpriced cologne, the booze on his breath. I felt the rasp of his stubble on my face. His disgusting tongue practically down my throat.

"He…he…he told me that I had to do it. That I'd only gotten hired to fulfill their minority quotient. That I wasn't any good but I looked good in my skirt. That I…had to let him fuck me. Or I'd get fired."

I heard Trent suck in a breath. Horrified that I'd actually told him, much less that I'd actually believed the sorry asshole, I tried to disentangle from him. But he wouldn't let me go.

"Afterward, he locked me in the bathroom without my clothes for the night. Then…before he'd let me leave I had to…suck his dick. Now do you believe me when I say I'm a fucked-up mess? That you don't need my crap in your life? Jesus. Let go of me."

I shoved his arms off me and turned around, gripping the counter behind me. Tears were pouring down my face, and my nose was stopped up and hurt like a bitch. "God, I'm gross. Get off me." I pushed his chest. He didn't budge. He grabbed a paper towel and held it under my nose.

"Blow."

I shook my head.

"Blow, god damn it."

I blew.

"That's good." He tossed it into the trash, got another one, held it under warm water and wiped my face. "That's better." He tossed that one too, then pulled me into his arms. "I'm so sorry all that happened to you, *bella*." His voice caressed the word in a way that made he all shivery again. "My poor, sweet *bella*."

I leaned into his chest, wrapped my arms around his waist, filling my brain with his smell, willing it to cancel out all the others that had haunted me for so long.

Chapter Nine

Trent's brain was spinning with so many emotions, he'd need months so sort through them all. Anger, of course. But pity. And disappointment with his fellow man. But mostly, a strong urge to sit with Melody in his arms, holding her close until the evil in her past no longer haunted her.

Of course, there was the lust. It was like the lingering, sharp smell after a gunshot. He tasted it on his tongue. And he had no idea what to do about it.

Melody was sniffling into his chest. They stood in her miniscule kitchen for a solid five minutes, while she calmed and he decided what to do. "Listen," he said, tilting her face up and swiping the tears with his thumbs. "Listen to me." She nodded, keeping her gaze on his. "I...I like you a lot. And I want to help you. Will you let me? Take care of you?"

She frowned. He groaned and stepped away. "Don't misunderstand me on purpose. Not now. I don't mean that I'm going to take over your life or be a sexist asshole."

"I didn't..."

"Yes, you did," he said. "But try to understand me. I'm... I have the sort of personality that needs to be in charge. I mean, mostly in the bedroom." Her lips turned up ever so slightly. He chuckled. "But that's only part of it. And we aren't there yet." He tucked her hair back behind her ears. "Why don't we start with this—you trusting me with your past. With all the bad stuff." He turned to the freezer. "I saw ice cream. I say we eat some."

She nodded again, reaching for some spoons.

He grabbed her hand. "You only need one spoon. I'm going to feed you." Her beautiful face flushed. He tried to control himself, but it took everything he had.

They sat on the couch, her feet tucked under his thighs. He clicked around until he found a real football game, then they shared the remains of a pint of double chocolate chip, one bite for her, one for him until it was gone. Her lips were so luscious, he thought as she took the last bite from the spoon. He could not wait to kiss them again. Among other things.

But he was okay with going slow. She had to learn to trust him. And he would not do anything more with or to her until she did.

A sense of contentment suffused him as she snuggled into his side, pretending to listen to his explanation of the American style of football. When he sensed that she'd fallen asleep, he tugged her around so she was lying across his lap. He pulled the blanket down off the back of the couch and covered her, then spent a half hour indulging in a fantasy by threading his fingers through the silky black strands of her hair.

At one point, he dozed, jerking awake when he realized Melody wasn't lying on him anymore. The TV was off. The room was dark. He rubbed his eyes as his brain caught up with his body. "Melody?"

He heard a shuffling noise from the back of her space. "Where'd you go?" Something in the air put him on edge. His skin prickled. The small hairs on his arms seemed to tingle. He rose slowly, his brain switching gears, moving into a space he understood, but wanted to avoid for now.

He smelled her before he saw her. That incredible taste he'd detected on her skin that had indeed been a heady combination of rich chocolate and exotic cinnamon was now swirling around him, wrapping him up, forcing him forward. "*Bella*," he whispered.

"*Si*," she answered, stepping into a shaft of light that pierced the blinds at the sliding glass door. Trent had seen his fair share of beautiful women. He'd seen them in various stages of dress, undress and everything in between. He actually had developed a preference, and one he fully acknowledged was an awful, sexist throwback that involved high heels, garter belts, silk stockings and leather collars.

But the vision before him drove pretty much every single thought from his head. Including the ones he'd been pondering before he fell asleep — the ones about going slow.

Melody — his Melody — stood before him wearing nothing but a smile. He swallowed past the stricture in his throat and took a step forward, taking her hand and pulling her closer. She moved easily, comfortable with her nudity in a way that made him dizzy. "Turn," he whispered. "Please."

She let go of his hand and turned slowly, looking over her shoulder at him as she did it. Her deep brown eyes shone. Her lips were wet, parted slightly, as if she couldn't catch her breath. Which made sense, as he couldn't either.

He sat back on the couch before he fell down, leaving her in the middle of the floor. As if she understood that she should wait until he said anything more.

No. No. No. No. This is not how you should proceed with her. You aren't interested in seeing how far she'll go with you.

He ran a hand down his face, around the back of his neck, tugged at the neck of his shirt. But he could not take his eyes off her, God help him. He'd developed enough control over himself that he could sit and do nothing more than observe her. But the control he'd established over other parts of his body had flown straight out of the window. His cock was ramrod hard. His balls tight, as if in a pre-orgasm state. It hurt like hell, trapped behind the zipper of his jeans. But he let if hurt. He needed to feel the pain. It kept him focused.

She stood stock still, letting him look to his heart's content. Her breasts were firm, high, tipped with nipples that resembled the world's most perfect chocolate morsels. Her hips flared out from her waist in a way that briefly reminded him of Evelyn's figure. But Melody was more compact, less showy in her beauty.

He took a long, deep, hopefully calming breath as he let

his gaze drop to her belly — slightly rounded, perfect in its imperfection. Her thighs were lean, her calves shapely. Her feet were small, with deep red toenails. Somewhat clinically, he noted that her pussy was not fully waxed. He'd not seen actual bush in a while. The sight — that of a woman's body, not of some fake pre-adolescent's — made a drop of sweat form on his temple.

"Why?" he asked, knowing she'd understand the question.

"Because I want you to make love to me." Her voice, with its lilting accent, hit him right in the libido. The pain in his crotch increased, making him grunt and lean forward. She took the few steps between them, took the hand he had gripping one knee and put it on her hip.

"No," he said, jerking away from her. "I won't."

Dude, what the hell? Yes. You will. You will get in there now.

He winced, ignoring his lizard brain as well as he could.

"Please, Trent," she said, pulling him up to standing as his vision dimmed around the edges. The deep bronze hue of her skin was all he saw now. All he ever wanted to see, for the rest of his damn life. "I need this."

"I can't... I'm not..." He heard himself stammering, felt his pulse racing so fast it alarmed him.

"Yes, you are. And you can."

See? She agrees with me. Go. Now. Take her to bed and show her how a real man treats women.

He let her pull him back to where her bed waited for them, a place he'd avoided contemplating all afternoon on purpose.

Slow, Hettinger. And with extreme control. Let her set the pace.

He licked his lips when she sat on the edge of the bed and reached for his belt.

"No. Not yet, *querida. Eres la mujer de mis sueños. Por mis ojos eres la mujer más guapa en el mundo.*"

Melody froze. Trent shrugged. "What? I know my way around a Spanish language podcast. And it's true. You are the woman of my dreams. In my eyes, you are the most beautiful woman in the world."

She raised an eyebrow. Trent pulled her back up to her feet. Keeping his hands firmly on her upper arms, ignoring the firm tips of her breasts that brushed his T-shirt, he used his strongest tone, trying to impart his real meaning. "If I do this, *angelita*. If we make love the way I want to right now, you have to understand something."

She nodded, putting her cool palm alongside his burning hot face. He covered it with his hand, closed his eyes and let himself take a deep breath of her—that intoxicating scent that he was within moments of being completely addicted to. Her hand slid down his neck, his chest and lower, making him shiver so violently he stumbled. This was beyond weird. He, Trent Hettinger, alpha male, Master Dominant, did not feel this way about anyone.

He opened his eyes and looked at her, as something in him seemed to slide into place. "You scare me, *bella*. But I need to... I want to..."

"Sh..." she said, pressing herself against him, arms up and around his neck, breasts smashed into his chest. "No more talking."

Chapter Ten

I'll be the first to admit that I have no idea what possessed me. I woke up, lying across Trent's lap. The TV was blaring away. The remains of our dessert pint of ice cream melting on the table. The tequila bottle and glasses alongside it.

Quivering with something I didn't understand, I got up, leaving the blanket over his lap. The booze bottle tempted, so I grabbed it and took another quick drink straight from it as the tingly sensations I'd woken with formulated into a plan.

Before I could talk myself out of it, I tiptoed back to the bathroom, stripped out of my clothes, including the possibly ruined Real Madrid jersey. Taking a moment to study myself in the mirror, I realized that, for the first time in my almost thirty years of life, I wanted a man. I wanted him to kiss me. To touch me. To make love to me. Yes…to fuck me. To drive out the demons that had hovered around me for so many awful years. Years I'd pretended that I was normal.

I bit my lip and cupped my heavy breasts in both hands. My nipples were so hard they hurt. I brushed my fingers over them, shivering at the sensation that hit me between my legs. Without a thought in my head, I wandered out to the bedroom, waiting, second-guessing, until I heard him. His beautiful voice. Calling my name.

And now, I was the one who had to make the first move, which made me feel even better about this crazy decision I'd made. At last, our lips met, his tongue teased, then got forceful, as I sensed something in him rise and meet me in a way that went beyond our bodies. Without breaking our kiss, he eased me back onto the bed, his hands now stroking my breasts, his fingers teasing my nipples.

The bolt of near pain hit me hard, making my back arch. He pulled away, concern in his odd-colored eyes. "No, no, please. I liked it. I just... Don't...oh... *Mi Dios.*"

He grinned and pushed me all the way back and lowered his face to my breasts. Lips. Tongue. Teeth. Fingers. All combined to drive me insane. I sensed my hips moving in a way that embarrassed me but that I couldn't stop. All the pain and pleasure in the world seemed to be centered in my nipples, and there was a line of nerves that connected them to my pussy. I spread my legs. Made strange sounds deep in my throat as he kept stroking, licking, sucking.

"Oh. I... It's..."

"Sh, *mi amor*," he whispered, letting his lips trail up my neck until he kissed me again, in that way he had, that shut out the world and made me want to cry. I clutched at him, trying to pull him over on top of me. My body needed more. It required a connection.

His hand dropped to my stomach, teasing me in little circles with his fingertips. My hips thrust up as he placed tiny kisses down my neck. I sensed myself writhing, forcing parts of my body closer to him. Driving out the voice that tried to interrupt my pleasure, to call me a slut, a whore and all the things I'd been called during all my previous experiences with sex, I grabbed his hand and shoved it between my legs. I felt his smile against my skin, which was now slick with sweat.

"*Quiero. Quiero que estés dentro de mi. Por favor. Mi...*"

Trent propped himself on his elbow next to me, and moved his hand back to my stomach. "Did you just say what I think you said?" His teeth grazed my earlobe. That hand I wanted elsewhere tickled its way up my torso and tweaked my nipple, making me gasp.

"Stop teasing me," I demanded. "I need..."

"I know what you need, *bella*," he whispered. "Relax. Let me work. Okay? Trust me."

I nodded.

"Now lie back, and lift your arms up over your head."

A shiver of anticipation joined all the other many shivers running through me. He was kinky, Evelyn had said. Kinky. I wasn't sure how I felt about that.

As if reading my mind, he smiled and kissed me gently, softly, without any rush or urgency. His hands cradled my face, slid into my hair. And any fear or worry flew from my mind. He kissed his way down my neck again, gave each of my nipples ample attention, making my hips thrust up again. *Shameless*.

Yes. Totally.

To my surprise, he began to kiss his way down my stomach, tickling me, shocking me, tantalizing me in ways I'd never felt in my sorry life. He was murmuring something in that musical voice of his. He shifted so he was on the floor, between my legs, which were already spread wide. The pulsing sensation between my legs got stronger, more urgent as his mouth moved across the mound of my hair. Fingers gripped my hips, digging in hard, pulling me down the bed, toward his face.

"Oh, no. I…can't."

"Yes, you can," he whispered. But instead of doing what I thought he was going to do, he bent one of my knees, gripped my foot, straightened my leg up and started kissing — starting at my instep, working his way down my ankle, spending some time sucking the skin behind my knee. I gripped the bed cover, trying to understand what was happening to my body.

I hurt, but I was also zinging with something strange. His lips moved again. He bent my leg up to my chest, then, of all things, sucked my big toe into his mouth. I watched him, fascinated by the many sensations slipping and sliding around inside me, all over me. He let go of my toe. His gaze met mine. I reached out to stroke his head, loving the soft skin under my fingertips. He let go of that leg and did the same thing with my other one, drawing out the extreme pleasure—pulling it like a bit of yarn he'd found on a sweater, tugging it until it lay between us, connecting us.

This time, after bestowing all that odd, yet incredible oral attention to the skin behind my knee, he kept going, nipping at the back of my thigh. Then, without warning, he tossed my leg over his shoulder and dove between my legs.

"*Ay! Papi!*" I yelped when his lips touched me in a place that made actual fireworks explode behind my closed eyelids. He had some part of me in his mouth and was sucking it. I was shoving myself up and into his face. My fingertips were dug into his scalp. When it happened, I screamed, I'm embarrassed to say. But at that moment, everything in me was focused between my legs, where my man was showing me what heaven looked like.

"Oh. Oh…oh…" My voice came from far away as my body seemed to settle back into itself. He stayed down between my legs, riding out my first orgasm ever. Finally, I lay gasping for breath, arms and legs spread. He rose, his smile wide. His lips slick. I refused to let embarrassment ruin this for me. Because I was not done. Not by half.

"Please tell me you didn't call me your daddy," he said, flopping back down onto his side with a small wince.

"It's a Spanish thing, *mi amor*." I stroked his cheek, then put my fingertips to my lips, tasting the delicious tang of his sweat. "I don't think you're my daddy, don't worry." I rose on my elbow mirroring him, and hooking my leg over his hips. "But you are my *papi* now, *guapo*. Deal with it."

Face pensive, he took a lock of my hair and put it to his lips. "I love everything about you," he said, his voice rough. "I don't believe in soulmates. But I think I may change my mind."

"Sweet talker," I said. But something in my chest expanded at his words.

"Too soon?" He smiled.

"Probably." I wanted to touch him, to stroke his flesh, to hold his cock in my hand. But I was frozen with shyness all of a sudden. "Thank you," I said, putting my fingers to his lips.

"Oh, *mi angelito*, that is only the beginning."

"Good," I said as my fingers touched his neck. They were shaking, which made me feel like a stupid fool. He grabbed my hand, kissed my knuckles and pushed my shoulder until I was on my back again.

"Would you like more?"

"I… I want to…touch you." He stood between my spread knees, still fully dressed. It was too dark for me to see much but I noted when his hand dropped to his belt. My mouth actually watered right then, which shocked me almost more than the force and beauty of my first orgasm.

"Not sure I'm ready for that, *bella*," he said, even as he lifted his shirt up and off. "But I'll muscle my way through it." The light from a full moon hit the side of his face, giving me a sense of how he really felt. His eyes gave him away every time. They were wide, shining, a bit wary. And I loved him for it.

He unbuckled, unzipped, pushed his jeans down. He stood there, looking sheepish in a way that made my heart pound. This man was waiting, holding back, for me. I sat up fast and yanked his underwear down—or I tried to. They got hung up for a few seconds, which made him chuckle and me horrified at my rookie move.

But finally, he was naked. And I could see he was exactly as I'd imagined him. Defined chest muscles, an honest-to-God six-pack. And his cock… I exhaled as I sat up, reaching for him.

I'd seen a penis before. I'd felt what it could do, ripping me from innocence forever. I'd had one in my mouth, as I'd told him. It had gagged me, made me cry and sickened me.

A wave of terror engulfed me as I observed this most intimate part of him. He stood still, not saying a word. Letting me draw my own conclusions, make my own moves. I hesitated, closing my eyes and reminding myself that this was Trent. This was the kind, gentle, perfect man who'd just bestowed a mind-bending climax on me.

He tilted my chin up so I had to meet his eyes. "We don't have to take this step yet, *angelita*. If you're not ready."

I blinked, parsing my emotions. I closed my eyes and felt something come roaring up and out of the mire of fear and disgust I'd inhabited relative to my own sexuality. I wanted this. I wanted him. I would have him—over and over again. This woman—the true Melody—had been cowering inside me for years. Trent had found her, pulled her from her hiding place. She took over my mind, my body, most specifically my hand, which rose again. My fingers wrapped around the amazing thickness of Trent's cock.

He sucked in a breath at my touch. I—and she, my new self—observed a bead of fluid form in the slit at the top. I took a breath, sucking in the essence of him—of his raw, masculinity. Time slowed to a crawl as I leaned forward, wanting to taste him. The new Melody urged me on. She was a healthy, sexual creature and we had a lot of time to make up for.

"No," Trent whispered as my tongue touched the tiny pearl of fluid.

"Yes," I—and she—whispered back. "It's fine," I said, before lowering my lips over the beautiful, most intimate part of him I held in my hand. His groan was low and loud and seemed to come from somewhere deep in his chest. His fingers twined in my hair. His hips thrust forward. I slid my lips as far down as I could, then retreated, loving the taste and feel of him.

I—me—because I was this new woman now. She and I had become one, finally. Thanks to Trent. I owed him so much. It was time for a bit of payback. I looked up at him as I teased the edges of the head. He was staring down at me, sweat beaded up on his face. My body was rising again, filling with blood, not unlike his erection.

I had so much to learn, I thought as I slid my fingers underneath his heavy balls. And I couldn't wait to get started.

Chapter Eleven

Trent didn't know what was worse — needing to come so badly he could taste it, or realizing he was about to come in her mouth. He wanted to come somewhere else. But her sweet, inexperienced lips and fingers were making him wild. His hips pumped forward, as he gripped her hair, grunting with the effort of holding back.

Then, she did it, shocking him to his core. The sensation of the head of his dick bumping up against the back of her throat, then actually entering it made his eyes open wide as his brain went into reflex mode, releasing the tight hold he'd kept. He cried out, barely hearing it but feeling every sweet pulse deep in his balls. But he held some back, having trained himself how to do that — so he could put his cock where he wanted it and finish. She slid her lips up and off his dick which sent him stumbling backward.

"Wait," he said, reaching down to tug the condom from his jeans pocket. He never went anywhere without one. Not that he did not love his daughter, but he had zero intention of having any more like her. Melody grinned as he rolled the thing down his cock. He ran a shaking finger down her cheek and tilted her chin up so he could look into her eyes.

She smiled, rising from the bed like a Latina Venus. *His* Venus. *His* Goddess. He grinned and launched himself forward with a low growl — a sound he didn't think he'd ever made before. He shoved his tongue into her mouth, gripped her ass, turned them and dropped back onto the bed. He tasted his cum on her lips, which mingled with the delicious taste of her that he doubted that he'd ever get enough of as she straddled his hips.

"Oh, *Mi Dios*," she gasped into his mouth.

"Call me *Papi* again, *bella*."

She rose, her hands on his chest, her dark eyes shining. *"Quiero que me des duro hoy, Papi,"* she whispered, shifting her hips. Her full, now slightly swollen lips parted. He held back, loving the sweet sensation of her clit, full and plump, rubbing against the head of his dick. He'd gone out of his way in the last few days to listen to Spanish language recordings. And had sought out some fairly specific terms and phrases.

"Oh I plan on it, *angelita*," he said, yanking her down so he could suck one of her huge, sensitive nipples into his mouth, roll it around in tongue. She sighed and pressed her clit harder against him. She was hot and wet and ready for him. But he wanted to make this a night she'd never forget. So he started reciting baseball stats in his head even as he sucked one of her nipples and pinched the other one, making her writhe harder on top of him. When her hips angled in such a way that he found himself entering her body, he gasped and dropped back on the pillow, gripping her thighs.

"I need to finish, *mi hermosa diosa*," he said, as his brain went into serious shut down mode. He felt her hand on the top of his head, surprising him with how sexy it felt to have her soft, teasing fingertips along his bare scalp. She ground down, taking him deep inside her, yanking him toward climax. Her pussy gripped him so tight it hurt. And he loved it. "Roll your hips," he said, clenching his jaw with the stress of not blowing, wanting to feel her orgasm on his dick first.

"I... I'm going to... I don't know..."

"Roll your hips, *mi diosa*," he said, pushing her up so he could cup her breasts. He was getting a sense of her triggers, her more sensitive spots. "Put one hand on my chest, the other one behind you and take whatever you need from me."

She moved faster in that position, and he felt it, smelled

her orgasm approaching, which caused his brain to fog over. He loved this, of course. What man didn't love to come inside a beautiful woman? But something felt different. Something scary was roaring up from a deep place inside his soul. "Don't hold back," he demanded, sensing her withdrawing, as if afraid of it too. "Don't you dare hold back from me, Melody. Give it to me. Give me all of it."

Her eyes were wide as she bucked and ground down on his body. He saw the tears forming in her eyes even as her walls tightened around his dick and a spasm inside her seized him, dragging them both into the bright light of a loud, glorious, climax.

Trent gripped her thighs as his hips thrust up, allowing himself the glorious release. Her mouth was open, but no sound was coming out of it. She shuddered from head to toe, even as her body kept a tight hold on him, pulsing over and over again.

Finally, a loud sound burst out of her, as if it had been trapped inside her somewhere. It was a beautiful sound – a cross between a sigh, a groan and a cry of pleasure. Trent had bestowed plenty of loud, wet orgasms on more women that he could even recall some days. And it had always been there, in the back of his brain, a point of pride and a reminder that he had purpose.

But now all that shit was gone, vanished, no longer important. Nothing was important anymore. He rose, keeping their bodies connected, and dragged her legs to either side of his hips. Her head was thrown back, exposing the long line of her neck to him. He pressed his lips to that delicious dip between her collarbones, and his palms into the small of her back as he rocked them, sensing his cock going even deeper into her body.

She draped her arms over his shoulders and raised her head. Her raven's-wing black hair was wild around her shining face. Her eyes were filled with tears. Her lips trembled. "I... I... I'm afraid," she said, even as her lips covered his and the small tip of her tongue breached his lips. He opened his mouth to her, opened his soul, opened his whole life to the beautiful creature in his arms.

He broke the kiss, brushed the tears off her face. "You never have to be afraid ever again, Melody."

Chapter Twelve

The nightmare approached, threatening and grumbly like a distant summer thunderstorm. I faced it, as I usually did. Head bowed, heart pounding, body tensed for the dream-memory of pain and humiliation. I waited, knowing that I'd get through it. Just like I'd gotten through the ugly actuality of it.

I raised my face to it. Wanting to move past it and get on with the dreamless part of my sleep.

But when I looked up, expecting to get slammed square in the brain with the odors, sights, sounds and sensations of that long-ago afternoon, all I saw, heard or felt was Trent.

In my dream, I blinked, trying to clear the fog in front of me, willing the evil to hit me. I deserved it, after all, acting like such a silly slut that afternoon. For trusting the shithead banker boss. I'd dressed in short skirts. Let my blouses gape open. Worn sky-high heels. What else did I expect from him?

The long years I'd spent after quitting the well-paying bank job, keeping my head down, trying to rebuild my own shattered psyche had meant years of reminding myself that I'd gotten exactly what I'd deserved. In the dream, I set my jaw, ready for the pain and horror, even wishing for it, in some sick and twisted way. It was all I'd known. All I had to anchor my sexual self.

I felt something on my arm, but I brushed it away. "Come on, god damn it," I yelled into the dream-fog. "Come and get me. I'm here. Yours for the taking. Hurry up. Get it over with." A loud, growling sound emerged from the swirl of mist around me. A face emerged. I glared at it, and stamped my foot. "Go away. You're not part of this. This is mine. I own it."

"Melody." The lips on the face moved, saying my name. "I'm here. Give it to me, *bella. Mi hermosa diosa.*"

"I can't," I yelled, my throat aching like it had for days after the gang rape. I had screamed. But that had seemed to make the boys want to hurt me even more. "I'm not your fucking goddess. I can't give it to you. It's horrible. I can't let you see it."

"You can. And you will. You already have, remember?" His kind, compelling eyes, softened. His full lips parted in a kind smile. "Come on. Come with me." His hand emerged from the fog. "Come with me, now."

"I won't," I said, backing away from him. "You won't want me. I'm ruined."

"I already have you, my love. Don't you know that?"

I forced myself to wake, gasping in the bright morning sunlight. My hands were balled into fists, gripping the soft fabric of my sheets. I shivered in the air-conditioned air, as sweat dried on my face. Terror slowly exited my consciousness, leaving behind a strange sensation of fullness. Followed closely by a distinct pain in some of my more intimate body parts.

Sounds and smells pierced my post-nightmare brain. Coffee. Bacon. Music. I blinked, clearing away the last fog of fear and rolled onto my side, curling into a shivery ball of naked skin. I hurt between my legs. My nipples stung. My lips felt swollen. But my heart was calm. I smiled, recalling the night. Remembering that odd but glorious feeling of finding myself — my true self — the pre-victim Melody that Trent had discovered and teased out of me.

With a sigh, I rolled onto my back, letting the sheet slip down to my waist. Every inch of my skin felt happy, tingly and satisfied. I bit my lip, my face flushed as the wash of recent memory filled my brain. Trent — his lips, hands, tongue. The way I'd wanted to taste him. How I had tasted him, pleasuring him, swallowing the head of his penis and making him climax.

I smelled the sex lingering in the room, then rolled and pressed my face to the pillow where he'd slept, sucking in huge lungsful of him. How in the world had I gotten here? Since when did I ever wake up happy, satisfied, dare I say still horny?

This was going to be fun, I decided, shoving aside thoughts of our age difference, among other things and getting to my feet. I limped to the bathroom, realizing just how sore I was between my legs, and took care of a few things including a quick clean up with a warm washcloth. There was some blood on the cloth so I kept cleaning myself until it disappeared.

I popped a few painkillers and ignored my still bruised face in the mirror, deciding to slip on my ratty robe at the last minute instead of putting on clothing. I didn't want anything touching me too tightly — because of the pain, yes. But also because I wanted my skin to stay exposed to the air, to relish this wonderful, after-a-night-of-lovemaking feeling.

"There she is," Trent declared as I wandered over to the kitchen where he stood in his jeans and nothing else. "Good morning, sleeping beauty."

I stared at the broad, muscular expanse of his back, wishing I had the nerve to walk over and wrap my arms around his waist and press my lips to his shoulder blades. But I held back, wary all of a sudden. He turned, brandishing a spatula. "I hope you like pancakes. It's my specialty."

I nodded, still speechless with wonder and a twinge of anxiety. His eyes narrowed at my expression. I turned away, seeking something to do with my hands. We had been so intimate. We had said and done things that went beyond this casual, morning-after scene. My pulse raced. My heartbeat thumped in my ears. I tried to pour a cup of coffee, but my shaking, stupid hands wouldn't cooperate and the mug crashed to the floor, shattering and sending hot liquid splashing everywhere, including onto my feet.

"Wait, don't move," Trent demanded, setting the spatula down and stepping over the mess. He scooped me up, tossing me over his shoulder like a sack of rice. I yelped in surprise, but the nearness of him, of his bare flesh, soothed me. When he dumped me onto the couch, I bit my tongue, hard.

"*Meirda!*" I covered my lips with one hand. "Ow."

"You're sort of a klutz, eh, *angelita*?" He kissed my cheek and reached back for a tissue. When he handed it to me, his eyes were soft. His face relaxed and happy. "Should have warned me."

"Then you wouldn't have come over for lunch…was that yesterday? Seems like a long time ago."

"Oh, you have your redeeming qualities." He winked. "Sit. Relax. I'll clean up your mess."

"No, no, I've got it." I tried to get up but he pressed me back.

"No. I'm taking care of you right now, okay? It's part of my thing. Some of which you haven't seen yet. But we'll talk more about that later?" His grin widened.

"Fine," I said, feeling like I could rip off his jeans and jump his bones with little more provocation than his musical, mildly erotic words. "May I please have coffee?"

"Yes, you may. Give me a few." He handed me the remote. "Here, go ogle some hot soccer man flesh. I'll let 'em fluff for me. I'm that confident."

"Fluff?" I blinked up at him, honestly confused.

He chuckled and ran his fingers across my lips. "Yes, *bella*. They will fluff you up, get you excited and ready for me. Then I will finish you and way better than any of those pseudo-athletes would ever do."

My face flushed so hot it made me gasp. "You are very bad," I said, loving how my body had gone from tingly to full-bore horny at his words.

"Guilty. Now, sit. Relax. I've got this."

"But…" I half-rose, then flopped back when he glared at me. My phone buzzed from the table, reminding me that

I'd gone for hours without checking it. I had a missed call and a half dozen texts, all from Evelyn.

I glanced over at Trent, who was indeed sweeping up the mess. I waited as directed while he wiped down the cabinets, poured me a fresh cup, added the perfect amount of milk to it because, of course he'd figured out how I preferred it. "*Gracias, guapo.*" I smiled up at him.

"My pleasure, *diosa*. Pancakes in about five, all right?"

"All right." I turned on the telly, then grabbed my phone as soon as his back was turned.

You need to call me, woman. I need to talk!!!

OMG, Mel. I need to talk to you!

Jesus. Woman. Please!

The other three were in a similar vein. I typed out a quick reply.

What? Sorry. Was busy. You know…

The little bubbles popped up immediately as if she'd been waiting for hours for my reply.

I sold with Austin Fitzgerald yesterday. I'm a wreck.

Frowning, I tried to figure out what this meant.

Why? Was he a jerk?

Her reply took a little longer this time. *No. That's the problem.*

He's pretty good-looking, if I remember right, I said, feeling her out a bit.

You do remember right. Oh shit, Mel. He's a trust fund asshole.

I should not be feeling this way about him. At all.

Doesn't he have a twin brother?

I think so. Anyway. I'm still trying to get over it. Tell me about your fun night!

I sighed, closed my eyes and relived a tiny corner of it before answering.

I'll tell you some other time.

Mel! Puta!

Hardly, I typed out. *I'll call you later, promise. Gotta go. I'm getting breakfast made for me.*

I hate you right now. But you know, I don't. You get into that, chica. You deserve every bit of it.

"Who's that?" Trent asked as he put a single plate on the coffee table in front of me.

"Evelyn," I said, before realizing how awkward that answer was.

"Ah," he said, as he sat on the floor, pulling me down with him.

"Is that weird? I asked as he picked up a piece of bacon.

"Is what weird?" He held the bacon in front of my lips. I smiled and took a bite. "That you're friends with Evelyn?"

"No...I mean. You know." I bumped his side, and picked up the fork. He bumped me back, hard. "Hey!"

"Hay is for horses," he said, snagging the fork out of my hand and cutting into the butter and syrup-drenched pancakes. The bite he brought to my lips made me frown.

"I am perfectly capable of—"

"Ah, ah ah." He waggled his finger at me. "I am not taking anything away from you by wanting to treat you this way. I think women are not only the fairer but the stronger and smarter sex. We will have plenty of time to debate and for you to prove it to me. But now…I'm feeding you. Because I want to. Now open up, *mi amor*. Let me take care of you for a little bit longer?"

And what red-blooded woman could resist that? Not this one.

I opened my mouth, took the bite, chewed and swallowed it. He touched the corner of my lips and put his fingertip to his mouth. I was starting to understand what the romance novels meant when they talked about wanting to swoon. He handed me bacon, then took his own bite. We sipped coffee in between our bites while the television droned on in Spanish.

"Can I ask you about Evelyn?" I said, once we'd finished and he'd put our dishes in the washer.

"Of course." His smile was wide as he returned to the couch and flopped down onto it with a sigh, rubbing his flat belly. "Damn, I'm good at that breakfast thing."

"You are," I admitted. He reached for me but I kept my distance. "About Evelyn…"

He settled into his end of the couch, looking way too comfortable considering the topic. "I told you, we went out a few times but agreed that we weren't a good couple, in that way."

"She told me about you," I blurted out, not even sure why I was doing it.

He raised a dark eyebrow but didn't reply. I swallowed hard and plowed on. I'd started this and it was something I wanted to be clear between us. "That you had…a kink."

"Yes," he said, keeping his gaze on me and his face neutral.

"So…why didn't we…I mean, you know." I jerked my chin towards the bed where we'd shared such an amazing experience a few hours prior. My face and ears were getting hot. He leaned his head to one side, as if studying me. "Never mind." My body was revving in a way that confused me. I rose, pulling my ratty robe around me like some kind of prude.

He stayed put, his eyes following my movements. And it was as if this alone was enough to make me want to do things—to do more things—with him. Now. My hands shook as I pulled my hair back and fastened with an elastic I'd left on the side table.

"Don't stare," I said, as anger flared up in my chest. "It's rude.

"Here's the thing, Melody." He rose slowly, gracefully, and stood within centimeters of me, his hands at his sides. My knees shook and as hard as I tried to do it, I could not meet his eyes. I stared down at our feet. Mine with their silly red nails. His—large, and capable-looking sticking out from the hem of his jeans. "I do have a preference for being in charge, in control. But I don't always manifest it by a specific sort of activity in the bedroom."

I closed my eyes, swayed a little, trying not to reveal how badly I wanted to launch myself into his arms. When I opened my eyes he frowned at me, which made me train my gaze on the floor again. For some reason, it felt right, natural. Which was so strange I had to choke back a nervous laugh.

"Just listen a minute while I try to explain it." He kept his hands at his sides. I studied them while he spoke—noted their size, the length of his fingers, their tidy, squared-off nails. "I do enjoy a certain level of kink, yes. If you want to call it that. I go to clubs. I choose partners who are strangers to me. These women have come of their free will and pay as much as I do for the pleasure of my company. We both enjoy our roles. We require it, I guess, to maintain our equilibrium in other parts of our lives."

He lifted my chin, as if giving me permission to look at him. His eyes were shining, his expression serious. "It's a part of me that I'll never give up—the need to control. But I'm not ever going to make you do anything you don't want to do, *bella*. You've been through too much. It's not the right thing for you. At least not yet."

"Maybe I want to decide that," I declared, sounding way more confident than I felt.

He frowned deeper, causing distressing lines to form on either side of his mouth. "No," he said, as if convincing himself as well as me. "Not yet. If ever."

"But if it's part of you, something you won't give up, how will I… I mean…" I dropped my gaze again, and gnawed at my lip, worried I was getting way ahead of myself.

He pulled me into his arms. I went gladly, wrapping my arms around his waist and lifting my face in eager anticipation. But he didn't kiss me. He just stared at me, as if trying to figure out how to proceed. "Never mind," I said, worried I'd upset my lovely new applecart and regretting every word.

"No, we'll talk more about it, I promise. But it's something that…bears taking a bit more time to ponder, let's say." He smiled, which sent relief pouring over me like a warm waterfall. He leaned into my ear. "Didn't you like what I did for you last night, *querida*? Was it not enough for you, my sweet little sex kitten?"

I giggled, and turned my head so his lips met mine. The kiss was slow, easy, perfect. It left me gasping and wanting more. "So, what is this then?" I leaned away from him, keeping my fingers linked behind the small of his back.

"This," he whispered, pulling me close again and opening my robe. As it slid to the floor at my feet, he cupped both my breasts reverently. "This," he repeated, brushing his thumbs across my already hard nipples. "This," he said, as one of his hands slid around to grip my ass. "This." His voice dipped lower as his other hand dropped between my legs. I stood, speechless, humming with need as he touched me all over, murmuring the word "this" over and over again.

He walked all the way around me, pulled the band out of my hair, pressed his face into the mass of it as it tumbled down my shoulders and back. I started to reach for him. But he stepped away from me. "No," he said. "I'm touching right now. You are to remain perfectly still and let me. Nothing more."

"All…all right."

I felt him against my back again, sliding his fingers through my hair until he reached my scalp. He rubbed, making my knees weak again with the perfection of his touch. "I don't want you to ever put your hair up when I'm around."

I started to speak. But he pressed a finger to my lips. "It's a simple request, *querida*. And a good way for you to understand that my needs are simple. But I expect them to be met."

His voice had that edge to it again. The edge that crawled up my spine, one vertebra at a time, and landed squarely in the part of my brain that I'd discovered the night before. The part that made me pant, spread my legs and want him inside me so badly I ached with the lack of him. He stayed behind me, cupping my breasts, teasing my nipples, kissing my shoulder and neck until my knees did give out. I fell back against him with a low moan.

"Touch yourself, *mi diosa*," he said, his voice low and clear.

"I don't…know what to do."

His fingers pinched my nipples, making me cry out. "Tell me a word," he said from behind me. "A word that you'll use when you want me to stop whatever it is I'm doing."

He kept working my nipples, but gently now, teasing them into even harder peaks. My hips were moving, like they had last night. I was on fire between my legs. I needed him to do more, not less.

His fingers clamped onto my nipples again. I groaned and reached down between my legs, requiring the relief so badly I was willing to find it myself. Even though I had never, once, done this.

"That's it, *mi amor*," he crooned in my ear, keeping his lips on my neck. "Touch that beautiful pussy. You'll know where."

I nodded, my breathing ragged, sweat beading up on my

skin. "What do I do?"

"Find your clit. It's that tiny little nub of flesh at the top. It should be firm right now, ready for you."

I gulped, and felt around my own anatomy, as he tugged my nipples, distending them, and making me want him so badly I thought I might cry. "I...c-c-c-can't." I reached back to cup his neck, but he took my hand and put it back where it had been, guiding my finger, showing me what he meant. When I touched it—that tiny little bud of skin that felt plumped up and sensitive—I cried out, crying *"Si! Si! Si!"* as he and I stroked me to orgasm together.

"Oh, *Mi Dios,*" I sighed, leaning back into him fully, letting him hold me up with his body. *"Mi Dios. Mi...Dios."*

He took my hand and brought it to my mouth. I hesitated. "Taste it, *querida.* Taste your sweet cream." I put my finger in my mouth. I tasted like the ocean—like the sweet, brine-encrusted breeze that I used to love so much as a child—not like the evil memory that its smell had invoked for so many years.

I tried to turn around, but he held me still. "A word, Melody. I need you to give me a word that's ours, only ours. A word that you know will keep you safe no matter what."

I nodded, still shaking all over from the climax. His hands were roaming over me know. Breasts, nipples, stomach, pubic hair, thighs, ass, shoulders. Everywhere he touched me I burned, like fire. Such a cliché. But true nonetheless. "A word, *bella.* Give me your safe word. I'll hold it close to my heart."

"Anything?" I was dying to get my hands on him and was arching my back, pressing my ass against his crotch, which promised much even as he withheld it from me.

"Anything." His fingers fluttered all over my skin.

"Mariposa," I said, reaching back to touch his scalp, knowing already how that made him react.

"Mariposa," he sighed into my neck. "Perfect." He pulled my hands off him, making me whimper. "I told you, Melody. I am doing the touching."

"Yes. All right."

"I want to feel inside you." His hand parted my legs from behind. He cupped my entire, pulsing sex in his large palm. "You feel so good. So ready for me."

"I am," I sighed. His other hand moved up my back to my neck and into my hair again. He tightened his fist, gripping hard, pulling my head back gently. I spread my legs wider, but he kept his hand still, giving me exterior friction but nothing more. And I wanted more. But I waited, knowing he would give me exactly what I needed.

Which had to be the weirdest thing I'd ever thought. My sense of unreality ramped up higher as I stayed still, so still I thought I could hear our heartbeats syncing up, matching rhythm. His breathing was soft, near my ear. I moved my hips, feeling the leading edge of another climax roiling up from the soles of my feet. His fingers tightened in my hair, pulling and bringing tears of pain to my eyes. But I wasn't afraid. I didn't want him to stop.

"Touch your breasts, *mi amor*," he demanded, his voice firm, in control. The sound of that edge, fully realized now into something new and exciting made me gasp and move my hips faster. "Stroke those nipples. Make them harder. Pinch them." His fingertips burrowed between my legs until he found my eager clit. "Ah, yes, you are so sensitive there. In those huge, delicious nipples. I love them," he said as he stroked me.

He was teasing me, of course. Not giving me what my body was clamoring for. And suddenly, he removed both hands from me, leaving me shaking and breathless. I wanted to turn and face him. But I didn't. I understood something of this now and was willing to let it play out, to see how much better it might be even though I could hardly imagine how it would.

His breathing was labored now. I could hear it, near my ear. I sensed him unzipping his jeans. I felt him press his erection into the cleft of my ass. "I need to be inside you, *querida*," he said, his voice gone hoarse. "I can't...control this. Not right now."

I smiled, loving his admission. Feeling even closer to him because of it. As I heard the crinkle of a condom packet opening, I took a few steps to the side, until I was behind the one large chair next to the couch, and propped my hands on it, arching my back and exposing myself to him. The sound he made, deep in his throat and chest, almost an animal growl, made the tops of my thighs even damper than they were. "*Bella*," he whispered, as he positioned himself behind me. "You are…you… are…ah…Jesus, yes."

He slid into me with one firm stroke, making us both groan. He buried one hand in my hair again, pulling hard, making me cry out as he pounded into me. "I'm going to come, Melody. I can't stop. Holy shit!"

"*Si, mi amor*," I said, even as I put my finger on that most tender, sensitive place he'd shown me, rubbing fast until I came again with a full body shudder and loud cry of happiness even as he was groaning behind him, shoving in deep, caught in his climax while I found my own.

He draped himself over my back. Our sweaty skin made us slippery as his hips kept moving against my ass. I yelped when he bit down on the spot where my neck met my shoulder, but didn't use my safe word. I didn't need to. I wanted him to bite me. To put his mark on me. He licked and kissed the bitten spot, then pulled out of my body slowly with a loud sigh of satisfaction.

I remained bent over the back of the couch, legs spread, face down on my arms, relishing the tiny aftershocks that were consuming my entire nervous system. When I stood again, he was there, holding a wet cloth. He helped me up and held it between my legs, where I was now aching. I gasped and winced, but the cloth was warm. He pulled it away, frowning at the pale splotch of red. "I hurt you, *bella*," he said, walking to the kitchen to rinse and rewarm the cloth.

I grabbed my robe, but he pulled it out of my hands. "No. We are going to stay naked the rest of the day."

I smiled at him, wincing again when he put the cloth between my legs.

"I'm sorry, *angelita*," he said, kissing both my cheeks as he removed the cloth. "I didn't mean to hurt you."

"You didn't," I insisted. "It's been years since I've had sex. I probably grew my...my..."

He chuckled as he tossed the cloth into a wash basket in the laundry closet. "No, I doubt you grew your hymen back, sweetness."

I flushed hot. He pulled me down onto the couch and dragged the blanket up over us. "I didn't mean to be a jerk or to patronize you just then."

"I know," I said, snuggling into his side, sucking in deep breaths of his scent—the sweat, combined with his cum, and all mixed with my own, suffused his skin. "I have to go work later," I reminded him. "At the diner."

He frowned down at me. "I think you should quit that job," he said.

I leaned away, glaring at him.

He held up the hand not already cupping my ass. "Never mind. Forget I said anything. Sometimes my mouth gets ahead of my brain. Sorry. Do your job. Do more jobs. Do anything you want. As long as you sleep with me every night."

"I think even that is getting a little ahead of things, don't you, *guapo*?"

He heaved a huge sigh as his eyes shut. "Probably." He kissed my hair. "But let me sleep on it a bit, here, with you."

"Okay," I said, settling in to watch him sleep and surprising myself by dozing right along with him.

Chapter Thirteen

Six weeks later

"Dad!"

Taylor snapped her fingers in front of Trent's face. He flinched, then blinked fast, pulling himself out of his trance. "Sorry, Tay. What did you say?"

"I said, it's time for us to head to the church. To feed the smelly homeless guys? I changed it this week, remember? You're not even supposed to be here. You have a fight with your latest gal pal, or what? You told me you'd be gone from Thursday to Sunday."

"Right. Okay. And none of your damn business." He got up, rubbing his eyes, his mind spinning with all that had gone down in the last few weeks. "Hey, uh, Taylor?" She was slipping her feet into her sandals at the one large hall closet. "I need to ask you something."

"Hmm?" She grabbed the keys. "Can I drive?"

"Yes. Listen, I…"

But she'd already slid open the large metal door and was headed for the elevator. "Come on, Dad. I have things to do."

He eyed her, suspicious all of a sudden. Ever since the incredible, scary, life-changing night he'd spent at Melody's apartment, he'd been more than a little checked out when it came to Taylor. She'd finished her two-week suspension, kept her room clean, her homework done and her mouth shut. Of course, she still spent most weekends with her mother, which freed him up to do whatever he wanted.

And he had. He'd taken Melody up north to his lake

house twice already where they'd fucked their way through every room—indoors, outdoors, on the pontoon. She kept angling for more from him, wanting him to release the full force of his Dominant personality, but he knew she wasn't ready for that. Nor was he. He kept it ninety-percent vanilla most of the time, which was perfectly fine. More than fine, really. Which, in and of itself, was strange. He'd always considered himself the sort of man who'd use vanilla sex to get past a woman's basic defenses. Then he'd show her how he really liked it.

But he liked it any way he could get it with Melody. Which was starting to freak him out.

He sighed and followed his daughter into the elevator. She babbled on about something he barely heard, until he realized she was asking him a question. Something about the lake house.

"What? No. Hell, no you are not going up there with a bunch of your friends without any adults. You know I'd never allow that, Taylor."

She climbed in behind the wheel of the Jeep. "I know. Just thought I'd try."

His suspicions rose again, making him feel even more guilty about being so absorbed in Melody that he'd almost forgotten about his own daughter. *Time to slow it down*, he thought as Taylor careened around corners on her way to the large Catholic church that housed a homeless shelter.

Yes, that would be best.

Three hours later, the giant kitchen was clean and the men who were taking refuge at the shelter were either smoking outside or sitting around drinking coffee. He and Taylor waved to the priest who ran the place and headed for the Jeep. This time he got behind the wheel.

"What did you want to ask me, Dad?"

He didn't answer for a bit. "I was going to ask you if it was okay if I invited my new…friend over for dinner. To meet you."

She frowned at him, then gave him a diva-worthy hair

flip. "I don't care. Do whatever you want."

"Well, I know I can do that. But..." He hesitated, then pulled into the underground parking garage. "I don't know if I'm going to introduce you quite yet."

"You're weird," she said, as she jumped down to the garage floor. "I pity you."

"Yes, pity me," he said. "How about a pizza tonight, kiddo?"

She glanced over her shoulder at him as she pressed the elevator button before she turned away. "Fine. Whatever."

"Great. The famous whatever pizza. I'm on it." He yanked her against him, hooked his arm around her neck and gave her a noggin noogie until she shrieked and shoved him off her. She ran into the loft and into her room, shutting the door softly behind her. He looked at it, hands stuffed into his jeans pockets. "I'll order it," he hollered.

"Whatever, Dad," she sang back at him.

"Yeah. Whatever. Dad." He sighed and slumped against the wall outside her room, his brain aching and his pulse racing with the need to call her, to hear her voice, to have her here, with him, sharing his whole life, not just a part of it.

He'd fucked himself up so royally once. He'd fallen hard for the painfully gorgeous Shelia after just a few weeks, too. Of course, two women couldn't be more unalike than the ex-Mrs. Hettinger and the feisty, unpredictable, gorgeous Melody Rodriguez. Not at all.

And yet...

He sat at the table again, stroking the light stubble on his jaw, his brain doing that thing again—the thing where all he could think about was Melody. Which rendered him useless. With a mild curse, he shook his head and reached for his phone. After ordering their favorite local pizza, with a side of garlicy breadsticks, he headed for the shower, hoping it would clear his head.

He wanted to call her even worse when got out, dried off and re-dressed. Despite his best efforts, he kept reliving the night before. He'd taken her to his favorite bed and breakfast, having rented the whole place out, not wanting there to be any limitation on how much noise they could make. She'd been pensive, something he'd picked up on right away but had left unmentioned.

They'd shared a nice dinner — salmon on the grill, roasted potatoes, spinach salad, expensive wine. She'd stayed quiet, answering in monosyllables and not giving back in her usual, snarky manner. Finally, after they'd taken a walk after dinner, hand in hand around the edge of Silver Lake and he'd convinced her to stop and make out a little while the sun set, turning the horizon a blaze of orange, pink and purple, they'd lain on their backs in the sand, fingers entwined.

He'd brought her knuckles to his lips, loving that now familiar combination of spice and cocoa that he swore she wore on her skin like a powder. She'd sighed and pulled her hand free, sat up and leaned her elbows on her knees. Reading her reluctance, he'd sat beside her, not touching her, giving her the space to cough up whatever had been bugging her.

"I want to know why you won't introduce me to your daughter," she'd said, not looking at him.

He'd put a hand on her shoulder. She'd shrunk from his touch inside the strapless excuse for a shirt he'd been ogling all day. "Are you ashamed of me?" She'd turned to glare at him. Her deep brown eyes had blazed in a way he'd come to recognize as the leading edge of a very angry girlfriend — a girlfriend whose anger could at times outmatch his own.

He'd smiled to himself and scooted forward so he was sitting next to her. He'd draped his arm around her shoulders and pressed his lips to her cheek. "Don't distract me with your damn kissing and…stuff."

He'd grinned into her neck. "My stuff, huh?" He'd walked his fingers up her bare thigh but she'd smacked his hand away. "I thought you liked my stuff, *mi diosa*." He'd loved the way the Spanish words rolled around his mouth as he said them.

She'd sighed and moved out of his reach.

"All right, I'll invite you over for dinner with my evil spawn."

She'd jumped up, brushing the seat of her shorts. "Don't put yourself out." Confounded, he'd watched as she'd stomped back toward the empty B&B.

"Okay," he'd said to himself as he got to his feet. When he'd caught up with her, she'd been busy opening another bottle of wine in front of the large bank of windows, overlooking the lake where they'd been sitting.

He'd sat, waiting for her to get a grip on herself and talk to him. But she'd simply poured herself a glass, grabbed a book off the shelf and headed into the bedroom, shutting the door firmly behind her. He had glared at it, anger pinging around in his brain as he knocked. "Melody?"

Silence.

He'd knocked again, firmer this time. "Melody. Open the door."

"Go away," she'd insisted, her voice devoid of emotion.

"I'm not going to operate like this. If we can't talk about what's wrong, then we…"

"Go away, Trent. Leave me alone."

"I won't go away, Melody. I haven't been keeping you from Taylor. It's just that…"

"That you're ashamed of me. Your silly *Mexicano puta*."

"You aren't—Jesus." He'd leaned his forehead against the door. "Why would you even think that?" Fury had built in his brain so fast his temples had pounded and his mouth had gone dry. None of these were signs pointing to a nice weekend away. "God damn it, woman, stop making me feel bad for something I never said or thought."

"I can see it in your eyes."

He'd groaned. "No, you fucking well can't."

"It doesn't matter. I don't want to meet her anyway."

"Well, she is a giant pain in the ass most days so I can't blame you there." He'd jumped back when the door wrenched open, revealing Melody, her eyes blazing, her color high, her hair in a wild tumble around her face.

"Don't you dare talk about your own daughter that way. Teenaged girls need their fathers." She'd shoved her finger into his face. He'd taken a breath and moved it aside with his hand. With the other hand, he'd grabbed her and yanked her close.

"I know that, Melody. I also know that I fucking love you, you moody bitch."

She'd shaken her head, still fighting his efforts to draw her out of her funk. To his surprise, she'd jerked herself away and stood glaring at him, her fists clenched at her sides. "You say that, Trent. But you don't really mean it. You're holding back from me. And I don't just mean your family."

He'd sighed and tried to rally, to purposely *not* understand exactly what she meant. Because it was rising in him now, rolling up his spine, filling his chest, clogging his throat. The need to dominate her, to show her what he really meant when he said he needed — that he required — control at all times.

Her eyes had flashed as if recognizing the shift in him. She'd lifted her chin.

But he'd shaken his head. "You're not ready, yet, Melody. Stop pressuring me."

She'd blinked and seemed to deflate. Which was not at all what he wanted. He required the full force of her, the Melody that he'd rescued from her inner, cowering, teenaged victim. He would not go full-bore on her until he believed she was all the way back, when she'd have no reason to fear him. When she could meet him halfway as his submissive. Not his victim.

"I'm leaving," she'd declared, stomping past him to the bedroom.

"Fine," he'd said, leaning in the doorway, impotent with rage and his own inability to explain it to her.

"Fine." She'd thrown her few items into her bag and shoved past him. As he'd turned to watch her, he'd realized that she had no way of leaving. He'd driven them and he still had the keys.

But she'd kept walking until she was out of the front door. He'd waited for her to return, smug in the knowledge that she'd have to, so they could hash this out...somehow. But after fifteen minutes, he'd followed her, reaching for the keys in his pocket, only to find himself gripping air.

"Holy shit." Half pissed, half admiring, he'd looked out where his Jeep had been parked, fifteen minutes ago. The sun had set. The night noises had filled his ears. He'd grabbed the wine she'd opened and sat in the warm summer air, drinking straight from the bottle until he'd passed out in the lounge chair and awoken to find himself covered in a scrim of dew.

He'd called a ride share car and made it home by nine this morning. Since then he'd written a dozen text messages then deleted them before sending. He'd held his phone to his ear after hitting Call by her number at least that many times, only to hang up before the first ring.

And now, here he sat, pissed off, hungry, horny, miserable.

His phone buzzed, startling him. He grabbed it, praying it would be her, knowing it probably wouldn't be.

It wasn't.

Hey, asshole. What did you do to my friend?

He sighed and tapped out a response. *Lovely to hear from you again Evelyn. How's Austin?*

None of your damn business. Why is my friend unhappy? I need her to help me make this damn Fitz Pub operate in the black. But she's fucking miserable and I know it's your fault.

He glared at the screen. Damn women. After dragging his hand down his face he got up and grabbed a beer from the fridge, popped the cap and sucked back half of it straight from the bottle, like a philistine, as Melody would say.

How in the world could you possibly know that it's my fault?

Because you are a man. Ergo, it is your fault.

He hit Call, his ears buzzing with a combination of anger and desperation.

"What?" she barked. He could hear the sounds of the bar behind her. "I'm busy trying to pull my friend out of her funk long enough to do the damn job I hired her to do."

"You hired her?"

"Yes, dumb ass."

"And you're working for Fitzgerald now too."

"Yes. Can I go now?"

"No, wait." He sighed. "Listen, Evelyn, I'm... I don't know..."

"Oh Lord, here we go."

"You aren't helping me. I helped you, you know. If it weren't for me, that putz Austin would still be standing in my store, ogling your ass as you stomped away from us, remember?"

"Yeah, yeah, whatever. So, what happened?"

"I... It's hard to explain."

"Hmm...is it maybe because you still haven't taken her to a real club, to show her the real you?"

"The real...what?"

"And that you keep her at a distance, won't share all of yourself, when she's told you all her worst secrets."

"I'm... I..."

"Oh, oh and this—you have yet to introduce her to Taylor?"

"Shit."

"Yeah. Dude. You had me at a club within two weeks. And I was enduring your daughter's laser stare of hate the week after that, remember?"

"Fuck."

"Exactly. So, sounds like you have some planning to do."

"Yeah. Thanks, Evelyn."

"Don't mention it," she said. "I'll tell her you said hey."

"I'll tell her myself, thanks."

"That's more like it, studly."

"Tell Austin I said hi. And if he needs any tips…"

"Fuck off, Hettinger."

"Your wish, my command." He grinned, realizing that she'd hung up already.

He got up, answered the door and set the pizza box on the kitchen table. "Taylor, food." He rapped on her door. She opened it and gave him a big hug.

"Thanks, Daddy," she said. He frowned.

"What do you want?"

"Cynic! I can't say I love you?"

"Not right now."

She blew him a kiss and flounced over to the table, popped open the pizza box and grabbed a slice. "Yummy. Thanks, Daddy."

"Yeah. Okay." He approached her, wary as hell. He grabbed a slice, ate it, finished his beer and watched as she devoured two pieces and drank a glass of milk, between chattering about school, her friends, way more shit that she'd ever said since she'd turned fifteen. His wariness ramped up by a thousandfold.

He glanced at his phone, reminding himself of his earlier resolve. But now…this whole weird thing with Taylor had him tied up in knots. He needed to figure out what she was trying to pull. What all this lovey-dovey, Daddy-you're-so-great shit was all about. She smiled at him. His anxiety tripled, then quadrupled.

"Okay, so, I'm going to Tina's. A weekend sleepover." She kissed his head. He grabbed her wrist.

"The whole weekend."

"Yeah. You told me you were gonna be gone, remember?"

"I remember."

Her smile turned sickly sweet. His frown deepened.

"A whole weekend?"

"Dad." She put her hands on his shoulders, meeting his

gaze with her mother's deep green gaze. "Chill. If you were…wherever you'd planned to be, you wouldn't even know." She kissed his nose and scampered to her room.

He sighed and grabbed another slice, stared at it then tossed it back into the box. Feeling more out of control than ever, he poured the second beer down the drain and drank a huge glass of water. Gripping the edge of the sink, he counted his breaths, trying to find something to focus himself.

"Okay, well, later, Daddio." Taylor skipped past him, heading for the sliding metal door.

"Wait," he said. "Stop."

She stopped. He saw her shoulders pull back, just like her mother used to do when she'd decided to stop pretending to be his submissive. He shook his head, forcing thoughts of that particular distressing scene out of his head. She turned slowly, her fake grin even wider. She batted her lashes at him. His throat constricted. She was up to something and he could sense it like a creeping fog on the horizon.

"What's really going on tonight, Tay?" He kept his voice light.

"A sleepover, Daddy. I told you."

"Where? Who's hosting it? I'll call her parents."

She rolled her eyes. "Tina. You have her mom's number, I think. From a few years back?" Her smiled shifted, turning into something ugly.

Trent would not be moved. So what if he'd dated her friend's mom for a hot second? That was beside the point right now. But she was playing him like a Stradivarius and he damn well knew it. "Taylor…"

"What?" She blinked fast, the picture of innocence.

"Fine. Go. I'm… I am going to go out tomorrow night. But I'll have my phone on me if you need…anything."

She rolled those beautiful green eyes again, making his heart clinch with a sick combination of worry and guilt. "I'll be fine, sheesh. You worry too much."

"It's my job. And rest assured I'm calling Tina's mom."

"Sure. Okay. Fine." She slid the door aside, then turned back to him, her eyes ablaze with something he didn't like in the slightest. "Going out with her again?"

"Who?" He gripped the chair to brace himself.

"The Hispanic lady."

"Her name is Melody."

Taylor waved a dismissive hand. "Whatever. They never last anyway."

"I know what you're doing right now."

"I'm not doing anything. Just leaving to go to my friend's for a damn sleepover and getting the third degree."

"Taylor." He let the edge of alpha slip into his voice. She blinked in the face of it. Then her fake smile re-emerged, widening by the second.

"Daddy, I'm sorry. I didn't mean anything. You should bring her around sometime. Like the blonde."

"Evelyn."

"Right. Her. I kind of thought she'd stick. Seemed like your type."

They glared at each other. "Taylor, I'm going to pretend you didn't just say that."

"Do whatever you want. I gotta go. Tina's here." She brandished her phone.

He closed his eyes, pulled between his desire to see Melody and his gut-deep feeling that Taylor was headed out to find trouble all over again.

"Go," he said. "I'm calling her mom now."

"Fine." She pulled the door shut behind her as he put the phone to his ear.

"Hello?"

"Hi, Moira, it's Trent."

"Oh, hello there." Her voice went flat. No wonder. They'd had two dates. He'd not called her again. No big deal. Just no connection. But he'd been made to feel almost as guilty about that as he had about giving Sheila the divorce she'd demanded, three months after Taylor's birth.

"Hey. So, uh, Taylor's coming over for a weekend

sleepover she says." He ran a hand along his scalp, nervousness making him wish that he'd skipped the greasy pizza.

"Yes. That's right."

She didn't say anything else.

"Okay, so, I was just sort of checking on that. Seemed a little fishy to me."

"No. Tina said Taylor was coming, and Beth and Jackie."

"All right," he said. All girls who'd been friends since grade school, still as thick as thieves. "Thanks."

"No problem." She hung up. Trent stared at the phone. Since when was he the kind of man women hung up on? Jesus.

He dropped onto the leather couch, his head spinning, his heart racing.

Focus, Hettinger. Control the things you can control. Taylor's accounted for. He knew Moira was nothing if not a hovering parent. She'd keep tabs on the girls.

Time to take a few other things in hand. He grabbed his phone and hit a speed dial number. Within fifteen minutes, he had the reservation set. Then he made another call, ordered some items to be delivered to Melody's apartment tomorrow morning. He rose, his mind calm for the first time in days—definitely since he'd heard Melody tearing ass away from the B&B in his Goddamn Jeep.

He sent a quick text to Evelyn.

I'm about to call Melody. If she's with you, please use your female superpowers to make her answer the goddamn phone.

He had his response within seconds. *You got it.*

He took a deep breath, opened his closet door then pushed aside the civilian clothes to reveal a second rack. He grabbed a crisp white shirt and a pair of tuxedo trousers. Polished black shoes were lined up beneath. His cufflinks rested in mahogany box along with a full money clip, and a solid black plastic membership card with his name embossed in silver. He ran his fingertip over the raised letters, giving himself a moment to ponder the reality of where he stood, right now, the options laid out before him.

Melody.

He believed that he loved her. And he needed to seal that deal. She was the sort of woman who required it. No more bullshit.

He grabbed his phone, scrolled to her name, stared at it for a half second then touched the screen.

"Hi," she said, her voice soft.

"I'm sending you some things tomorrow, delivered to your place."

"Oh?"

He pressed his fist against the doorframe, pushing hard, so he felt pain to center himself. "Yes. A car will pick you up tomorrow night. Nine o'clock."

"How do you know that I don't have plans?"

"Cancel them."

"Trent...what is this about?"

"You'll see soon enough. Be ready." He ended the call and pressed the phone to his forehead for a few seconds before he set it aside and headed for the spinning bike, ready to put in some serious mileage to clear his head.

Chapter Fourteen

"You need to get ready," Evelyn said. "You only have a few hours."

I stared at the computer screen. "I'm not going."

"The hell you aren't." She slapped the laptop closed. We were in the office she'd assigned to me in my new job as general manager of the Fitz Pub. "You are going. But not until you get your ass home for a clean-up." She raised an eyebrow. "Did you ever get to my wax artist?"

I put a hand to my face.

"All right. Well. Get on home and take a shower. Do you have a nice dress? I mean, something super dressy?"

"Yes. He sent a dress. And shoes. And…a kind of a… mask."

"All righty then. He hasn't lost his edge. So, let's go." She snapped her fingers and smiled at me.

"Go where?" Panic was settling into my psyche. I'd spent a lot of energy in the last couple of days being mad at Trent. I wasn't quite ready to let go of it.

"It's wax time, *puta*." She handed me my purse.

"We have work to do."

"It can wait."

"That's not what you said to me this morning." I crossed my arms, leaning back in my rickety chair.

"Yeah, well, scratch all that. Hang on." She pulled her phone from her pocket. "Hey. Yeah. I gotta go help Melody with something. I'll be back in about an hour." Her face reddened. "Yes, I know." She turned away from me and muttered something more, then ended the call. "Whew. All right. Come on. It won't take long."

Two hours later I was home, staring at myself in the mirror. I put a hand to my neck, turning my head left, then right, admiring the semi-casual updo and the subtle makeup. I held out my hands, checking out the bright red nails. Between the primping, buffing, waxing and everything else, they'd even found time to get me a shower at that crazy spa.

I glanced over at the bed, where the simple, cream silk dress lay alongside a cream-colored garter belt, real silk stockings and a gorgeous, matching bra. The shoes were a work of art—sky-high heels, open toes, satin ribbons to wrap around my ankles. Everything was the perfect size. Of course.

I sat, fingering the creamy mask. It was intimidating, yet beautiful, edged with intricate lace. My fingers trembled as I held it to my face, then dropped it onto my lap.

You wanted this, Melody. You demanded it from him. Do not be that woman who, when her man gives her what she wanted, suddenly changes her mind.

I willed myself not to cry and screw up the expensive makeup job. As I was fastening the stockings into the belt, my phone buzzed from the table next to my bed. I smiled when I saw I was Evelyn.

Mel. Just relax. It will be fine. He loves you.

I sighed and looked at the ceiling before answering. *I'm not sure about all that. He wants to tie me up and spank me. That's not love. That's kind of crazy.*

Don't worry. If you don't like it, tell him. He'll stop. He'll do anything for you. Lighten up a little.

There was a brief pause, then another text from my friend. *You're going to blow his mind, chica. Own it.*

I covered my lips with my hands. There was no denying it—I was flat out terrified. I wanted this. Or I thought I wanted it. And now I definitely had to own it.

Noting the time, I stood slowly and pulled the dress with me. The fabric was like a lovely soft sheet draping my body, magically clinging to all my curves. I ran my hands across my stomach, down my hips, admiring myself in the full-length mirror.

With a frown, I started pulling at the pins and whatnot that the hair guy had used to give me the glamorous up-do. My man wanted my hair down. I ran my fingers through it, which reminded me of the way he loved to do it — gently at first, then when he'd close his fingers in it, tugging and pulling...

I shivered, and I smiled at myself, noting how my makeup looked better since I wasn't ghostly pale behind it anymore.

We'd parted badly. And I'd taken his Jeep. Granted, I'd left it in his garage, keys in the gas door. But I had taken the man's car. It had been a bold move. Or a shitty move. I still hadn't decided. But now, if Evelyn was to be believed, this night would be The One. The night I would get the full force of this whole BDSM Thing. Take it or leave it.

I swiped a bit of gloss over my lips — he'd also told me he preferred the taste of this particular brand — with a full three minutes to spare before I was to be collected by some mysterious entity. Damn the man. He was too fucking perfect.

But did I really want this? Was I ready? Would it be too demeaning? Some of the books I'd read really made it sound like abuse, or worse. Of course, most of the women in those books were beyond silly to begin with.

I leaned on one of the tall bar seats, clutching my fancy new purse. My body was zinging from pillar to post, reminding me that I'd gone without direct, intimate attention for a solid thirty-six hours.

Spoiled much, Melody?

Yes, thanks. I am.

At the appointed time, I grabbed my keys, shut the door and headed up the steps, teetering on the precarious heels.

I stopped at the top of the steps, my mouth hanging open. The car was a long, black limo. The driver was standing by the open back door, smiling at me.

I slid into the soft leather seat. There were ice cold bottles of water, but nothing else. I took one and sipped while the car cut through the traffic, repeating an inner mantra — *Keep an open mind. Be ready for anything. Understand that this is what you asked him for. This is Trent.*

The car stopped after about forty minutes in front of a mansion with columns and a large, wooden front door. I took the driver's hand and got out, squaring my shoulders.

This is Trent. He would never hurt me.

"*Mariposa*," I whispered under my breath. I had the mask in my hand still, unsure what the protocol was for it — or anything else, for that matter. The door opened. I walked in, deafened by my own heartbeat. Soft string music played. It smelled like sandalwood and leather. A handsome man in a tuxedo and a black mask met me as I stood in the entryway.

"Hello, Miss Rodriguez. Welcome."

He pulled aside a filmy curtain. A soft puff of air washed over me. I took a step forward as my eyes adjusted. The room was full of people, which was my first shock. I thought this thing was *mano a mano*, not a group project. My skin pebbled in the chill air as I hung back, taking in my surroundings. It was a ballroom, or something like it. A crystal chandelier hung in the middle. Velvet curtains were closed over what I assumed were windows.

But it was the people who were the most amazing. Every woman looked as if she'd stepped off the pages of a magazine. Every man was drop-dread gorgeous. I swallowed hard, reaching behind me for a doorknob. This was not for me. I was not one of these exotic creatures. I didn't want this. I wanted to go home.

The mask I'd been gripping slipped out of my sweaty, nervous hand. With a mild curse, I bent my knees to reach for it. But someone had already retrieved it for me. I rose, and my eyes met his. My heart ceased its pounding. My pulse slowed. The rest of me reacted in other, more primal ways. Ways I'd come to recognize, and welcome.

Even though a pitch-black mask covered his eyes and the top of his nose, I knew who he was. I'd know those lips anywhere.

He held out his hand with the mask in it. I turned around, and he slid it over my eyes, fastening it behind my head. Someone took my bag as he placed his warm palms on my bare shoulders, calming me, soothing me, revving me up in ways I wanted to act on — immediately.

"Are you ready for this, Melody?" His deep voice zinged through me. And as afraid as I was of this whole thing, as bizarre as this entire scene might be, I knew I was safe. That he was giving me everything he had. He was giving me the depth and breadth of him, just like I'd asked him to. No backing out now.

Music swelled. He turned me slowly and held out his hands. "First, this, I think," he said with a wide grin. I slid into his arms and we danced.

It was, to put it mildly, the most fairy-tale-like thing I'd ever experienced. Trent led but I knew what I was doing. We'd chatted about our mutual ballroom dancing experiences before. He knew this was one of my favorite things. I bit my lip as the music changed and we switched directions. His lips remained curled into a small, sexy smile. We didn't speak. But oh, how we danced.

Finally, after four turns around the floor, surrounded by the beautiful people, I held up a hand. "I need some water, please."

He nodded and pulled me out of the group. As he fetched us some cool, cucumber-infused water, I sat and held my hair up off my neck. The crowd continued to move around us as we sipped and sat, unable to talk due to the music.

After about five minutes, he rose from his chair and held out his hand again. I put my palm in it, and at that precise moment, the music switched. A sexy, very familiar opening note hit my ears. I smiled as he whipped out a deep red rose, and put it between his teeth.

"Oh no, we are not," I said, even as he was tugging me back into the middle of the group which had parted, forming a circle around us as the strains of the tango filled the air.

"Oh yes, we are," he said, clear as day as he yanked me forward, his warm thigh now shoved between mine.

To say that this particular dance is sexy was like saying the Pope is a little Catholic. This dance personified sexy. It *is* sex, played out between two people on a dance floor, in carefully choreographed steps. My face flushed hot as I kept my eyes on his, the mask only adding to the charged atmosphere. The music filled me. I let it happen.

This man…this amazing, confounding man. He even knows his part of this, very much female-centric, dance.

After a few panicky moments when I realized what a spectacle we were about to make of ourselves, I let go of that and let the familiar moves take over my body.

By the time we were through, I was breathing heavily and not because of the dancing. His hands were where they were supposed to be, but I wanted them elsewhere. I had the rose in my teeth now and we stared at each other. His eyes glittered behind the mask. And I sensed how much he wanted to move this public dance of intercourse somewhere else. It was like waves coming off him, desire, lust and a sort of animal need for me that I was responding to in kind.

The applause faded. We got to our feet, our hands clasped, our eyes locked. I handed him the rose, which completed the dance. "That was amazing," he said. I stared at his lips, and nodded, unable to speak.

"I want you," I said as the music flipped to something else yet again. The dance around us filled as couples began to grind against each other to the sounds of the latest hip-hop. We hadn't moved. I was frozen in place, pinned by his gaze, my body on fire. But my mind was oddly, completely calm.

He yanked me to him again and we joined the crowd.

I lifted my hands over my head and smiled as he ran his hands up my sides, then around to my ass. I felt his erection, pressing against me from behind his fancy tuxedo trousers. His thumbs brushed my nipples which were straining the thin bra and dress fabric. His lips landed on my neck. I closed my eyes and let it all happen.

I knew he was in control of this night. And it would be perfect.

Chapter Fifteen

Even as he was mentally grateful for the time he'd put in learning how to tango, Trent wished he and Melody were alone. He'd set this whole night up, course. At no small amount of expense. His Melody loved to dance. He'd arranged for that. His Melody would look great in Dior. He'd arranged for that. If she'd said she wanted to dive into a chocolate fountain and let cherubs lick off the excess, he would have figured out a way to make that happen, too.

He was on dangerous ground, approaching crazy country, and he knew it. But he was about to turn forty-one years old and had spent the last sixteen years in a turmoil of regret over his first—and last—deep dive into what he'd thought was love. Emerging with his princess of a daughter—whom he truly had worshiped for most of her life and was now having to deprogram—had been part and parcel of all of it. He would do anything for Taylor. But he needed something more. Something to make him whole as a man again.

Melody Rodriguez with her smart-ass mouth, her four-lane-wide independent streak, her soft heart and her keen mind—not to mention her hot, tight, perfect body—was it. He would have her. And he would fulfill every fantasy she'd ever given a passing thought to, if that was what it took.

He smiled down at her, watching as she undulated to the sexy thrum of the bass. He had no idea what this music was, or who was singing it but he'd told the club manager what he wanted and the man had delivered, in spades. He'd nursed a hard-on from the second he'd spotted her which made dancing a challenge. But this was how it was supposed to be here — not that limp-dick, useless, sick feeling he'd had the last time he'd been here. He was supposed to be on a knife edge, about to blow, immersed in the erotic sights, sounds, scents and tastes of this exclusive locale.

Melody's face was alight. She was in her element, dancing sinuously around him, letting him grind his aching cock against her body, while everyone around them did the same. He sensed the couples slipping away one by one as the music kept thumping away and his precious Melody kept at it, her energy boundless, her olive-tinted skin shining in the dance floor lights.

Finally, he grabbed her elbow and pulled her close. "Look around you," he demanded.

She stopped and turned her head left and right, noting that that over half the couples had disappeared. His heart seemed to stop for a second when she gazed up at him, then it stuttered forward. The fear was back. He smelled it rolling off her. But if anything, that reassured him. He had to show her this life. To see if she'd take it on with him, alongside him.

"It's all right," he said, taking her hand and putting her knuckles to his lips. The delicious taste of her filled his mouth, firming his resolve to make her fully his tonight.

"Is it?" Her voice made his body tingle all over again.

"*Si, mi amor.*" He pulled her off the dance floor and over to a curtained-off hallway. He held the heavy velvet aside, then motioned for her to enter. She hesitated. He put his hand firmly in the small of her back, hoping she could sense the strength of him, that she knew to lean into it, because it was hers for the taking.

She walked forward and he let the curtain drop behind them. The hallway was a sort of mini-initiation rite. It led to his suite, the one he preferred and was given every time he came here. But before they reached it, she needed to see some things. She stopped at the first open door, her mouth hanging open. He put his arm around her. "Watch," he said as she started to turn away.

A woman was on a St. Andrew's cross, naked, spread-eagled, her wrists and ankles clamped. A man dressed in a tuxedo circled around her, touching her here and there with his fingers.

"Tell me what you need," the man said, smiling over at his audience.

"I need you to lay hands on me, Sir," the woman said.

"In what way?"

"Softly, please."

A sharp sound came from the next room, making Melody flinch. Trent took her elbow and guided her to the next open door. A man was on his hands and knees, bound and naked with a ball between his teeth. A woman in full Domme gear cracked a bullwhip in the air around him.

He kept her moving, hoping this wasn't making her more afraid. The next room held a threesome — a woman, bent over a spanking bench. A fully dressed man stood behind her, using a crop on her bare ass. Her wrists were bound in front of her. Another man stroked her hair, crooning to her, even as he released his cock so she could grab it in her bound hands.

"Please, Sir. Please I must have it."

"Ask again," the man behind her with the crop commanded her, giving her a soft smack.

"Please. Sir, I need to suck his cock."

Melody leaned into him. He looked down at her still masked face.

"S-s-s-sir," she said, her perfect, full red lips saying the word that almost made him come in his tux trousers like a teenager.

"Yes," he said, tilting her chin up as she tried to avert her gaze.

"Sir, please...I need you."

He motioned to a woman standing nearby. She unlocked his suite door with a smile and disappeared. Trent pushed Melody forward and she walked in.

She turned to him, surrounded by all the things he wanted to share with her — the swing, the overhead bindings, the bench. He was not a fan of the cross so the keen staff always made sure it was removed from this room before he entered it. She ran her fingers over the table covered in dildos. She picked one up, then another, then touched the crop with her lovely, red-nail-tipped fingers.

Trent sensed himself fading, going into his zone, but knowing this would be a long, wonderful night, for both of them.

"Go there," he said, pointing to a raised platform underneath a pair of dangling leather straps. He saw her swallow and licked his lips, eager for the taste of her skin. She went and stood, waiting for him. "Take off the dress."

She hesitated, then slid the straps off her shoulders, unzipped it and let it fall to the floor at her feet.

"My god," he breathed, taking in the soft cream underthings that were, as he'd hoped they'd be, in ideal contrast to her brown skin.

She smiled, then held up her arms, reaching for the straps. He was at her side in a second, fastening her wrists and sliding his hands down her back. She was shaking. He smelled her fear again.

"I am going to do some things to you and there are two rules," he said. She nodded. He walked around her, not touching, just looking, drinking her in with his gaze. "If you use your safe word, I'll stop. Otherwise, you don't speak."

She nodded. He touched her lips, smelling something else rolling off her now. Something he was going to own, and soon. "I'm going to make you want to come, to climax, to scream. But you aren't allowed to — not until I say so."

She nodded, but was frowning. "I don't —"

"Sh…remember?"

She nodded again, but her jaw was clenched. He pressed his lips there, then kissed his way down her neck, making her sigh and her nipples peak high and proud. He reached for the crop and trailed the ends of it along her skin. The handle fit perfectly in his palm and calmed him. He gathered himself mentally and forced control over his body. His dick wouldn't cooperate and soften like it usually did but this was a special night. So he cut himself some slack.

He flicked the leather along her legs, up her torso, and on her arms, keeping it light. When he moved around to her back, he did it a little harder, his mouth watering at the sight of the tiny red marks he left. "Remember, my love, safe word anytime."

She nodded, but stayed silent. He gave her sweet, bare ass a hard bite of the crop, once, twice, then again. Then he dropped it and slid his hands up her body from behind, tugging her nipples the way he'd learned she liked, drawing a low, loud groan from her. He let it pass. But he withdrew, taking a seat in the giant leather chair in front of her.

She squirmed. Her lips opened and closed. He smelled her lust curling around them. He needed to take a break or he wasn't going to be able to fulfill this scene.

After about ten minutes during which she remained admirably silent, she whispered, "S-s-s-ir?"

He rose and went to her, sliding his hands into the mass of hair that he loved so very much, gripping it and tilting her head back. "Sh," he said, as he lowered his lips to her neck. "No talking."

He kissed her shoulders, sucked at her nipples, then slid his hand between her legs. She thrust at him, eager. Too eager. He withdrew again.

"I want you to trust me, Melody." He grabbed the nipple clamps, and popped open her bra, letting it hit the floor as he caressed her breasts. "I want you to listen to my words, breathe slowly and trust me."

She nodded, hissing but not crying out as he put the clamps on at the same time. A tear slid from underneath her mask. He licked it away. "Safe word, *bella*. Say it, and we stop." She shook her head. He slid his fingers between her legs again, feeling her heat. He put his fingers to his lips, tasting her need.

He stood back, looking at his work, cupping her full breasts, kissing her neck and shoulders but keeping himself under strict control. She whimpered a little, but didn't say anything. He grabbed the crop again, teasing her skin with it, admiring the way she seemed to relish it. He striped her ass once more, almost coming again without even touching himself.

He dropped the crop, and reached for ice. "Are you hot, my love?"

She nodded, licking her lips, her arms staining against the bindings. He trailed an ice cube down one arm, to her shoulder, across her neck. Her skin pebbled in its path. He put another cube in his mouth and kissed her, loving it when she sucked it into her mouth and bit down on it.

He put another ice cube between her legs, feeling how badly she wanted to come, stroking her firm clit a few times, before stopping and leaving her whimpering again. He released the clamps and pressed ice to her distended nipples, covering her lips with his and taking her moans of pain into his mouth. Sensing the tension in her arms, he reached up and flipped open the wrist cuffs, holding her when she slumped against him.

"May I...Sir?"

"No," he said, picking her up and carrying her like a child to the large leather seat. He was losing it, and he knew it. He had to do something...something to distance her. That was the only way he'd make it tonight.

He dropped into the chair, still cradling her close and wondering, for the first time since he'd begun this sort of rough sex play, why he felt the need to keep her at a distance. He wanted her closer, closer than any woman.

She was not Sheila. She wasn't a gold-digging, neurotic faker.

He guided her gently off his lap. "Stand there, in front of me."

She sniffled, but did as he asked. He leaned back, using all his self-control not to unzip his trousers. She was trembling all over. Her skin was flushed from head to toe. For the first time in almost twenty years, Trent was at a total loss.

He jumped up and strode over to the box where he kept ropes and the whip. He ran his fingers over them both, pondering the possibilities. "Come here," he demanded. She turned and joined him next to the box and the swing. Something primal rumbled around in his gut, pressing up into his chest, making his throat so tight he could barely breathe. She was emanating some kind of pheromone, he decided. Something deep, dark and needy. Something that was blinding him, deafening him, sending him into the subspace that he prided himself on bestowing.

He groaned and pressed his fists against the top of the now-closed box. Everything in him was yowling, clamoring for her, needing to be in her and nowhere else. This had never, ever happened to him before. He used all his mental tricks, everything he'd taught himself about orgasm control, to no avail.

"I...need you, Melody," he croaked. She touched his cheek, then pulled his mask up and off, before doing the same to hers. "I...don't understand what's happening to me."

She smiled. He fixated on her lips for a few seconds. "I'm here for you, *mi amor*," she whispered. "I am yours." Her hand was cool against his face.

He nodded, swept her up and tossed her down on the huge, silk covered bed, looming over her, unsure and yet, never more sure of anything in his life. She lay still, spread out for him, her hair an ebony fan around her face.

"Sit up," he said, his voice still croaky and weak. "Unzip me."

She rose slowly, her firm breasts with their slightly elongated nipples his focus now. With a small smile, she unbuttoned, unzipped and shoved his trousers down to his ankles. "Closer," he demanded. She moved forward, her face tilted up to his. "Between your breasts."

She cupped her breasts, pressing them together and he

slid his aching cock between them with a loud groan. He felt her fingers under his balls as he grabbed her hair and kept fucking her glorious tits like some kind of a vanilla rookie. The orgasm roared down his spine but he choked it, holding it off, only allowing a small release of liquid. She licked it off him, making him groan at the effort not to give her more.

She pulled away from him, leaning back on her hands as he stood, shuddering and quaking, confused and unable to speak.

"Sir," she said, making him open his eyes and meet hers. "I need something from you. May I? Please?"

Still speechless, he pressed her back on the bed, his focus regained. He lowered his lips to her clit, sucking it hard and making her scream before sliding two fingers into her, angling them forward and feeling the pulse of a full-body climax grip her. He rode it out, gasping along with her.

Her smell, her taste, her cries of pleasure, all blinded and deafened him. He crawled up her body, licking and sucking and biting and shoved into her hard, making her groan even as she was still coming. Without a single thought to his unprotected state, he pounded into her, needing to come, to fill her, to imprint on her in way that frightened and thrilled him. She wrapped her legs around him, digging the heels of the shoes he'd bought into his back. The pain drove him even faster.

"I'm going to come," he ground out against the sweaty skin of her neck. "I can't stop. I want…to… Ah god!" His mind went blank. A whiteness descended over all his senses. He looked down and could see her beautiful face, her o-face, her lips moving as she babbled in Spanish like she always did when she came. But he heard nothing.

They lay in a head, tangled together, her lips on his scalp, kissing and crooning. He shook so violently he thought he was hurting her but she kept her arms and legs around him. Saying nothing and everything to him in Spanish. His body finally stilled. He rose on his elbows and stared down at her.

"That was sort of not how I wanted this to end."

She smiled and touched his lips. And at that moment, Trent knew.

"I love you, Melody. Thank you."

"For what?" She yawned and grinned up at him, stretching her arms over her head.

"For proving something to me about all this." He pulled out of her and flopped onto his back. Pulling her against his chest, which was still covered in the tuxedo shirt, albeit a sweaty one. She untied the tie.

"This was what you looked like the first time I saw you," she said, kissing him gently and unbuttoning his shirt. "This is what I wanted to do to you then. Indulge me?"

He nodded, speechless, watching her fingers move. She kissed his chest as she opened the shirt, bit each of his nipples, then hiked her stocking-clad leg over his thigh. "I'm not done, Sir," she whispered, biting his earlobe.

"I can tell," he said, sliding his hand up her thigh then pinching her nipple. "What would you like from me?"

She pointed to the line of sex toys. Trent grinned and grabbed a couple, then pushed her onto her back. "I am all yours, no charge for the batteries."

She grinned, and bent her knees. "Show me," she said, grabbing a tube of lube that lay helpfully on the side table. "I want to feel you in my ass."

He matched her grin, sensing his dick harden at her words. "Hmmm," he said, flipping on one of the toys. "I think that can be arranged."

Chapter Sixteen

As we lay, piled on top of the now damp and disheveled silk coverlet on the giant bed in the strange, dark, sexy room, I had an epiphany. I'll admit that I'd done some research into this lifestyle after Evelyn had told me about Trent's kink. I'll also admit that most of what I read I didn't like. It seemed demeaning on too many levels. As if being a woman in a man's world wasn't hard enough, why subject yourself willingly to this kind of thing?

I'd even bought a few of the dollar romance novels in the BDSM category online, finding many of them poorly written, and some of them pretty hot. But I still had the feeling that the fantasy of having some guy tie you up and spank you a bit on the throwback side of things.

But you did this anyway, you silly hypocrite.

Yes, because I will freely admit that I was curious to figure out what about it appealed to Trent. He and I had had sex in so many fun ways already, without all this stuff, I had to know why I sensed that he was holding something back from me. Something that my friend Evelyn had even gotten to experience — not that I was jealous.

Okay, I was. Just a little. But she was neck deep with Austin Fitzgerald now, and if rumors around the brewery were to be believed, with a guy named Ross Hoffman as well, somehow.

This Hoffman was an old friend of Austin's from their brewing institute days. He was, apparently, German, and a serious hottie, in a Viking kind of a way. The three of them had spent some quality time together out in Denver, again if one were to believe the rumors swirling around my new workplace, the weekend that Fitzgerald Brewing had won Midsized Brewery of the Year.

I rolled onto my side, about to say something until I saw that Trent was sound asleep, his arms up over his head, his gorgeous, sculpted chest covered in a light sheen of sweat. I ran my fingertips along his scalp, allowing myself a few minutes to enjoy simply looking at him. His prominent cheekbones, his aquiline nose, his full, oh-so kissable lips.

This man…my mind refused to wrap its woozy self around what we'd done. How he'd made me feel. Cherished, protected, loved and most of all safe. The small pains he'd inflicted on me, giving me time to adjust to each of the new experiences had proven to me that he wasn't interested in demeaning me. He was interested in my pleasure, pure and simple. And he knew how to bestow it—even if it were in ways I'd never imagined would be pleasurable.

I lay my head on his chest, near his shoulder, listening to his heartbeat—steady and strong. That moment when he'd stared at me with pure anguish in his eyes and admitted that he didn't understand what was happening to him will be something I never forget. The fun times we'd shared—mostly having sex but also watching movies, sports, going on long walks before more sex—had been intense. But once I realized that he'd freed me from the scared little girl I'd been for so long, shown me how I deserved to live as a sexually healthy woman, I knew I was way over my head in love with him.

And now, I'd seen all sides of him. He'd shown me what he liked—what he really liked—when it came to sex and I was all in. I rolled to my other side and sat up slowly, gingerly. My nipples hurt like fire and my ass was sore but I'd never felt more sated or happy. Nothing would ruin this. I had a job I loved working with my best friend and her man—both her men, I guessed—and now this? It seemed a bit decadent, like I was being handed too much at once.

But that was my grandmother's old superstitions talking. She'd spent a lot of time with me as I'd recovered from the attack at home. She was the one who'd demanded that my mother take me to a doctor to make sure I was neither pregnant nor the recipient of any nasty diseases. I wished wholeheartedly that she were alive now, so I could tell her about my man, my new life. I glanced over my shoulder, needing to see him again, to ensure that I was not dreaming.

His eyes were open. His smile wide as he regarded me. He held out his hand. "I didn't hurt you did I, *querida*?"

"Nothing I didn't ask for, *guapo*." I got up and limped to the bathroom. "I need a shower. I don't suppose they have food in this weird place? I am starving."

There were two showers, both with a million heads at all angles. Hot steam filled the room as the water ran. I stepped into its warm embrace, only emerging after my fingers got pruney, vaguely aware that Trent had spent a few minutes cleaning up in the other one. Wrapping myself in a huge, soft towel, I sniffed the air with a smile.

"You are too good to me," I said, walking out to find him with a towel around his waist, uncovering a plate. "How did you know that's what I was craving?" He motioned for me to climb into his lap. I needed no more encouragement.

He cut the filet mignon and fed me bites in between taking his own. The rich, tender protein slid down my throat and filled me with a different kind of warmth. The potato had the perfect amount of butter and salt. The green beans were crisp, yet warm and flavorful. I sighed and snuggled into him, not even having a twinge of doubt about what all this meant.

He flopped back with a sigh of satisfaction after we'd each drunk a bottle of water. "No wine?"

"Not here. It's against the rules."

"You'll have to fill me in a little more. Maybe...show me some more...sights?"

He chuckled and kissed the top of my head. "Ah, a little voyeur as well as an adventurer, are we, *mi amor*?"

"Well..." I finger walked around his firm, lightly furred chest. "It was *muy caliente, si*?"

"Si, bella. Si."

I drifted, and so did he, our bellies as full as our hearts. I woke with a jerk. I was even more sore this time, as I rose and limped to the door where I thought I'd heard something like a doorbell. Without a thought to what I might find, I opened the door. A man stood there — a very tall, very good-looking man with deep black hair and blue eyes. He was dressed in a tux. He held out a flat, square box. "Mr. Hettinger ordered this delivered." He handed the box to me, then walked away.

I stood, staring down at it, curious and still sleepy. Trent was stretching, and the towel had slipped, revealing a part of him that I never thought I could become addicted to — but I was. I smiled and cocked my hip, holding the box like a drinks tray. "Something came for you. A *muy guapo* young man delivered it just now."

His eyes narrowed. *"Muy guapo,* eh?" He grabbed my wrist and dragged me down to large leather chair, his lips locked on mine as he maneuvered us so I was straddling his lap. He broke the kiss, leaving me breathless. "I don't like it when you use that word on anyone but me, *bella.*" He poked the tip of my nose. "Give me the box."

I held up over my head. "Well, he was," I said, smiling as I felt his dick harden beneath me. He growled and grabbed for it. I tossed it between my hands, loving the play of his muscles as he moved and the direct pressure his erection now put against my very sore but still eager pussy.

With an evil grin, he tugged my towel down and sucked one of my nipples, hard, making me squeal and drop the box on his head. He grabbed it, pushed me up then turned me so I was plunked down in the seat he'd just vacated. I snagged my towel, re-wrapping myself, and blew my hair off my face. He'd moved the plate and water bottles aside, and was sitting across from me, looking way too serious.

"What?" I said, irritated, but trying to stay neutral. "What is it?"

By way of answer, he lifted the lid off the box, revealing

a thick, silver, ropey necklace, with a heart-shaped locket. It was nestled in a deep burgundy bed of velvet. He held it out to me, his gaze lowered. "In exchange for your trust, I ask that you wear this. To show the world what we are to each other."

I lifted the chain. It was heavy and didn't seem to have a clasp, like it was an endless loop of a precious metal. It slid through my fingers as I studied the odd locket. There was a single, very large diamond set in it. I hadn't seen that as the locket had been turned over inside the box. It caught the light from the bathroom, blinding me.

My hands shook as I laid it back in its velvet nest. "Is this...a thing?"

He smiled and took it, motioning for me to join him. I turned and sat between his legs on the ottoman, lifting my hair and feeling him settle the weight of if around my neck. It was tight, almost like a choker. He kissed the nape of my neck, then my shoulder. His hands were warm and comforting on my bare arms. "Yes, *mi amor*. This is a thing called a collar. But don't get your *feminista* hackles up. It's not like that. And we can call it whatever you want. As long as you understand what it means."

I moved so I was sitting in the chair again, facing him. I took his hands and kissed his palms, then placed them on my chest, over my beating heart. "*Ah guapo. Estoy desesperadamente enamorado de ti.*" I felt the tears slip from my eyes. "I will wear this, if it means something to you." I touched the locket. It lay almost exactly in the cleft between my collarbones. It was heavy around my neck. But I didn't care.

"It does, *bella*. It means a lot." His eyes were shining. "But now, I say we head home."

"Home?" I shot him a look. I had yet to stay at his place more than one night. I'd only been there on weekends, when Taylor was at her mother's.

He grinned and opened a case I hadn't noticed near the bathroom. He pulled out jeans and a T-shirt for him, and one of my favorite, lightweight summer dresses and sandals for me. I rolled my eyes. "And here I thought we had to do the walk of shame out of here in our dress-up clothes." He tossed me the dress. "Undies?" I held out my hand.

"No need," he said, waggling his eyebrows as he stuck his long legs in the jeans.

I pulled the dress over my head, letting it flow down my body, getting that too-perfect sensation again. Like this was all way too much wonderful for one silly Latina to enjoy. He dropped to the ottoman again and helped me do up my sandals, kissing my ankles, then my knees, then my thighs. I spread my fingers on his scalp, relishing the sensation of his bare skin against my palms. But he stuck his head out from under the dress before getting to the top of my legs, leaving me a little pouty.

"Yes, home. To my place. The spawn child is on a weekend-long sleepover, or so she claims. I checked with the other girl's mom and it's legit."

I watched him pull the shirt down over his bare chest, already relishing the anticipation of a night spent in his arms, in his loft downtown instead of my tiny studio, listening to the marital discord, screaming babies and barking dogs through the paper-thin walls. I touched the locket again, pondering the next steps. I got up and found my dress, stockings, bra and garter belt from the various locations in the room where I'd left them. As I was picking up Trent's trousers and trying to locate his shirt and tie, he put a hand on my arm.

"We don't have to do that."

"What are you talking about? These are expensive clothes."

"I know. But part of the deal here is the clean-up. These things will get returned to me, dry cleaned and ready to reuse."

"But..." He took the trousers out of my hand and dropped them on the bed, then kissed my forehead gently.

"No buts, my love. Let's go. My bed awaits your presence."

I stood, staring at him. He crossed his arms. "What?"

"This…" I waved my arms around. "This is just…too much."

"Too much what? Too much awesome? Too much great?"

"Too much, I don't know, pure fantasy. It's ridiculous. There are people starving to death in the streets."

He grinned, then chuckled, then pulled me into his arms. "I love you," he said.

"What does that have to do with this present line of conversation?" But I closed my eyes and sucked in a deep breath of him.

"Everything." He pulled me back, gripping my arms. "You have a lot to learn about me, *bella*. I'm not a spoiled rich asshole. I earned every penny I have. But when I spend it, I expect to get full use of it."

"I didn't say…" He put his finger to my lips.

"Humor me. Let me get the full value of the money I spent for our night here, okay?"

I nodded, grabbed his wrist and sucked his fingertip into my mouth.

He smiled. I bit down, hard. He winced, and yanked me closer, keeping his finger where it was. "Better watch yourself, *angelita*. I'm not done with you tonight." He pulled his finger out and gave my ass a hard smack.

I squealed and jumped away from him, already tingly with anticipation, rubbing my smarting backside. He put on his watch and grabbed his wallet and keys then held out his arm. "Your wish," he said, his smile lighting me up from the inside out as I tucked my hand into his elbow. "My command," he whispered, sending a jolt down my spine.

We walked down the hallway. All the rooms we'd seen earlier had velvet curtains drawn over them. The large ballroom was chilly, but when our feet touched the dance floor, Trent pulled me around and twirled me under his arm again and again, making me dizzy. When I fell against him, he laid one of his toe-curling kisses on me, then leaned away, as if studying my response.

"Are you trying to blow my mind with this over-the-top fairy tale *mamadas*?"

"Did you just call the date night I arranged *bullshit*?" He slapped a hand over his heart.

"*Si, guapo*. I did."

He sighed. "I guess I'm going to just have to try harder."

I hip bumped him as we made our way across the large room toward the foyer and the front door. "Guess so."

He harrumphed. I giggled. He gave me another hard ass smack on my way out the front door. His Jeep was waiting, already running in the circular drive. I sighed. "Seriously?"

"*Si*, my love." He opened the passenger's side door and bowed low. I flicked his earlobe then climbed in. "Every pain from you is worth it. So far, anyway."

I stuck out my tongue as I fastened my seatbelt. But I had never felt so happy in my life. I tried not to feel too lucky as we drove the forty minutes back to Grand Rapids. I threaded my fingers through the ones he had on my leg. He glanced at me at one point. "You all right?"

"Never better," I claimed, kissing his knuckles and focusing forward, willing myself not to cry.

When we were on the elevator up from the parking garage, he pressed me up against the cold metal wall and kissed me so hard I saw stars. He broke slowly from my lips when the doors opened into the hallway outside his loft. His hands cradled my face. His body was warm against mine. Our lips were mere inches apart.

"What are you thinking about right now, *bella*?" He traced my lips with his thumb. "Talk to me."

"I'm thinking that I am the luckiest woman in the world."

"Liar," he said with a smile. "You'd never think anything so clichéd and I know it."

I shrugged, but I honestly never wanted him to move, to never let go of me, to never stop kissing me. "You are so unbelievably beautiful."

"*Gracias*. You're not too bad yourself, *guapo*."

"I want us to be together, Melody."

"We are, silly man." I put my fingers on the locket. But my heart was doing that weird flippity-flop thing again. Like it had done at our first date, when I'd made us lunch.

He propped his hands propped on either side of my face, but looked away from me, down at our feet. "Listen," I said, tilting his chin up like he'd done with me, many times before. "I'm going to warn you now — I'm not always a ball of fun. I can be a little, um, bossy. Sometimes I'm moody. I have a bit of a short fuse. It's the Mexican in me."

He grinned and pecked the tip of my nose. "Oh, I think you'll find us pretty well matched in the temper department. As for you being bossy, well…we can balance that out a little bit, I think. If you're game to let me try."

I wrapped my arms around his neck. The elevator door had given up on us and had shut again. "I'm game to let you try anything."

"All righty. That's more like it." He pressed the button and doors slid open once more. I'd only been in the space for a few seconds before he scooped me up and tossed me over his shoulder. "Trent is feeling very cave man. Cave man want to fuck." He smacked my ass all the way back to his bedroom.

I yelped and bounced when he tossed me onto his bed — a giant expanse of green and blue covered softness. I threw pillows at him as he dodged and weaved. When he leapt on me, pinning my wrists over my head, grinding his crotch against me, I growled at him. "Feisty," he said, shoving his other hand up my dress. "I like it. Now…let's find something you like, shall we?"

He pressed fingers inside me, keeping his thumb on my clit. I shoved my hips up, not even believing that I could want more, but wanting it nonetheless. He lowered his lips to mine, owning me, possessing me even while giving me what I wanted. I came hard, moaning into his mouth. I flopped back, gasping, my eyes closed as my body pulsed. "How do you do that?" I asked, when he put the fingers he'd had inside me to his lips.

"I'm a bit of a miracle worker. You may call me the orgasm whisperer if you like."

"Bragger."

He let go of my wrists and I took the opportunity to shove him over onto his back. "Now, let's see what I might have in my magician's hat for you." I unzipped him and tugged his jeans down and off. His cock was ramrod hard, jutting upward, a pearl of cum glistening at the tip. I licked my lips and crouched between his knees. "Lay back, whisperer. Let me work."

I sucked the fluid from his head, making him groan low and loud. I wrapped my fingers around the base, and slid my mouth down his length. He tugged at my hair as I took him deep, then released him, then swallowed him as much as I could. Even as I felt his balls tighten in my palm and his thrusts took on an urgency that I recognized, he pulled me up and off him, tossed me onto the bed and crawled up between my legs. *"Bella, bella, mi amor,"* he crooned as he angled his hips and penetrated me slowly, deliciously, filling me and making us both groan. I arched my back, as he moved faster. I reached back and grabbed the wooden headboard, tilting my hips so I could feel him all way inside me.

He slowed, using external friction against my clit and latching onto one of my nipples, making me shiver and cry out. "Come inside me. I want to feel it. Fuck me, *papi*. Fuck me hard."

He let go of my nipple and stared down at me, his expression one of wonder. "I...I need to..." He gasped and pounded fast and hard against me. I wrapped my legs around his waist, as the climax rose in me, bringing a cry of pleasure to my lips. He matched my cry with his own.

We shivered in unison. A drop of his sweat hit my lips. I smiled and licked them. He was still shaking when he pulled out of me and dropped onto his side. "Come here," he said, pulling me close. "Oh my God, Melody. You gotta stop calling me *papi*. I come so fucking hard when you do that it's just sick and wrong."

I smiled and touched his nose. "Don't be so anglo. I don't think you're my real *Papi*. It's just...what comes out of my mouth. You're only my *papi* when you make me come so hard I can't see, all right? It's a figure of speech."

He sighed and nodded. "I gotta sleep a little."

"Me too. Bathroom first."

I slid out of his arms and headed for his bathroom. I'd been here before. We'd christened his kitchen, his living room and his shower already. But I didn't have to sneak out tonight before his daughter came home. Tonight I would sleep in his arms, in his house, under his roof. I used a wet cloth to clean up, then grabbed one of his black T-shirts out of a drawer full of them folded so perfectly I giggled. He muttered something and rolled onto his belly, stuffing his hands under the pillow. His muscular ass was awfully tempting. I wanted to bite it.

I shook my head at myself, touched the heavy locket like a talisman then headed for the kitchen, seeking water and maybe a snack even as a tiny tingle of regret over the night's full round of non-condom sex hit me between the eyes. I hesitated, counting the days in my head, then shrugged, figuring I was in a safe zone but making a mental note to discuss it with him.

His giant, double-door fridge was packed full of yogurt, protein drinks, fruit, veggies, milk, OJ and the usual condiments in the door. I grabbed a handful of grapes and a yogurt, then poked around until I located a spoon. I flipped on the teapot and sat, munching on the grapes while the water heated. I stared around the large combination living and dining room, noting that he used the edge of the big wooden dining table as a home office. It was cluttered with his laptop, piles of papers, files, pens and handwritten notes.

I took a few bites of the yogurt, trying not to be too nosy. I knew he had a big project in downtown Kalamazoo he was trying to get approved. As I studied his neat, tidy, left-leaning handwriting, the teapot dinged.

As the fragrant Earl Grey steeped, I snooped a little more, moving papers aside and checking out income statements for his various businesses. I clutched the mug close to my chest, getting as much out of the aroma as I would the flavor, noting that his most profitable enterprises were, without a doubt, the three liquor stores. He had partial ownership of two restaurants and a coffee shop. Damn guy was loaded, if these P&L sheets were any indication.

A low, insistent buzzing sound hit my ears. I knew it was a phone, but I'd turned mine off hours ago. I set my tea down and went on a seek and find, locating Trent's phone, deep in his jeans pocket in the bedroom where he was still snoring away. I pulled the duvet up over his naked butt, after giving it a proprietary little pat. I glanced down at the screen. He'd missed three calls and a bunch of texts from Sheila. His ex-wife, Taylor's mother.

As I was staring at it, trying to figure out what to do, since Taylor wasn't with her mother this weekend, it buzzed. I almost dropped it in surprise. This time it was Taylor herself. I put the phone to my ear. "Hello, Taylor. It's Melody."

"Uh...so...where's my dad?"

"He's asleep right now." I could hear noises behind her — party noises. She sniffled. My trouble radar pinged. "Are you all right?"

"I'm...no. I'm not. Shit."

"Okay, so is there something I can do?"

"Maybe." She sniffled again. "I don't know."

"Where are you?"

"Um...that's kind of the problem."

"Oh?" I grabbed my tea and took a sip. Maybe I could help her and she'd try to not hate me.

"Yeah. I'm...not where I said I'd be. I'm up north. At the cabin."

The tea shot down my windpipe, making me splutter and cough. She waited me out. I tiptoed back to make sure Trent was still snoozing, then headed for the kitchen, pulling the sliding door shut behind me. "What in the hell are you talking about?"

"I'm up north. At the cabin." Her tone made me want to reach through the phone and snatch her hair out.

"I heard that part, Taylor. Your dad thinks you're at a friend's for the weekend."

"Yeah, obviously, since you're answering his phone right now."

I chewed the inside of my cheek to keep from biting her head off, and determined not to be so judgmental when Trent would call her the devil spawn. I was beginning to see his point. "And so, is there something I could do to help you?"

She heaved a sigh. "Well...could you come up here, maybe? My friends got in a big fight and one of them drove off and left me here without a car."

I glanced over my shoulder, expecting to see Trent any minute. "That's kind of a long way. And you don't sound like you're alone."

"You know what, never mind. It's really none of your business anyway." Her tone had gone sharp again.

"Your mother has called here a few times."

"I called her."

"Well, she's obviously trying to reach your dad and tell him."

"Shit."

"Is everyone there safe? No one's hurt? No police or anything?"

"No. It's just me, Tina and a couple of our friends."

I heard a feminine squeal and some masculine guffaws behind her. I frowned and switched the phone to my other ear. "Taylor, you snuck up to your father's house after telling him you were at a friend's and threw a party?"

"Well..."

"Holy shit, *chica*. You've got some *cojones*. I'll give you that."

"Are you coming, or what?"

"Yes. I'll tell your dad I had to go see my mother, that's she's sick or something." My head was pounding and my inner, much smarter Melody screamed at me that this was a Massively Bad Idea. But I was caught up in it now. I wanted the damn girl to like me. I needed her to like me. Ergo, I was prepared to lie to Trent and save her sorry ass. Apparently.

"It's a solid three hours so I expect you to clear the house out of partiers before I get there, do you understand?"

"Yes." She sounded contrite. I should've known better. But I didn't.

I scratched out a quick note to Trent, then called for a ride home, biting my lip so much on the way there it was a bloody, ragged mess by the time I climbed into my car. I plugged in the address of Trent's cabin—a huge, six-bedroom, six-bath mansion on Lake Michigan, with a gourmet kitchen and a deck stretching across the back. He'd bought it right after his divorce, he'd claimed. A sort of up-yours to his greedy ex who'd always wanted a lake house. But he never used it as much, he claimed. Too busy working.

I didn't dare stop more than once for gas and a huge cup of crappy coffee. As I approached the house, I saw the tell-tale flashing lights. Praying there was an emergency at the next-door neighbor's, I sucked in a breath and spat out a string of my best Spanish cuss words at the sight of the police car, the small fire truck, and the ambulance parked in the long drive at Trent's house.

I parked on the street and jumped out, then ran up the drive, heart in my throat. The medical types were gathered around someone lying on the grass in the back yard. I stopped, hand over my mouth. But I spotted Taylor, standing on the bottom step, talking to a policeman. I ran to her, grabbed and hugged her in relief. She stayed stiff in my arms. I released her and turned to the cop.

"Thank you, Officer."

He frowned at me. "Are you this girl's mother?"

"No," Taylor and I both said at the same time.

143

"Well, we need a parent here. She's underage and that house," he pointed up where lights shone out of every single one of the many windows. "That house is full of booze and pot and teenagers." He held up a tiny, glass pipe. "That kid is lucky to be alive." He pointed to the boy who was on his back, getting his leg checked out.

I stared at Taylor, horrified. Mainly because I was officially out of my league. I had to call Trent. "I have to call your father."

"No, please no." She gripped my arm. Tears made her green eyes sparkle. "Oh God." She dropped to her heels, hand over her eyes. The cop shot me a moderately sympathetic look and snapped his notebook shut.

"Better call him," he said. I nodded, shivering in the cool night air. The EMTs had the injured boy on a gurney now. He moaned in pain as it rolled by me. I gripped Taylor's arm and hauled her to her feet.

"What in the hell happened to him?"

"He was walking on the railing or something stupid."

I glanced up, confirming what I recalled about the deck railing and its relative distance from the ground. "Fucking-A," I muttered, gripping my phone and trying to get up the nerve to call Trent, which would of course reveal my own complicity in the basic wrongness of this whole scene.

Taylor was sniveling and shaking. Fury clouded my vision. The sheer stupidity of this whole thing made my head ache. I touched the quick dial and put the phone to my ear at the precise moment I remembered that he'd had minimal battery on the thing when I'd first talked to Taylor. When my call went straight to his voicemail, I closed my eyes and leaned against the flight of steps.

"What?" She yanked my phone from my hand. I snatched it back.

"Oh no you don't," I said, marching her up the steps where the cops were talking to the other girl and boy who both looked like they were about to throw up. If they hadn't already. "You listen to me, young lady. You dragged me into this and now I have to tell your father that I lied to him to come up here and save your sorry ass." I shook my finger in her face. She seemed moderately contrite. "Now, guess what? Your dad's phone is dead so there's only one other person you can call. I suggest you get her on the line, now."

Nodding, she took her phone from her pocket, touched the screen and put it to her ear. "Mom? Mommy? I need you to come up here. I can't get hold of Dad."

I turned away from her, my face burning hot as I tried to imagine how any of this would end in any way that would possibly work in my favor. I got a whole lot of nothing. I watched as the ambulance doors slammed on the moaning deck-railing-walker and as the vehicle drove away, lights and sirens going full force. I sighed and slumped into one of the lounge chairs. Probably the one where I'd made love with Trent a few weekends ago.

I groaned and put my head on my knees and prayed like mad for a miracle.

Chapter Seventeen

Trent's dreams were of soft sheets, pillowy clouds, fields of flowers that smelled like chocolate and cinnamon, and of the full, delicious lips of his new girlfriend.

His. Girlfriend. His. Melody.

He saw her, felt her, held her, made love to her over and over in his mind. He also smelled leather and candle wax, something else he couldn't wait to try with her. She was staring at him through the cream-colored mask, her expressive brown eyes shining.

She was knocking on something, making a huge racket all of a sudden. He glanced around, trying to figure out where the loud banging noise was coming from. It was getting louder, breaking in to his pleasant, sexy dreams.

"Hey, open up, god damn it!"

His eyes opened. He rolled out of the bed and scrambled to his feet. After grabbing a pair of shorts, he stumbled out to the door and slid it open, rubbing his eyes and trying to figure out where Melody was. "Sheila," he said, shocked and more than a little dismayed at the sight of her. Every time he laid eyes on her, he was reminded of what a total fool he'd been for her, about her, with her.

"Well, it would seem as though your daughter managed to slip through your overprotective clutches, Trent." She crossed her arms. Her green eyes shone with something way too close to I-told-you-so for his taste. He sighed and leaned against the doorframe.

"Speak English please. You woke me up."

She glared at his bare chest, then into his eyes, her lips turning up in that smile that had once captivated him, and now made him want to put his fist through the wall. "Well?" He tried to keep the edge out of his voice. Taylor. Something was up with Taylor.

"Are you going to let me in?"

"No, I'm not. Tell me what's going on."

She sighed. "She's up north, Trent. She threw a party or something at that fucking obnoxious cabin. Some kid fell off the deck. The cops need us there."

"What in the hell?" He stepped back. "The cops? A party? Off the deck?" He knew he was babbling but none of it would compute.

Sheila stayed in the hallway, glaring at him. She glanced at her phone, then put it to her ear. "Tay?"

"Give me that fucking thing." He grabbed the phone out of her hand. "Taylor? What the fuck? Where are you? What were you thinking?"

The girl was sobbing so much he could barely hear her.

"Cut the shit, god damn it. Talk to me."

"I…I'm sorry, Daddy. I'm s-s-s-sorry. I didn't mean to…"

He saw the note with his name on it and snatched it up, as he tried to formulate an answer to his beautiful, God-awful daughter. Knowing he had to own this, that he'd been the one to take his eye off the ball with her, he read through the note, then crumpled it in his hand. Wishing Melody was here, but knowing her mother was a priority for her and when she called, Melody went running, he tossed it in the trash.

"Put someone on the phone. An adult." He was expecting it to be a policeman. But the voice he heard stopped him in his tracks.

"Trent? Honey?"

He put a hand on the kitchen counter to keep from keeling over. "What…are you doing there?"

"She…I…you were… *Mierda*."

He closed his eyes. "A simple answer is all I require. Why are you there, and I'm here, staring at my ex-wife who has just informed me that Taylor threw a motherfucking

147

party at my cabin and some kid is now in the hospital." His vision was going wonky. The sound of his own heartbeat deafened him.

"She called. I answered it. It wasn't…it wasn't this bad then. She just needed a ride home—"

"A ride home. From fucking Petoskey?" He was yelling now. But he didn't care.

"Well, yes. But…"

"Melody, just stop. Right there. I have to think. I have to get some clothes on. And, best of all, I have to drive all the way up there with the ex-Mrs. Hettinger."

"Trent…I'm…"

"You had no business doing whatever it was you thought you were doing. Do you understand?"

"Yes. Without a doubt."

"God damn it, Melody, don't you dare get snippy with me."

"I was only trying to help."

"No, you lied to me so you could suck up to Taylor. And it backfired on you." He held up a finger when Sheila held out her hand for her phone. "I have to go. I… We will be there in about three hours."

"They're taking all of them to the police station, so you should go there, not to the house." Her voice was tight. He felt immediate regret for being so harsh. But fuck him to hell and back, this was beyond the pale. What in the name of all that as holy made her think doing any of this without telling him was a good idea?

"Melody…"

"No, no, you're right. I have no business. None whatsoever. I'm going home now. Your daughter and her friends will be in police custody. The kid who fell only broke his leg. Good luck."

He opened his mouth to answer, but the line was dead.

"Fuck!" He clenched his fists on his knees for a few seconds.

"Where is my daughter, Trent?" she demanded as she

caught the phone he tossed her.

"Our daughter is in police custody, Shelia. Hang on. Give me five minutes to get dressed."

They were in his Jeep in seven minutes, pointed north. He did his best to ignore her all the way up, keeping the music cranked and providing her with enough monosyllabic answers to give her the hint that he wasn't in the mood to chat. By the time he finally parked at the small police station, he'd ground his teeth so much his skull ached. He wanted to lay eyes on Melody. To reassure her that he didn't mean to be a dick. But he'd blown that, big time.

He jumped down to the asphalt and ran to the front door, shoving it open and calling for Taylor, letting Sheila fend for herself.

"Can I help you?" A tall, unformed man stepped in front of him.

Trent pulled up short. "I'm Taylor Hettinger's father. She's here. The one with the…the house party?"

"Yes. This way."

Sheila caught up with him. "I'm her mother."

The officer opened a door, indicating they should head through it. Trent rubbed his temples, willing the headache away as he followed Sheila down the hallway. As they turned a corner, Trent pulled up short.

Taylor sat on a bench, her eyes red, her legs shaking. She was flanked by Tina—she of the not-terribly-observant mother—on one side. And Melody on the other. When she met his gaze him, his heart expanded at the sight of her beautiful brown eyes.

"Melody."

She rose, lifting her chin. He saw the set of her jaw. Recognized the flash in her gaze. "I'll leave this for you, now. I think my level of understanding of the situation has been exhausted." She glanced back at Taylor. "Next time, think twice before lying to your parents."

She walked up to him.

"Who's this, Tay?" Sheila was beside the girl now,

brushing her hair out of her face and glaring up at Melody.

"That's Dad's new...friend," Taylor said, keeping her gaze on the floor.

"Then maybe the better question is, why is she here?"

Trent shot Sheila a hard glare. She met it halfway. "It's a legit question, Trent. Who does she think she is, coming up here before us?"

Trent swallowed hard, hearing the gist of his words to Melody spit back at him. He looked from his ex-wife to Melody, then back again. By the time he met Melody's eyes again, she was holding out her hand. When he didn't move, she grabbed his arm and dropped the necklace — her collar — into his palm, and closed his fingers around it.

"Wait, Melody. I'm sorry. I was..."

"No, it's all right. You were just speaking the truth. I had no business. So, I'm divesting myself of your business."

He attempted to arrange his face in please-be-calm lines. "You're overreacting. Now is not the time..."

She smiled at him, brushed her fingertips along his cheek. "Goodbye, Trent."

She walked out, leaving him holding a piece of jewelry that to his mind was for all intents and purposes, a wedding ring, surrounded by his hell-cat of an ex-wife and his sixteen-year-old daughter who was being held by the cops on charges of breaking and entering and possession of booze and pot. He took a long, deep breath, shoved the necklace into his pocket and turned to the officer who was watching this particular trauma drama play out.

"All right. Tell me what happens next."

Chapter Eighteen

Four weeks later

In the time between that horrible moment at the police station in Petoskey and now, I'd never been more grateful for the coping skills I'd developed. As I re-inhabited that space — somewhere between sleepwalking and brutally focused on anything but myself — I even admitted to myself how much I'd enjoyed it. That its warm, familiar contours, corners and edges were something I'd actually missed, in a sick way.

Luckily, the work at Fitz Pub was a near twenty-four-seven challenge. Evelyn had put me in charge and left me alone to run it the way I saw fit, which meant first drilling down to see why the place was hemorrhaging money. That meant poring over daily reports until my eyes crossed. But it also meant I could not think about Trent.

"I need some space to think about what happened," I'd told him in the one and only communication I'd allowed since that night.

"I need to see you," he'd pleaded. "Let's talk about this face-to-face."

But I'd left it at that. Easily the hardest thing I'd ever done, and I'd done some hard things in my life.

"Hey," Evelyn said one evening a solid month since that bizarre, amazing, horrible weekend. She used to come down a few nights a week for a beer after work with me. But that had turned into every night, now that she and Austin were on the outs.

"Hey yourself," I said, pouring her a stout and myself an

IPA. I turned my laptop around to face her. "I found the leaky spot. Your ex-manager was siphoning cash. Pretty easy to do when deposits are made daily. I want to change that system. Keep more cash on hand so money isn't being handled every day like that."

"Fine." She put her head on her arms. I patted her shoulder. My sympathy for her was real, if tinged with a bit of frustration. She was being way too stubborn and I'd told her as much. But she also had a side bonus to distract her, which made me jealous all over again.

"How's the hunky German?"

"Oh, he's...fine."

"Evelyn," I said, sitting beside her and taking a sip of my beer before continuing. "You look awful." I lifted her face and inspected it. Sallow skin, dark circles under her huge, blue eyes. Even her hair was stringy and wrung-out. "Why won't you just call him—?"

She smacked my hand away, frowning as she pulled her beer closer. "You have no room to talk. My friend Trent is beside himself and wearing me out asking about you."

I sighed. She sighed. We smiled at each other and lifted our glasses for a toast. "To us," I said. "And our stupid, bull-headed personalities." I spotted Ross Hoffman, the new brewer for Fitzgerald and the man doing the Evelyn-distracting. He was indeed Viking-like in his appearance— very tall, broad-shouldered, long blond hair he kept tied back, light reddish beard along his jaw. His smile was usually mischievous. I liked him, on a certain level.

"Ladies," he said, sliding into the seat on Evelyn's other side. She sighed and leaned into him a second, then pulled away fast, in case anyone had seen her do it. As I sipped and observed them, I saw how their shoulders touched, the way he put his arm around her, briefly, brushing her hip with his fingers. They were sleeping together, of course. Evelyn had told me that. I didn't get it. But she was my friend so I didn't pry.

"Trent finally got his approval on the city block in K-zoo,"

Evelyn said, eyeing me for a reaction.

"Good for him," I said, unable to stop the rapid flutter in my chest at the sound of his name again. "That will keep him busy."

"I suppose. Whatever happened with Taylor?"

"I don't know. Stop making me talk about him. I don't make you talk about..." I leaned on the bar and caught Ross's eye. He raised his eyebrow at me. "About him."

"Fair enough," she said, hopping down off her barstool. "Ross, I have to finish up some work upstairs. Meet me later?"

He nodded, kept drinking and ignoring me. I noodled around with my sales projections, then snapped my computer shut. Time to start the third half of my day. The part where I avoided going home, since all I could see, smell or hear in my space was Trent.

Why won't you talk to him? You've had your damn space. It's been a month. You miss him. You probably love him. Get over yourself.

I shook my head, clearing it of my inner advice column. I smiled briefly at Ross, then headed around the bar, aiming for my small office behind the kitchen. I figured I could stretch out the work from today well into the evening, with careful planning. "Hey, um, Melody?"

I turned at the sound of the brewer's German-inflected voice. "Yes?"

He looked almost as bad as Evelyn at that moment. The usual light had gone out of his eyes. His shoulders slumped. His cheeks were gaunt under the facial hair. "Can I ask you something?"

I hesitated. We hadn't really talked much beyond the basics. I admired his professionalism, managing his own staff in relation to mine. He kept a super tight ship and a stringently clean brewery, which mattered, since I planned to double our income once I convinced him to make a few funkier, trendier brews just for pub consumption. But we were hardly buddies. The awkward fact of his presence and my knowledge of how he, Austin and Evelyn had been a real live threesome for a while made my face flush.

He grinned that boyish, troublemaking grin, which put me at a bit more ease. "So, um..." He fiddled with the coaster under his beer. "What's the word? I mean, the gossip. You know about me...and...her."

I crossed my arms and stared at him, a little surprised by this question. He'd not struck me as the sort of guy who gave a shit about gossip. "Well, it didn't help that Amy walked in on you guys a few weeks ago...up in her office, you know?"

He actually blushed as he looked up at the ceiling. "Yeah. Guess not."

"It's not a secret, Hoffman, if that's the fantasy you're indulging. She and Austin broke up but he left her and you in charge here while he runs his father's food supply company. You guys were...ah..." I put my hand to my neck. I did that a lot lately, feeling the phantom weight of Trent's collar that I'd worn for all of six hours.

Ross slumped even farther. I patted his arm, not at all surprised by the bulky muscles under my palm. Guy was built, there was no doubt about it. He ran a hand around the back of neck, then across his bearded jaw. "I don't want it to be...bad, you know? Nasty talk. I'm not just...um... with her, physically."

"You mean you're not just fucking the boss for shits and giggles?" I grabbed his glass and refilled it, leaning forward on the bar, eager to talk as it allowed me to drag my evening make-work out even later.

His eyes narrowed at me, then he chuckled. "Yes. That. You have a lovely way with words." He held up his glass to me, then took a long drink.

"So I'm told." I studied him a few seconds. "How is Austin?"

"He's...not great." Ross ripped the coaster in half then crumpled it in his fist. "God damn it."

I peeled his fingers open and retrieved the soggy cardboard.

"Those cost me money, Adolf," I said, hoping to lighten the mood. The last thing I needed was more downers.

He gave me a half-smile. "All right, *señorita*. Sorry." He slid off his barstool and stretched his long arms up, then out to his sides. "Gotta go. The boss lady summons me."

"I'll just bet she does. Lock the office door this time, hot stuff."

He waved a hand as he headed around behind the bar and back to the back room that led to the old brewery space, and Evelyn's office.

I was half-sorry for, half-jealous of my friend all over again. I believed that she loved Austin Fitzgerald — that they were meant to be together. That she was using Ross and his admittedly useable body to deflect from her heartbreak. But who was I to criticize? I was using work. Not quite as nice, but still. I propped my elbows on the bar and watched the staff doing their thing, aware of my presence. I honestly believed the same thing about me and Trent Hettinger but I would be damned if I'd let him talk to me like he had that night.

"We have matching tempers," he'd said to me. I'd laughed it off. But it was pretty damn clear to me now that he'd spoken the truth. I held my phone out, staring at the screen, willing myself to stop being such a total butt-head about this. If I were in one of the novels I'd read as part of my research in the BDSM lifestyle, readers would be screeching at me right now and throwing their e-readers against walls.

I gathered up my laptop and headed to my office, checking in on the night's cook, already concocting excuses to stay later in my head.

* * * *

The next week was more of the same. The following, just another set of days where I kept my head down and my brain focused on my job. I'd fired some people, hired a few more, including a new chef for the kitchen. Convincing

Evelyn to let me pay him a going rate had been almost too easy.

And finally, a Friday came where I didn't feel like I had to stay and watch everything like a hawk. Which both thrilled and depressed me. I would have to go home. Alone. And stare around at the space where I'd been so happy for a few, short weeks. As I was packing up my laptop and a few papers, I heard raised voices coming from the back hallway. I peeked around to tell them to cut it out, that their constant squabbling was scaring the natives. The voices got louder, but I couldn't see anything.

The Evelyn and Ross Show was, on one level, highly entertaining. They were well-matched in stubbornness, pride and their willingness to have loud, public arguments. I could tell that their dynamic included the ongoing friction. I knew my friend well enough to realize this. But I also knew she was miserable without Austin. Something had to give. Ross was falling right off a cliff over her and it would end nowhere but in a hole of shit, which would not help this company one bit.

The gossip was loud and moved fast through all sides of the brewery. Ross was a prickly guy when he was at work—particular about every aspect of brewing as he should be but many times too impatient and overly critical of his staff. That had only gotten worse in the past two or three weeks. Now that I was established as a sort of go-between from the staff to Evelyn, as she'd made herself into something scary and unapproachable, I heard it all—the stories of thrown office supplies, screaming matches and, of course, the sex. Those two would go at it just about anywhere. Making up, it would seem, was just as important as the daily breaking up.

I burst through the main brewery doors and found them, their faces inches apart, yelling at each other, neither of them doing a second of listening to the other. "Hey!" I clapped my hands to get their attention. "Cut the shit!"

They stopped, turning to look at me. Their faces were

flushed, eyes bright, but they were both in a steep personal decline over this, robust, daily sex or not. I put my hands on my hips and gave them my most stern, boss-lady glare. "To your corners."

"I... He..." Evelyn spluttered.

"I don't care. Go upstairs to your office and cool off. I'll be up there in a minute."

She glanced at Ross. I pulled her away from him. The fury was rolling off the man in waves, almost physically palpable against my skin. She headed up the metal steps at a run. "And you," I said, turning back to the man who was now leaning against a fermentation tank, his smirk firmly in place. "You need to find some other outlet for your frustration. This is killing her. And you. But I'm more concerned about her right now."

He rolled his eyes and tried to turn away from me. I wrapped my hand around his arm and dug my fingertips in. He glared down at my hand, then at my face. His expression had gone from red-faced furious, to up-yours fuck-off, to almost helpless and anguished so fast it took me a second to process it. I let go of him. He stood there, staring at me, his handsome face fallen, his entire body slumped in an utterly defeated posture.

"I have to get them back together," he said, his voice hoarse. I blinked, not expecting this.

"You are not responsible for them." I backed away from him. "That's crazy, Ross."

"No, it's not." He pressed his hands against the stainless-steel vessel. His head dropped low, between his shoulders. "I have to do it. She is not for me. As much as I want that. I can tell. We...we make love and I see another man's face in her eyes when she looks at me."

I felt my face flush hot at his words.

"But it's a man who is my good friend. Who brought me into this, with her. I've got to fix this." He shoved past me, muttering in German, and stomped to the exterior door, slamming it shut behind him. I stood, watching the night shift assemble itself around the daily drama. The shared looks, the sideways glances, they all knew. And if they didn't, they sure as hell did now after that confessional moment.

Deciding to let people come to their own conclusions, since they would anyway, I headed up the stairs to the office Evelyn used, overlooking the main brewery floor. I hesitated outside her door a few seconds, gathering my thoughts, wondering what in the hell I could possibly offer by way of advice. When I heard her suck in a breath and let out a sob, I decided that advice was not required. She just needed a friend.

I shoved open the door and found her, crumpled in a wrinkly-suited heap on the floor, weeping as if her heart were truly breaking. "*Ah, chica,*" I said, dropping to the floor next to her and pulling her into my arms. "*Ésta bein, mi amiga. Todo estará bien.*" Everything was fine. Everything would be all right.

I sighed and quelled my urge to join her in the weep-fest and wondered if I even knew what I was talking about. After a few minutes, she swiped at her eyes. I handed her a tissue. She got slowly to her feet and blew her nose, looking for all the world like a sad little girl dressed in her mama's clothes.

"Come on," I said, grabbing her purse. "Let's go find some ice cream."

"I want a pizza," she said, following me out, contrite, crushed and not like my usual feisty friend in the slightest.

"Your wish," I said, holding on to as she wobbled down the metal stairs. "My command."

I heard his voice in my ear then. But I shoved it aside. This was not about me right now. I bundled her into the passenger's side of her car and climbed behind the wheel. She'd given back the super sporty German sedan Austin had bought her and was back in her POS Honda. This was familiar ground. We'd been here plenty of times before, when we were working together at the distributor and pissed off after dates. Well, when she was pissed off after them. I didn't date. Suppressing the strong compulsion to head downtown so Trent could help me with this, I bit the inside of my cheek instead, hard, drawing a satisfying drop of blood.

"My place or yours," I asked, praying that she'd want to go home.

"Yours. Ross is at mine and I can't look at him right now."

I put the car in gear and headed to my place in silence.

"Fair warning," I said, unlocking the door and having to give the Trent-memories an extra shove so they'd cease harassing me. "My place is trashed. I haven't spent much time here lately."

She sighed and slumped against the doorframe as I opened it, then stumbled in, heading for my couch. I'd been sleeping out here for weeks, unwilling to wash the Trent-smell out of my pillows yet unable to tolerate them against my face. I dropped my stuff on the cluttered counter between the kitchen and the rest of the space and looked around, my anxiety at being here making my gut churn.

Evelyn flopped face forward onto my nest of blankets, pillows and wadded-up tissues. A cloud of dust rose, reminding me that I really ought to clean a little. I made a quick call for pizza — bacon, feta cheese, spinach on thin crust, our usual go-to — then checked my alcohol supply. Deciding that this warranted a good bottle of wine instead of a few low-octane beers, I popped the cork on one of the two I still had from one of Trent's wine deliveries — an Italian blend which likely retailed for seventy-five bucks — and grabbed a couple of stemless glasses.

I sat near Evelyn's head and meted out two healthy pours. Nudging her shoulder, I tried to keep my urge to advise, to tell her what she should be doing right now instead of sobbing into an expensive serving of ripasso. "Here. Drink."

She sat up, grabbed a tissue from the box on the coffee table then took the glass. After taking a sniff, she whistled and held the glass up to the light. "Damn. Let me guess.

Something Trent picked out."

"Yes. And that is your one chance to say his name. No more. Please." I held up my glass. She clinked hers to it and we sipped, both of us smacking our lips in appreciation afterward. Italian wines were my favorite, as he had discovered. There really was nothing like them in terms of richness and full-bodied flavor. Evelyn took another drink then cradled the glass to her chest, curling her legs beneath her after kicking off her high-heeled work shoes.

"Thanks," she said, her voice small. "I needed this."

"I know," I said, brushing her hair off her face. We sipped in silence. When the pizza arrived, we ate it out of the box, staring at a brainless thriller I'd found, passing on all the rom-com options.

"You need to talk to him," I said, as I poured the last drops from the second bottle into our now-greasy glasses.

"Fuck you," she muttered, knocking back the wine like it was water. "I don't have to do anything."

"Okay, fine. But you will admit that all this extra drama you and the hot-head brewer cook up every day is not good for company morale. They're already freaked out since Austin vacated his office. And Ross is a pain in the ass enough already, on a good day." She shook her head. I kicked her thigh with my bare toe, hard enough to make her yelp. "You know I'm right. Get a handle on this shit or at least have your fights—and your fucking sessions—at home. I am ears to the ground, *chica*, and I am telling you people are getting weirded out and worried that Fitzgerald Brewing might fail."

"Fail?" She jumped up, swaying a little until she got her bearings. "That's bullshit." She dragged fingers through her hair, staring down in dismay at the handful of strands that had pulled loose. I got up and grabbed her hands.

"You're losing it, Evelyn. So help me I don't know what you should do about Ross but I know one thing—you have got to get Austin back."

"But...Ross is..." She bit her lip and other tear slid down

160

her face

"I know what he is. And he does too. He said today he wanted to get you guys back together. He gets it—it's fun and all, fucking your brains out on every available surface, but it's not something that will last. You and Austin...you will last."

She sucked in a breath. "Water? Please?"

I grabbed some while she headed for the bathroom. We drank and talked a little about the logistics of a threesome, which made my face hot and my body a little too tingly. She was so matter-of-fact about it, but her face told the real story. She loved them both. But she needed Austin in her life.

We called her a ride share, since she was in no shape to drive. She was determined to talk to Ross tonight, to hash out the real issues underlying their constant bickering. As we sat silent again, the TV droning on and filling the air with gunshots, expletives, car crashes and random explosions, my phone buzzed with a text. Thinking it was the ride share, I opened it and saw that it was, instead, from Trent.

I'm outside. Please let me in.

A sharp rap at the door made me yelp and drop the phone. Evelyn got up and opened it, the distinct non-surprised look on her face making my blood boil. I stood between them, pushing Trent back even as I got that usual melty all over feeling at the sight of him. "No. Sorry. You are not allowed to let him into my place."

"Melody—"

I whirled on her. "Your ride is here. Go on and mind your own business for a while. God knows it needs some minding." She grimaced and reached out to give me a tentative hug. "I know you did this. I'll let you know if I ever forgive you."

We stood side-by-side, watching her head up the stairs,

like a pair of over-anxious parents seeing our precious girl out on her first date.

I blew out a breath, and turned to him, arms crossed. "I'm not interested in talking to you. I'm sorry you wasted your time coming here."

He clenched his jaw. As I was noting how miserable he looked, I began closing the door, determined to stand my ground, to not get any more mixed up with him than I had — it was already going to take months of mental deprogramming to get him out of my head. His hand shot out. He stopped the door, sending it crashing back against the wall. After taking a single step, he was in my space, looming over me. I glared up at him.

He held up his hand. I glanced at it, saw the thing dangling from it and began backing away. "No," I said, my voice as firm as I could manage.

"This isn't for you," he said. He pulled out the plain, ladder-backed chair I had next to a tiny table that doubled as a desk. "It's for me." He sat, and handed me the pitch-black blindfold. "Put it on me. And then start asking me questions. Ask me anything you want. Hell, do anything you want. But just fucking talk to me."

I took it, pulling its silkiness through my other hand. My ears were buzzy, the way they always got around Trent.

"You owe me one good reason for ignoring me for this damn long." He pointed to the blindfold. "Make me as vulnerable as you want. This is your chance."

Without a word, I put the cover over his eyes, and fastened it in back with the long ribbons, giving it a tight yank for good measure. He put his hands on the chair arms and wrapped his long fingers around the ends. His jaw kept clenching, unclenching. I could hear his teeth grinding together.

I pulled another chair over and placed myself in front of him, our knees and toes nearly touching. Resisting the worst possible urge to touch his face, to soothe and calm and reassure, I leaned forward, elbows on my knees, studying his face — or as much of it as I could see. "Tell me about Sheila."

He sucked in a breath, blew it out and seemed to deflate all over, like a day-old party balloon. "We met at a party, not unlike the one I took you to, with dancing and masks and expensive clothes. I was twenty-four years old, a raw rookie at the scene but one with promise, I was told. I had my first liquor store going gangbusters and was trying to scrape up a loan to buy the second one. I was basically living in back of the store for the time being, saving as much money as I could. But spending it on the things I loved. Like the Dom and sub parties." He took another breath. "Sheila was trolling for a rich husband, as it turned out, but she was good at faking it. She snagged me. We had some...some admittedly amazing times together." He slumped back in the chair, as if it hurt to admit it.

"But she lied about birth control. And within a few months, after we went out on real dates and she had her hooks in me good, she broke the joyous news. I was not overjoyed. But I am a man who does the right thing. So we got married."

He blew out a breath. I waited.

"I grew up without a mother — or more precisely without the attention of the one I had. My therapist says I project my need to be nurtured onto the wrong women — at least one wrong woman. I was shuttled around between my mother's sisters for years. They all hated her, resented her for being the prettiest one. And they took it out on me after my father had her committed to an asylum."

I bit my lip. My hands were itching to touch him. But I kept my distance.

"I remember her in snippets. Her hair — it was long and blonde. Her smile which was wide and sweet. Her voice, a beautiful voice, she used to sing me to sleep. Or maybe I'm just making that up, who knows?" His breathing was getting ragged. "My father..." He stopped and swallowed hard. "He was a fucking asshole." Trent shook his head.

I could tell he wanted to pull off the blindfold. I admired his control, keeping it in place. "He used to beat the living shit out of me and my half-sister, Kayla. Then when she started to look less like a little girl and more like a woman he...he..." Trent stopped. I held my breath. "Anyway, she ran away when she was seventeen and I was almost thirteen. That's when my mom lost it and my father had her committed."

I got up and walked to the window, closing my eyes at the thought of his sister at the mercy of a horrible bully — the one man in the world who is supposed to love you unconditionally. My father had loved me, but my mother had shielded him from the ugly truth about me — for his health, she'd claimed.

"My mom got out of the asylum when I was nearly seventeen. I'd lived with cousins and aunts for years, never made to feel welcome. Always knowing I was this giant burden to them. But she got out and I thought...I thought everything would be fine. Kayla was long gone. My father had left, supposedly to work on an oil rig. It would be me and my mom and we'd be fine. That lasted about a month."

He shifted in the chair, gripped the arms ever tighter. "I was a good student and a few of my teachers knew my home life was shit so they'd made a project out of me. They were bound and determined to get me into a good college, on a full scholarship. So I wrote essays and took practice SAT exams on weekends, when I wasn't playing football, of course."

I looked at him. His beautiful mouth was turned up in a smile. "Then one Saturday I stayed later to do another practice reading session — not my strongest subject. When I dropped my bike on the lawn, I saw a strange beater truck in the drive." As I watched, his Adam's apple bobbed as he swallowed a few times and he licked his lips, as if trying to get rid of a nasty taste.

I knelt next to him, laid my head on his knees, my need to prove something to him vanished like so much smoke.

He didn't touch me, stroke my hair or in any way indicate he noticed I was there. He was so tense, like a violin string, pulled tight. I ran my hand down his calf, cursing myself for being so selfish, for thinking I was the only one with the shitty backstory.

"He was...hurting her. Right in the living room. He had her..." He gulped and lifted his face to the ceiling. "He had her pinned on the floor and was beating on her, like some kind of a sick animal. There was blood...everywhere. She yelled at me to leave. I yanked him off her mid stroke and beat the ever-loving crap out of him — my own father."

A bead of sweat rolled down his forehead. I tried to touch his face but he flinched away from my fingers. "No. I'm going to finish. You won't ever understand me otherwise."

I laid my head back on his knee, keeping my arms around his legs.

"He was lying there, not moving. My knuckles..." He lifted his right hand to his lips as if smelling the blood there again. "My knuckles were shredded. When I turned to check on her, she was lying in a heap, not moving either. I remember...I remember standing there between them, thinking who in the *fuck* lives like this? Hand to mouth. Going to bed hungry or feeling guilty for taking a bit of food from a cousin's plate. Always afraid that my father would come home drunk and beat on me or molest my sister or...or..." His voice broke. His head hung low. "I swore to myself, right then and there, that my life would be different. I would work harder, reach higher, be successful and, above all, rich. Rich as fucking God, I thought as I stood there, trying to decide which of my parents were dead."

"*Mi Dios,*" I said with a sigh.

"I was going to be rich, successful and most of all I was going to treat women the way they were meant to be treated. Not like shit. Not like...like a hole to stick my dick in and run off. I would be fucking different." He bit off these last words, spitting into the room. Veins stood out on his neck. His cheeks were flushed red.

I got up and lifted the blindfold from his face. He grabbed my hands, stopping me. "No, god damn it. You have to hear the rest and I need this privacy. You're the only one who knows all of it. But I can't look at you while I tell it."

I ran my fingertips along his jawline, willing him to relax. He shivered and leaned into my hand. "My mother died a week later, from a cerebral hemorrhage." He wiped trembling fingers across his lips. "My father... He...he died too. I killed him. I guess. He lived about a week longer than she did, in a coma. I sat with him, watching him sleep, hating his guts and wishing I had the nerve to cover his face with a pillow and finish the job."

"In the end, he died when I wasn't even there, the old fucker." The chuckle that burst from his mouth was not a pleasant one. "I got there one morning to sit my vigil and his bed was empty, stripped, erased. I stared at it for a while, then I told them I didn't have any money and I didn't care what they did with his body.

"I rode my bike home and sat in the cold, empty house for a few days, as if I were in a coma too. Then I got my ass in gear, went to school and focused even harder on getting into the best college possible. I did it too. I lived in that rat hole of a house as long as I could, before the authorities came and booted me out. But I was eighteen by then, so they couldn't stuff me in a foster home or anything. I lived out of my car for a while, then a friend took me in and let me crash on his couch for a year."

"I worked three jobs while I went to school in Ann Arbor and graduated in three and a half years with a business degree and a great job as a manager of the liquor store. And I worked and worked and worked my ass off and when the old man wanted to sell the place, he let me buy it off him — he even financed me. The rest, well, I got into the scene, thanks to that same friend who let me live on his couch. I started going to parties. I made more money. I met Sheila. She got pregnant. We married. We divorced. She got Taylor at first, which killed me. But she left the house one Friday night, drunk off her ass, seemingly forgetting that our baby was still in her crib. I got custody and not by being nice, either."

He slumped back again, still not touching me or acknowledging me in any way. He sat, silent, all his words spent, it would seem.

"I didn't know what I wanted out of life. I mean, I had fun. I got to have sex the way I preferred it. But I never let myself get close. I rejected closeness. Went out of my way to keep my sexual partners at a distance." He put a hand on my head. "Until a few months ago, when I walked into a diner after bolting from one of my so-called parties. And I saw the most amazing creature dressed in an awful pink uniform shirt with her name on it, holding a pot of weak coffee and flirting with a roomful of truckers.

"I'm about as fucked up as they come, Melody. But so help me I do love you. I made a decision about you. And I don't make decisions lightly. I *need* to know why you won't let me back in your life."

I got up slowly, pulled him to his feet, wrapped my arms around his neck and kissed him, and kissed him and kissed him. I lost myself in him, praying he'd feel my strength, sense my willingness to be here, present, fully with him. He kept on the blindfold as he sat back down and tugged my super not-sexy flannel pants down my hips, pressing his lips to my belly and wrapping his arms around me. I stroked his scalp, ran my fingers down his neck and back. Tears poured down my face as I made nonsense sounds, trying to soothe him.

"I need you," he whispered, sliding his hands up my shirt and flipping open my bra with one practiced flick of his wrist. "I need to feel you."

He lifted my shirt up and off, leaving me standing in nothing but panties. His nostrils flared. "Ah God, Melody. You scare the living shit out of me but I don't care. I can't care anymore. I want you."

"Sh...sh...*mi amor*," I said, pulling him to his feet. I

unzipped his jeans and shoved them down, didn't bother with the buttons on his shirt, just ripped it off him like some kind of crazy person. "Sh...sh...sh..." I kept saying as I led him to the couch and pressed him down, straddling him and taking him inside me with a tilt of my hips. "Ah...yes."

He gripped my thighs and thrust up, leaning forward to take one of my nipples in his mouth. My tears wouldn't stop even as the exquisite pleasure of having him inside me again, the sweet bite of his teeth on my nipple, the noises he made deep in his throat all combined to bring on a soul-shattering orgasm. I heard myself yelling as I ground against him, while tiny explosions went off behind my eyes.

Finally, I lifted the blindfold. His eyes were bloodshot, but his smile was wide. "Oh, Melody — my love," he whispered, lifting me as he kept our bodies connected, then laying me back on the couch, muttering to me in Spanish and English. He stroked into me, making us both groan. I lifted my hips, wrapped my legs and arms around him. "I'm yours, *mi amor*."

When he cried out into the dark room, his entire body shuddering with his climax, I tried, and failed, not to cry. I still owed him a direct answer to his question — why had I held him off for the last month, why I'd not let what I knew in my heart to rule my behavior. But for now, all I wanted was to feel his body against me, above me, inside me. The rest would, no doubt, come in due course.

Chapter Nineteen

Trent rolled over and pulled Melody close, burying his nose in the tumble of her fragrant hair. She sighed and curved against him, fitting her head into his shoulder as he stretched his arm underneath her. He dozed, until the sun slanting into his window woke him fully. After kissing her shoulder and disentangling himself, he rolled and sat, rubbing his eyes.

He glanced over her shoulder at her, the lovely hourglass shape under a sheet, the tumble of hair. With a smile, he ran a hand down the swell of her hip. She didn't move. She was easily the hardest sleeper he'd ever met—or slept with—in his life. As it was Sunday, he decided to try his hand at a little breakfast in bed action.

She was still snoozing away when he emerged from a shower and put on jeans and a T-shirt. The summer months had ushered in a cooling trend, and they'd left the windows open the night before. The breeze on their bare skin had been invigorating as he'd taught her a thing or three about how much fun a bit of candle wax play could be. But now as he went around the loft shutting them, he realized that time, as it tended to do, was marching forward. And in the weeks since reuniting, they'd spent way too much energy tiptoeing around the elephant in the room—the sixteen-year-old one with the ongoing disdainful looks and rolled eyes.

Taylor had decamped to her mother's house—the house he still paid the mortgage on—after her four-week mandated house arrest, combined with expensive court appearances and lawyer meetings. It had been determined by Sheila, with some agreement from himself, that a change of environment for the balance of the summer might do her some good. Now that his ex seemed to have gotten her act together, maturity-wise, he didn't worry about the two of them like he used to do.

And it left him free to move Melody in to his home, installing her where he wanted her to be, with her own part of the closet, dresser drawers and bathroom space. He hummed along with the Rolling Stones as he scrambled the eggs and added cilantro and crumbled chorizo the way she'd taught him. He sipped coffee, waiting for the oven toast to crisp, then put everything on a tray.

She was on her back, one lush breast exposed, arm over her eyes to block the sun. He sat on her side of the bed and put the tray down, then gave her nipple a hard pinch. She yelped and smacked his arm.

"Time for breakfast, sleepy head." He poked her leg. She moved so he could sit next to her, the tray across his lap. "Well, more like time for lunch. But it is Sunday." He handed her a cup of coffee, expertly mixed with milk and a dollop of sugar the way she preferred it.

She sipped and sighed, cradling it to her sheet-covered chest. He took a bite of the eggs. "Mmm…perfection if I do say so myself." He held a forkful to her lips. She smiled and ate it, then sipped some more. He fed her bites of toast, letting her lick the butter from his fingers. She'd gotten used to this little quirk of his — that at times, all he wanted to do was feed her, watch her eat, observe her enjoyment of something he provided.

She waved away the last half of toast, her mouth pursed. She sipped, frowned, then set the cup down and leaned back. "Ugh. Did we really drink all that beer last night?"

"Yes, my love. We did. It was fun, remember?" He grabbed the candle he'd used from the nightstand and waved it at her. If he weren't mistaken, he was feeling a little frisky again, now that he had some food in his belly. "Want some more?"

"No," she said, pushing his arm aside and lurching out of the bed. "Oh my God...I gotta..."

She barely made it to the bathroom where he found her, huddled over the toilet, her face pale and sweaty. He ran a washcloth under cool water, then handed it to her. "Jeez, if you don't like my cooking all you have to do is say it." He crouched down next to her, noting the glazed look in her eyes. "Come on. Back to bed."

"No...no...I have to..." The sound of her hurling was not the sexiest thing in the world. But he waited, holding her hair to keep it from trailing into the mess. She flopped onto her butt, wiping her lips.

"All done?"

She nodded. He flushed, then pulled her up. She swayed a little, moaning into his chest. "Need to brush my teeth." He handed her a toothbrush. "You're hovering."

He backed out, worried that she might have picked up the stomach flu that had laid several of his sub-contractors low, which meant more delays in his block redevelopment. Which had led to his need for lots of beer and rough sex the night before. He heard the shower come on so he took the tray back to the kitchen and tidied up before opening his laptop to study the latest bad news on his project.

She emerged a half hour later, looking a thousand times better. Her hair was up, but he let it slide. He was neck-deep in trying to reschedule inspections and other crap around all the incessant delays so barely noticed when she slid into the chair next to him and put her head on his shoulder. "Hang on, babe, I gotta deal with this a few more minutes." She kissed his shoulder.

"It's all right. I need to head to the bar."

He glanced at her, but was too distracted by an email from one of his investors about a potential tenant for the building to pay close attention. "Today? Something wrong over there?"

"No. Well, maybe. Tia didn't show up for work, so we're short."

171

"But it's Sunday. How busy can it be?"

"Busy enough," she said. He blinked, hearing the somewhat breezy tone of her voice. He knew that tone. It was the 'I-have-something-I-want-to-say-but-won't-because-you-need-to-read-my-mind' one. He was no rookie in the woman game. But for this woman, he made the effort. He grabbed her arm and pulled her into his lap, kissing her nose, cheeks and lips. She let him but he sensed her withdrawal.

Deciding that since they had spent more or less every night together for a month, plus plenty of day time — she'd surprised him once, showing up at his office wearing nothing but a black raincoat, and he'd reciprocated, demanding that she meet him in one of the suburban parks, where he'd plied her with deli-prepared lunch, and they'd made out like teenagers under the trees — she was getting to a point where she needed some space. Not that she'd said anything like this but his female-mind-reading skills were keen and he believed that he had her mostly figured out.

"Okay, *chica*, go on. Pour the beer and flirt with the young dudes for a few hours. I'm good here, all by my lonesome." He pretended to pout, hoping to pull her out of her looming funk. She licked her lips, started to say something then just kissed him instead. "I love you."

She nodded and touched her neck where his collar lay, making the only statement he wanted about them right now. They'd agreed at least on that — no big showy engagements or weddings. Neither of them required it, at least, not yet. He would eventually, but he was willing to give her the time and space she required first.

The Taylor thing still had to be addressed. She lived with him during the school year, and would be moving back in a few weeks. They had not discussed this in any depth and needed to do that, soon. But he saw she was still a little wobbly from her bout of puking this morning. Today was not the day to bring it up.

He stared her, noting that she was pale under light coat of

powder. "Are you sure you feel all right?"

"*Si, guapo*," she said, reassuring him. She only used her pet name for him when she was in a good mood.

"All right. Want to take the Jeep?"

"Um, no thanks. I need to get some gas in my car before tomorrow anyway."

He frowned. "You know how I feel about that piece of shit you call a car, right?"

"*Si, guapo,*" she called from the kitchen. "You know how I feel about not wanting you to be my sugar daddy, right?" She stood in the doorway, putting the lid on her water bottle. "That car has seen me through some times and it has plenty of life left in it." She flicked his head with her fingers, kissed him and smiled. "Stop hovering."

"Yes, ma'am."

She picked up her purse and keys. He heard this but didn't see it as he was back at work, composing a response to the investor about the potential, big-name tenant. That damn lease would pay the principal on the construction loan. He felt his pulse racing at the prospect and barely heard the metal door sliding shut behind her when she left. It was a solid three hours before he emerged from the intense back and forth on the lease, triumphant, exuberant, ready to celebrate, and remembered that she'd left.

On a whim, and without a second thought, he opened Melody's laptop and found her sign-in page for her credit card. He'd observed the number over her shoulder once before, made a comment and been treated to the full force of a string of Spanish curse words. The loose translation of which was: "Mind your business. I've got this, asshole." But he'd also noted that she never signed out of that account.

Today, he was a master of the motherfucking universe. And the master wanted to bestow a gift upon his woman. With a few strokes, he erased her five-figure debt on one card, eliminated her mother's overdue hospital bills and paid back the loan she'd taken out on her paycheck back when she was working at the distributor. After informing those assholes that if they called her number again now that it was paid back with usurious interest he would call the fucking cops, he checked all her balances. The shiny zeros made him smile.

Noting that it was nearly five and that his stomach was rumbling, he put on shoes, grabbed his keys and headed down the elevator, eager to share the news about his new tenant and see Melody.

You're a sap, Hettinger. She is not going to like that you did that.

He shook his head to clear it of the negativity. She'd be mad and cuss him out in Spanish for a bit, but at the end of it all, she'd be debt-free. The best gift any woman could get, really. Then they'd make up. The thought of that made him smile even wider.

He parked and hopped out of the Jeep, waving to a few people he knew lingering in the parking lot on the perfect, late summer Michigan day. As he shouldered his way into the Fitz Pub, he got a text from his investor stating that the lease had been sent and should be in his inbox as of now. His phone dinged with an incoming email.

Trent gave a whoop and glanced around, seeking the pair of eyes he needed. After a few seconds, he took a seat at the bar. The bartender, one of her new hires, Trent figured, since he'd never seen her before—an attractive, if haunted looking woman—would barely meet his eyes as she put a coaster down.

"Hi. I'll have the double IPA. Is Melody around?"

The woman's eyes darted to his left, then settled somewhere near the top of his right ear. He frowned, his scalp prickling in a way that made him nervous. He waited, impatient, but sensing the woman's apparent nervousness. Finally, she raised her gaze and met his. He blinked, noting the unique shade of her eyes, the squared-off jaw, the distinctive nose. And her hair—a light brown with hints of blonde.

"Trent," she said, her voice barely above a whisper. Tears

welled up and slid down her gaunt cheeks. "Oh my God. She said you'd be here one of these days."

"I...don't know what you..." But he did. He tried to breathe, but his throat had closed up and his chest wouldn't cooperate. He stumbled off the tall bar chair, bumping into some guy's shoulder. With a quick apology, he dashed around the end of the bar, took the girl's hand and pulled her into the kitchen. He glared at her, his heart whamming around in his chest. "Kayla. It is you."

She nodded. "It's me. Melody found me a few weeks ago, maybe three or so. I was cleaning hotel rooms, and...other things. Living in a shelter. I'm clean though, Trent. I swear to God. I have been for a year now."

He took in the yellowish tint of her eyes and sallow skin. "Kayla, my God. Where have you been?"

"You don't want to know," she whispered.

"How did she find you?" His heart was racing now, galloping along so fast it made his head hurt and his ears clog up. "Kayla," he whispered, remembering the last time he'd seen his older sister, her nose broken, her eye black. She'd pulled him into the closet and told him stay there until their mother got home from the store, to not tell her what their daddy had just done. That she was leaving for a while. That he had to watch over their mother now. She'd kissed him. He'd cried for hours, going hoarse from it, eventually dropping into sleep out of pure emotional exhaustion. Their mother didn't get home until the next morning. And by then Kayla was long gone.

"Trent?"

He glanced over Kayla's shoulder and spotted Melody. Alarmed because she looked like hell—even sicker than before—he could also tell she was more concerned about this. About how he'd react.

"Why didn't you tell me?" He let go of his sister and tried to get hold of his emotions.

"Don't blame her, T," Kayla said, using the nickname she'd used years ago. "I wouldn't let her. I needed to do this on my terms."

"Where are you living?" His mind wouldn't stop spinning. It careened from awful memories of hearing her screams and cries into the night, to fond ones — of her reading him stories, making him peanut butter sandwiches on white bread and eating them sitting outside behind a row of bushes, hiding from their father. He glanced over at Melody who was leaning on the bar, her eyes closed.

"I have a place, don't worry. I already did, before she found me."

"I...don't know what to say." He swallowed hard, studying how old she looked, how rung out, how ruined. Fury flared in his chest. "I want to kill him all over again."

"I know, T. I know. It's all right."

He blew out a breath, and pulled her tight, holding her until she put her arms around him. "You don't have to tell me it's all right, K. I know it is. I made it that way for myself." He let her go and stared into her eyes again. "I will help you. I'll make things better for you, I promise."

She sighed, and glanced over at Melody, who shrugged in an I-told-you-so way. He stood straighter. "You should have told me."

Kayla gave his arm a weak punch. "Leave her alone, T. I mean it."

"Great, now one more woman to boss me around."

"Best I can tell, you like it that way."

He nodded, rendered speechless by the sight of her, his K, his big sister he'd loved so much and lost. Standing right here, in his girlfriend's bar with a job.

"I need to get back to work." He nodded, still dazed. When Kayla ducked back into the bar, he was left staring across the kitchen at Melody.

"Oh, *bella*," he said. She held up her hand, put it to her lips and ran for the bathroom.

Trent watched her. When he glanced at the kitchen staff, worry was etched on all their faces. They adored their boss. She was the perfect balance of in-charge and friendly, of concerned about their wellbeing and focused on the bar's bottom line. It engendered fierce loyalty, he realized, as he also realized that the head chef, a tall, ex-Marine, African American man named Walt could very possibly kill him with his glare.

Confused, Trent headed for the bathroom, but was waylaid by some of the other staff. "Not now, *pendejo*," one of the guys said, pointing him back toward the bar. "Give her some space."

He was about to shove his way past the smart ass little fucker, his danger radar going into high alert all of a sudden, when he saw Melody's mother emerging from the bathroom holding a wet cloth. "*Hola*, Trent," she said, wiping her brow. "I was helping out in the kitchen today. My Melody knows I get bored. So she lets me—"

Trent held up a hand. "Hello, Josefina. I'm sorry but I need to check on—"

"Oh no, *mi'ijo*. Not now. She's very sick. She doesn't want you to see her."

"But...I'm..." The woman, a force to be reckoned with he knew, turned and guided him away from the bathroom with a soft but firm hand. "I need to check on her."

"Oh, no, no. I will handle this. You go and sit. Go on." She gave him a hard shove for such a petite woman he actually stumbled, not expecting it. The staff tittered. He straightened and headed out, knowing he'd catch up with her and figure out if she needed to go to the hospital or something.

He made a quick decision and sent Taylor a text, telling her he needed her to meet him here, then sat and stared at his sister as she worked, still so flabbergasted that she was actually here, he got tongue-tied more than once. Once the teenager arrived, she took one look at Kayla and squealed in delight, then, thankfully, dominated the conversation a while. Once he felt that Kayla had been put at ease, he had another beer and talked with his investor on the phone, firming up a few details on the new lease. Finally, around seven-thirty, Josefina appeared, smiling and looking so much like her daughter, it made Trent smile back at her. Even though he anticipated her words before she said them.

"I have sent her home to her apartment. She needed to sleep."

Trent sensed himself getting angry, but tamped it down, knowing this woman's legendary temper would only match his if he crossed her. "Oh, all right. I'll go there and check on her." He motioned for his check. Melody's mother put her small hand on his arm, pinning it in place. "Josefina, I don't want to argue with you."

"We are not arguing, *mi'ijo*. I just want you to go home to your house and wait for her. She needs to rest. She doesn't want you hovering."

"I will hover when I feel like it, god damn it." He yanked his arm out from under her hand, threw some money down and stood. He was approaching a full-blown panic attack. "And for your information, I think she needs to go to the hospital. The flu going around shouldn't be ignored. She might need an overnight stay, for hydration, or something." Both Kayla and Josefina were staring at him now, making him feel like a toddler having a tantrum in the grocery aisle.

As he was opening his Jeep door, anger still pinging around in his brain, he felt a tap on his shoulder. "Trent?" It was Josefina. She was wringing her hands and looking worried.

"Yes?" He crossed his arms. As much as he wanted this woman to adore him, he was not about to let her boss him when it came to Melody.

"*Mi'ijo*…" She bit her lip. "I told her that you are a good man. That she should tell you. That you wouldn't care or mind. But she is *muy terca*. So damn stubborn. I'm sure she gets it from her father."

Utterly confounded by her words, Trent leaned back against the Jeep, studying the woman as she spluttered and curse in Spanish. Finally she grabbed his arm tightly. "You will love her, right, *chamaco*? I mean…she loves you so very much but this…I don't know. This might kill her."

Trent rose to his full height and took Josefina's hands in his. "*Señora* Rodriguez, I would do absolutely anything that your daughter asked me to do—I'd do it twice to make sure she was happy—whatever it is. Please believe me. I adore every inch of her and want to spend the rest of my sorry life with her. Now please, *por favor*, tell me what's wrong."

She pulled away, hand over her mouth. "I cannot. I swore to her I would not." Tears slipped out of her already bloodshot eyes.

"*Por favor, mi suegra. Estuviste llorando. ¿Qué tienes?*"

"You really don't know?"

He shook his head.

She sighed. "*Mi'ijo*, she is pregnant."

Trent's brain went on high alert. "No, no, that's not possible. I can't, you see. I had the…operation after Taylor was born." He stopped, his face flushed hot.

The woman was staring hard at him. He took a step back, his rational mind clicking in and taking over before he started screaming and running around the parking lot like the *pendejo* the kitchen guy had called him. Yes, he'd had a vasectomy right after the horror of Taylor's actual birth. But since then, he'd never once forgone condoms, until Melody. And with her, he'd been foolish at first, too eager and blind with lust to worry about diseases but his days worrying about having another oh-my-fucking-god-Trent-I'm-late conversation were well behind him.

He'd told her as much, after they both had a full gamut of tests, and could compare positive sexual health reports over a bottle of wine. He'd said to her, "I don't regret it," when she'd asked him, her huge brown eyes earnest. He'd said, "I don't want any more kids. It's too much work, emotionally, physically and financially. It's not practical at my age anyway." He'd even said, "Thank God we don't have to worry about me knocking you up, eh, *chica*," more than once. And by God he'd meant it.

He groaned, pressing the heels of his hands into his eye

sockets. He heard Melody's mother muttering something in Spanish nearby. He caught the words "sperms" and "boss man" and "stupid," the last one more than once. When he looked up, she was gone.

He got into his Jeep, turned the key and put it in gear. Then he sat, stunned on so many levels he felt as if someone had just run over him with a semi, then backed up and done it again. His hands shook as he gripped the wheel tighter, coming to terms with all he'd learned in the last few hours. His sister — not only alive, if not exactly well, here, working for Melody after she'd found her, without telling him a word about it. And Melody — pregnant. Carrying his child. Bun in the oven. Knocked up...somehow.

He ground his teeth and fought with his inner self. He should go to her. But she didn't want him around. They had to talk. He should go and get his swimmers tested. If he'd been playing with fire for almost seventeen years, he really ought to be aware of that fact. It had been a step he'd skipped, since at that time, in his immature mind, he honestly believed he'd never have sex again. Not if the possible results were the screaming, bleeding horror show that had finally ended, after three days, in an emergency C-section. His head was pounding. His mouth bone dry. The beers he'd drunk made his esophagus burn as the memories of those days Sheila had been in agonizing labor hit him square in the gut.

He peeled out of the parking lot and was outside her building within a few minutes. But the longer he sat, the more he knew that she had to come to him with this. He'd come to her the last time. If she wanted to have his baby, then he would, of course, support that.

But a long-buried part of him was rising up, waving its arms and saying "Stop! Halt! No! You said no more kids. You say what you mean, Hettinger. Now you have to mean what you say. Let her come to you with this. Then, you'll sort it out together."

He groaned and pressed his forehead to the steering

wheel for a few minutes. Then he put the Jeep in reverse, and headed home.

You're a shit head, Hettinger.

No. She wants space. I'll give her some. Then we will talk. I'm sure of it.

But he also knew that she wouldn't come to him. And that he'd just made one of the worst decisions of his life. He drank four more beers in his empty loft, then passed out with his nose pressed into her pillow.

Chapter Twenty

I knew I was pregnant the night it happened.

But one of my best, or worst, abilities is how I can pretend otherwise, ignore the painfully obvious, hope it will vanish on its own thanks to the sheer force of my will.

But I knew.

Any woman who loves a man the way I love Trent Hettinger would know. I think I knew the moment it happened.

It was the night of his horrible confessions to me, about his past. When I learned about Kayla, and how awful his life was as a little boy and young man. When we reunited, bittersweet at first, because I felt I needed to do something to comfort him, to show him how much he was loved. Then later, again, when he took over and showed me how much he wanted me back.

And how.

As I sat in my dark, chilly apartment, sipping cold water with slices of lemon for the nausea — something my nosy, yet observant mother had told me to do when she'd sent me home — I blushed and shivered and sensed myself getting aroused by the memory of that night. He'd carried me to my bed after our first go-round and a brief nap. I'd been sleepy, groggy, exhausted after weeks spent ignoring him and convincing myself it was what I wanted.

He'd lain me down and kissed me from the tips of my toes to my fingers, then down the opposite way on the other side, giving ample attention to my most sensitive parts. As I'd been panting and eager, begging him for release, he'd used the blindfold on me, forcing me to be silent and listen to only his words.

He'd said the dirtiest things to me—shocking me as I'd been expecting romance. But he'd not touched me as he spoke. He'd only whispered, first in one ear, then the other. He'd told me what he wanted to do to me. What he expected me to do to him. At one point, I'd gotten so worked up I wanted to touch myself.

"No touching, *bella*," he'd reminded me as I felt the warmth of my own sex against my fingertips. "I'm want to see if I can make you come with only this." He'd blown a puff of breath on my ear. "I want to watch you get off from the sound of my voice."

I had. And it had been the oddest, yet most erotic thing I'd ever experienced. Some of the things he'd said still rolled around in my head at strange times. He'd never done it again, but I knew it for what it was—proof that he had the sort of power of me that I was happy to relinquish.

As I'd lain on my bed, crying out with pleasure when he'd finally given in and bit down on my earlobe which is what finally sent me over the edge without a single touch anywhere else, he'd rolled me on top of him and shoved into me with a loud groan. I remember looking down at him, staring into his eyes, taking in everything I loved about his face, his neck, the perfect roundness of his head, the smooth skin of his scalp and coming again, or maybe I just kept coming.

But he'd reveled in it, using his voice to tease me even further. He pinched my nipples as he encouraged me to yell or scream or anything I wanted. There was something in the room with us then. Something primal and urgent and raw that I loved.

He'd rolled us over, pinning my arms up over my head and pounding into me so hard it hurt. But I loved it, I welcomed it, and when he'd come inside me then, I knew what had just happened.

I put the water glass down and raced for the bathroom for the millionth time that day. I had nothing left in my stomach but water, but it made its reappearance, leaving me shaking and weak, sitting on the floor gripping the toilet.

Trent had no interest in any more children. He'd made that abundantly clear to me. And at the time, I'd had no beef with that. I'd never really considered myself the motherly type, although my nature tended toward nurture. I never got gooey-eyed over babies, that I could recall anyway. I never wanted to hold one, much less carry one in my body. Right now, of course, I wanted to die from misery. The nausea that had clamped own of me from out of the blue that morning had not released its grip, not once.

I'd run to the bar to get out of his way, so he could work and not make me confess what it was. Not that he'd think anything of the sort, of course. He'd had the operation. But I'd looked it up on my laptop in my office between bouts of throwing my guts up. It happened. It wasn't likely but it wasn't impossible or unheard of, either.

I'd managed to ignore the lack of my period for a month, chalking it up to stress. Which was patently ridiculous. My cycles were as regular as clockwork, rarely varying in timing or intensity. The only thing I'd noticed that was different or obviously indicative of any hormonal shift was a serious ramp up of my libido.

I mean, I was horny before. Once Trent had freed me of the old, scared, asexual Melody costume I'd been wearing for self-protection, he had woken a monster. But one I could handle. I could do my work during the day without being overcome with heavy, inappropriate rushes of raw lust. The most innocuous thoughts about him—what I might fix for dinner, or if he'd remembered to pick up more wine—would send me spinning, leaving me panting and wondering if I could get away with masturbating in the bathroom.

I felt heavy with need, full, ripe like a fresh summer tomato. It was simultaneously irritating and exhilarating. Trent had no complaints of course. He was delighted. The night before I'd woken up with my next, most obvious symptom he had dropped over after several hours of rough play, ending with a loud climax for him and yet more skin-crawling need for me saying "uncle".

We'd laughed it off.

But I had known then. And by noon today I had no doubts.

Another confounded tear slipped down my cheek. I got up, flushed away what little I'd managed to lose, and shuffled back into the main room. My bed was a mess. Clothes were strewn everywhere. The shower was growing things in the corners and the kitchen would horrify my tidy-minded employees.

With a burst of energy, I got to work and didn't stop for a couple of hours when I looked around and smelled bleach and the pleasant violet-scented floor cleaner I recalled from my growing up years. My stomach was rumbling, which distracted me briefly from the low-lying, ever-present nausea. It was nearly nine o'clock, which surprised me, since I hadn't heard from Trent yet.

Hoping he was spending some time talking with Kayla, I gave myself yet another mental pat on the back for tracking her down. It hadn't been that hard once I did a little digging using her name and last known location in Kalamazoo. Say what you will about the maid mafia, the network of Hispanic cleaning staff is vast and tight knit. I'd put her description out on the vines and within days had her triangulated.

As an adult, she'd not made it any farther than Detroit, gotten busted for prostitution, held for a while and released thanks to the overcrowded court system. She made her way back to the west side of the state, she claimed, so she could check on her little brother. Keeping her distance and getting clean had kept her busy. But she'd found a job cleaning rooms at two different crappy hotels. I'd gotten her two jobs — my old diner one and behind the bar at Fitz Pub under the strict promise that she'd stay clean. The first sign of tweaking or anything else and I would cut her loose.

It had only been two weeks, but so far, so good. I'd wanted to take her straight to Trent, unwilling to hide anything from him ever again. But she'd insisted we wait. That she'd go to him when she was ready.

Today had come early in that plan, I figured. But I hadn't expected him on Sunday and so had scheduled her for times when we were rarely around. I peered into the sorry depths of my fridge, cursing myself for playing house with Trent for the last month. I'd have to wean myself off that soon enough, since Taylor would be back.

A cramp hit me low in the belly, forcing me to bend over and take deep breaths. It faded as quickly as it appeared, leaving me reeling and dizzy. I shut the fridge and leaned against it, willing myself not pregnant.

That didn't work. I put my hand on my stomach, trying to sort through the stew of emotions. My mother had figured me out within seconds, of course. Given me a brief lecture, then asked when the wedding was going to occur. Which had not helped one bit.

I grabbed my phone and sent Evelyn a text. I had, of course, forgiven her for not telling me that Trent was coming over that night. She'd not shown much improvement, personal-life wise, but at least she and Ross ignored each other at work. Not great, but better than loud fighting.

She didn't reply right away. I grabbed a box of plain crackers and plunked myself on the couch, holding the box, a tissue and my phone, feeling sorry for myself.

Fucking Trent and his fucking superman sperms. This was not supposed to happen. Neither of us wanted it. I winced when another mild cramp came and went, leaving me free of nausea long enough to get up and find a can of tomato soup. But once it was heated and ready, the smell of it made me gag. I wanted Trent so badly right then I could practically feel his arms around me. But I resisted it. He needed time with Kayla. I'd drop this little bombshell on him later. A lot later.

Not much later, chica. *The little shrimp won't stay that size for long.*

And that's if I even decided to keep it.

I shivered at the thought. *It* was a baby. I'd always believed that, even though I would never impose my views on any other woman's body or life.

Groaning, I choked down a few more crackers, drank more water and dropped to sleep on the couch, fully dressed, the TV blaring away into the room. I woke in a tangle of blankets, sweaty all over. When I sat up, the nausea caught up with me, slamming against the back of my throat and forcing me to half run, half crawl to the toilet again.

I took a long, hot shower, and checked the time. It was already seven, an hour after I usually woke on work days. I also noted that Trent had not sent me a single text or called. With a sigh, I dried my hair, skipped makeup since the smell of it made me dizzy, got dressed and headed for the pub. I was determined to get on with my life. Women get pregnant every day, hell, every hour. They go to work and do what has to be done. It's not an illness. It's a condition and one that some women would give anything to have.

I was sitting in my car, puffing out breaths to keep from throwing up before I even got into the building, when my phone buzzed with a call. I knocked it into the floor in my eagerness. But it was Evelyn.

"Hey," she said. "You at the brewery yet?"

"Yes." I gathered up my stuff, determined not to let my disappointment show. "What's up? You here yet?" She was usually one of the first ones to arrive during the week, powering up the various coffee machines and setting out bagels, fruit and yogurt in all three of the break rooms.

"No. I'm not feeling good today."

"Oh." I unlocked the front door of the pub instead of going through the old brewery. I could already tell that the strong smells in there were going to be unfathomable to me for a while. "Okay. What do you want me to do?"

I did the coffee making and took delivery of donuts and other stuff from the deli down the street, setting them out in the break rooms and trying to not look as pregnant as I felt. Once that was done and I'd chatted with Amy, Evelyn's assistant, for a while over a donut that seemed to quell my nausea for the time being, I headed for my office. I was implementing a new entertainment schedule next month, once the summer was officially over, and had some calls to make and graphics to order.

At noon, with still no peep from Trent, a thrill of aggravation shot down my spine. Hormones, certainly, but more than that. He was never this stand-offish. He must really be pissed about me keeping the fact of Kayla's existence from him.

At five-thirty, that thrill had turned into a flat-out fury, filling my chest, throat and head. I'd managed to eat a few peanuts, and was now craving, of all things, eggplant parmesan. Without thinking, I put my hand on my still flat stomach then took it off, pressing both of my palms on the desk, sweating my way through a wave of dizziness.

"Oh, *jefe*," Walt, my head chef, said, sticking his head around the doorway. "Evelyn is out here, asking for you."

"Thanks, Walt." I ran a hand over my lips, wondering if I would ever not feel sick again. This was so all-encompassing, enveloping me in a way any other stomach illness never had. It scared me a little, to tell the truth.

"You all right? Need some more water? My Melinda claims that you should put cucumbers over your closed eyelids and lay in a totally dark room for this." He waved his hand up and down, vaguely indicating my general condition.

"You ever think she says that so you'll leave her alone in a dark room for a while?" I eased myself up, hoping the latest surge of nausea would fade.

"I wouldn't put it past her." He chuckled, then grabbed my arm when I stumbled, nearly falling off my own stupid shoes. "Whoa, there. You sure you're all right?"

"Yes. I'm fine. Thanks." I straightened my back and attempted to regain my dignity as we walked out into the pre-dinner kitchen.

"No problem. I need to go over the kitchen staff schedule

with you real quick."

I nodded and focused as hard as I could on the grid he put on the counter but the names and numbers swam in front of my eyes. Finally, I leaned away from the counter. "I'm sorry, Walt. I'm sure you have a handle on this. It's why I hired you after all. I need to sit down."

"Here, let me help you."

"No, no, I'm not fragile. I'm just…" I sighed and bit back tears.

"*Señora* Josefina told me," he said, his voice low. "I didn't say anything to anyone else but the guys who were here yesterday figured it out, I think."

"Crap." I leaned forward, my elbows on the stainless-steel surface, which helped alleviate some of the dizziness.

"I sure wish he'd taken it better." He was patting my shoulder with his giant mitt of a hand. "*Señora* Jo was right pissed off when she got back in here. She's kinda scary when she's pissed off."

I blinked, trying to make my sluggish brain comprehend this odd conversational curveball. But even as I denied it, I was taking it in, processing, and realizing that the reason I was being ignored today was not due to his general unhappiness over how I'd handled the Kayla thing.

I was being ignored because I was pregnant. My meddling mother had told him. And he'd spent the last full day in radio silence.

My heart seemed to sink straight down to my shoes. Walt's patting was irritating me now, but I didn't want to be rude so I stood. "Evelyn's here, you say?"

"Yep. And she looks about as good as you do."

"Okay. Fine. Good. Thanks, Walt." I slapped a saccharine smile on my face to reassure him, then turned on my heel and headed for the bar. I saw her leaning forward, nursing a soda. In the weeks since I'd last seen her she had lost weight, which made her cheekbones stand out, and her eyes seemed to glow in their deep-set sockets.

"Hi," I said, pouring myself a ginger ale — my fifth one that

189

day since it did calm the raging need to puke everywhere.

"Hi." She sipped but didn't meet my eyes. "I'm pregnant."

I choked on my soda.

"Oh," I said, wiping my streaming eyes with a napkin. "Great. Me too."

She narrowed her eyes. I nodded and held up the ginger ale. "And if one can die of morning sickness, I will do it." I sipped. She sipped. We stared at each other.

"What are you going to do?"

I shook my head and put the half empty glass down with a *thunk*. "Not sure." My voice was firm as resolve rose in me. If he didn't want to see me or talk to me about this, then I would, by God, handle it on my own. One way or another. "You?" I knew it had to be Ross's baby, which was a complex wrinkle.

"I have no idea." Tears rolled down her face. I patted her hand. "I mean, I'm going to have it. But…"

I sighed.

"Do you need me to come with you…anywhere? You know I will. If you want me to."

"I know. I'll let you know once I decide."

"What about Tre—?"

I held up a hand to stop her from saying his name. Ice was forming around my heart and I let it. It was the only way I was going to get through this. "He knows. He hasn't spoken to me since he found out."

"Oh. I'm sorry. That doesn't seem like him."

"Well, apparently, it is." I slammed my glass into the rack for the dishwasher, as anger covered the hurt that was forming. Which was just fine. I would be angry. But I would not allow him to hurt me. I wouldn't allow any man to hurt me. "I'm sorry."

Evelyn smiled at me and fiddled with her straw. "Me too," she said. "Look at us, will you? Two grown women who should know better…"

"Knocked up like a couple of teenagers on prom night."

She chuckled, then covered her lips. "I shouldn't laugh at

that."

I shrugged, as the ice coating spread up my spinal column to my brain. It helped a little but by the time she'd left and I was sitting at my desk, I sobbed like a baby. The catharsis I should have felt never came so I slouched home, dropped onto my couch and fell asleep, my stomach rumbling from hunger, my eyes burning with tears.

The next few weeks were a blur. Between throwing up, crying and trying to act normal around people who had no business being affected by my poor life choices, I was asleep every night by nine, and had to drag myself out of bed every morning. Trent maintained his distance. And I met him halfway, not even allowing myself to type out texts or anything so I could stare at them before I erased them like I'd done before.

He was serious about this, it would seem. I was on my own. He'd made that clear.

Despite my best efforts — maybe in spite of them — I did think about him almost nonstop. I knew that Taylor would be back, going to school, doing her community service, playing piano and guitar. I also kept tabs on the Kalamazoo block development. He'd hosted a pre-opening opening party and the sight of him in a suit, his smile fixed and his eyes shining had sent me into a three-day tailspin.

I'd still not managed to eat much, which made my blood sugar spiral and turned me into a stark raving bitch. My mother had taken to showing up in the kitchen, to run interference between me as I sat crouched in my office, snarling, sobbing or puking, and the rattled kitchen staff. I worked some bar shifts and avoided Kayla as much as I could. Seeing her only brought it all roaring back in one giant wave of regret.

At least one thing had changed. Austin was back. Evelyn was ecstatic. Ross was somewhat less so, but I could tell he knew it was for the best. They were all back together, as three, best I could tell. But I had no energy to inquire about it, much less get any details. She looked positively radiant and I felt like I was withering away, drying up, empty even as my body was doing some truly weird things to remind me that *empty* was the opposite of my issue.

I'd developed a near constant craving for potato chips — something I'd never eaten before. It was as if my salt intake needed to triple to get me past the daily nausea. And I wanted a glass of dark stout every night — although *wanted* didn't give the gut deep craving for it justice. I skipped it of course.

The date moved closer. I ignored it. Then one morning I realized that this was it. This was the Rubicon that I would either cross or step back from, depending on if I kept a certain appointment, made for two p.m., with Evelyn on stand-by to take me and drive me home. I sat, staring out into the cloudy fall sky. Wind whipped at the trees, stripping them of their show-off red, yellow and orange adornments. *A lovely day for an abortion,* I thought, allowing that word to sit in my brain, flashing neon, reminding me that I believed in a woman's right to choose, but not at all sure that this was my choice.

I didn't want a baby. Trent didn't want a baby. Of course, this was the right choice.

A tear slipped from my eye and hit my hand. I stared at it as the usual morning roil of hunger for a bag of the greasiest possible chips warred with the need to throw up. I picked up my phone and made a call.

"Hi, Melody," Evelyn answered. "Are you ready for me to pick you up?"

"No. I'm not going. I can't do it." I wiped my eyes and sniffled.

"All right. So, let's get you an appointment with my OB, shall we?"

"Okay. Thanks."

"Don't mention it. We can compare our weight gains and shit."

I smiled, dropped back onto my bed and put my hands over my stomach. "We've got this, kid," I whispered. "You and me."

Chapter Twenty-One

Four weeks later

"Yo, Trent! Watch out!"

He ducked just in time, managing not to concuss himself on the bookcase that was being shuttled across the floor. "Thanks," he hollered up to Gabe, his construction manager. This project had been the most gut-wrenchingly stressful of anything he'd done. But it was almost finished. The whole place was rented out and within weeks of being ready. The loans were covered. And he was being touted at the next Dan Gilbert.

Which was a laugh. He'd never touch that guy's personal wealth level. But he was proud of having pulled this off and was already being courted by a new set of investors eager to rehab spaces in Grand Rapids. He had even made money off this project—a shit ton of it. And since his corporation would manage the building, collecting leases and handling all the maintenance issues, he'd keep making money on it. He'd hired six new people, including an admittedly hot woman who was doing her level best to make sure he noticed how hot she was, whose sole jobs were to manage this city block. Even with their solid, living wage salaries and benefits, he would still make money as long as it stayed rented.

But almost getting brained by a damn bookcase was emblematic of his bigger problem. He only got about four hours of sleep every night. Food turned to cardboard in his mouth. Beer or wine to vinegar. He would sometimes catch himself sitting and staring out the nearest window and picturing her. His hands would clench on his knees as he fell deeper into the fantasy of it—her hair, her lips, her ass, her long longs and her sweet, talented mouth.

His heart would seem to stutter-step, then speed up. Sweat would bead his face. His gut would roll and turn in around on itself as the next thing he'd see was her mother's face when she'd told him. He'd see the pavement that he'd stared at for so long after that. Then he'd see her building, where he'd waited, frozen and useless, unable to face her because of his own deep displeasure over the fact of a pregnancy.

"Trent," a female voice hit his ear, making him blink back to the here and now. "Could you come over here a minute?"

He rubbed his eyes and headed in her direction. The woman—God what in the hell was her name—stood at a work table, pointing down at some papers. Her long hair gleamed in the overhead lights. He looked down at the papers, ignoring the way she stared at him. This was not helping him. Not that he was interested, but fighting her off was sucking away what little energy he still possessed.

After okaying whatever it was she needed, he turned to his other youthful staff who also waylaid him with their details. The massive space that he was converting into his new HE LLC management company was making him nuts. He needed air. He shoved past the people scurrying around installing electronics and desks and bookshelves and shoved his way out into the cool fall air.

Propping his hands on his knees, he sucked in deep breaths, shoving aside Melody and the potential of their child—something that still wouldn't take hold no matter how much he tried to make it—and focusing on what still had to be done. He had to get through this. He needed to call her. But he wouldn't. Something held him back and he knew that the longer he waited, the less likely she'd be to ever talk to him.

His phone buzzed with a text from Taylor.

Don't forget my doctor's appointment.

He groaned and leaned against the building. Sheila had dropped the whole birth control thing in his lap last week, demanding that he get her to the doctor so she could get a damn IUD. He'd obsessed over it the last few nights, wishing like hell he could talk to Melody about all this.

But no. He'd fucked that six ways to Sunday.

"Right. Okay." He shoved the phone back in his pocket and ground his teeth, willing himself stronger, braver, anything but what he was right now — miserable, exhausted and missing Melody Rodriguez like a fucking phantom limb.

"Trent?" He turned around, about to bite the woman's head off out of self-defense. But she was holding out a phone. "It's for you."

"Thanks." He took it and put it to his ear. "Hettinger."

"Oh my God, Trent, where...?" Some kind of racket started up behind him from the office so he shoved his finger in his other ear and headed down the street away from the noise.

"I'm sorry? Who's this? I can barely hear you."

"God damn it...sorry motherfucker..."

"Oh, hi, Evelyn." He stopped at the corner. "What's up?"

"...you sorry ass, it's Melody."

"I can't hear you. What about Melody?"

"...Grant Hospital...blood loss...miscarriage."

"What the fuck?" He was already running for his car, keeping the phone pressed to his ear. "What are you talking about? Where is she? Speak up, woman!"

"She's in Grant Hospital. I found her at home when she didn't come to work this morning. She was... Oh shit. Just hurry up and get here."

He was already in the Jeep, pulling out into the heavy, late-afternoon traffic. Ignoring the honks and waved middle fingers, he screeched onto the freeway, his heart racing and his ears full of the sound of Melody's voice.

He parked and shoved past the crowds hovering at the elevator of the garage and ran down the stairs. When he hit the main desk, he was breathing heavy but focused. "Melody Rodriguez," he said, trying to smile at the old guy sitting at the computer. "Please." He tapped his fingers impatiently while the guy looked her up.

"Yes, she's in room seven eighteen."

"Thanks." He ran off, leaving behind the words "But wait, sir...you can't..."

He hit the elevator, punched the seven and held the door close button, shrugging his apology to the older couple who'd tried to join him before the doors shut in their faces. He kept wiping his lips and tapping his foot as the damn thing crawled up two, three, four. Then stopping at five and letting a bunch of people in scrubs on, and disgorging them at the next floor. Biting back the words "couldn't have taken the stairs, guys?" he gritted his teeth until the doors slid open on seven and he ran out, nearly colliding with a nurse carrying a stack of computer tablets.

"Excuse me," she said, snippily.

"Seven eighteen? Please?"

He must have resembled an honest-to-God crazy person—or somebody who was worried about a sick loved one—so she pointed helpfully down the hallway teeming with people in scrubs and lost civilians like himself. He took off at a run, heart in his throat, as if his proximity to her was ramping up his panic. He skidded to a stop outside her door, took a breath and knocked.

Evelyn appeared, her face haggard. She slipped out the door into the hall and gave him a tight hug. "Oh God, Trent. She's...it was awful."

"What happened?" He peeled her off him. "Talk to me."

She took a breath. "She was late for work which never happens. I called her. I texted. I sent someone over to beat on her door. He said no one answered but it didn't feel right to me. I knew..." She bit her lip and closed her eyes. "I knew something was wrong. Anyway, I got in my car and drove to her place. I talked the manager into unlocking the door. We found her in the kitchen, unconscious. There was so much blood. Jesus." She slumped against the wall.

Trent glanced at the closed door. "The baby..."

"She lost it. Not that you care." She seemed to recover herself, standing and wiping her eyes with a tissue. "Shit. She's gonna kill me for calling you." She glared at him. "She lost the baby and nearly died. Her placenta was in the wrong place or something and it ruptured. She must have fallen and hit her head on the kitchen counter. She was... The EMT guys said her body temperature was so low she was practically dead when I f-f-f-found her. Oh Jesus." She looked up at the ceiling. Trent tried not to yell. He used all his abilities, all his well-honed control skills not to shake her.

Instead, he moved her aside and pushed the door handle down. "No, wait," she said, moving in front of him again. "She's not...awake."

"Move," he said, not meaning to sound so gruff but not caring at the same time. "I need to see her, Evelyn."

She made one more effort, holding out her arm. He pushed it down gently, moved her aside once more, and opened the door. The room was dim but he could make out a bed and some beeping monitors. He froze for a few seconds, his mind flipping through all the reasons he'd left her alone for the last month. Which all boiled down to one thing—he was a total, weak-kneed loser. That broke his trance and he stumbled forward toward the bed and staring down at her.

She was asleep, or unconscious. Had an IV line stuck in one hand, some kind of clear tube under her nose. Her cheekbones were so prominent he cursed himself all over again for being such a lame ass. His hand shook as he stroked her arm. His fingers trembled when he touched her face. She didn't move. "Is she all right?"

He glanced over his shoulder. Evelyn was standing by the door, hand over her mouth. "I don't know. They moved her up here from the ER. They tell me she's got to have more surgery."

"Surgery," he said, under his breath. "For what?"

"I don't know. Do I look like a damn doctor?"

He rose, his ears ringing and his vision tunneling. An alarm went off somewhere and the room was flooded with people in scrubs, shoving him aside yanking off the sheet that had been covering her. Evelyn had tucked her hand in the crook of his elbow and was pressing her face against his shoulder. He put his arm around her and watched while the medical crew rolled Melody out, hollering about opening up an operating room, stat.

The next two hours were a living hell — and one purely of his own making. He kept his fingers locked together and his head down, staring at the floor until his eyes crossed. Evelyn patted his shoulder in between bouts of pacing. At one point, he grabbed her arm. "You're pregnant too?"

She nodded and leaned into him. "Please tell me she'll be all right."

"I wish I could," he said, his voice breaking. "Why didn't she...ever call me?"

She leaned away from him, her eyebrows raised. "Dude, don't even."

He sighed and resumed his study of the floor at his feet.

"I'm willing to forgive you," she said. "If you promise to never make me into a giant liar ever again."

He glanced at her, his fingers clasped so tight it hurt. "How did I manage that?"

"You disappeared," she said, bumping his shoulder. "I mean, I get it on one level. But on another, much more mature one, I would just as soon gouge out your fucking eyeballs as look at you right now. She was so fucking miserable. She hardly ate anything. She couldn't keep anything down at all. Our OB had her on those gross liquid supplements like for old people or little kids."

"Jesus," he muttered, pressing his forehead to his hands, willing himself back four weeks, or five, so he could just go to her and hold her and take care of her...and their baby.

Dear Lord. The baby.

His vision blurred. He closed his eyes tight.

"Why didn't she...never mind." He ground his teeth. "Just never fucking mind."

She leaned into his shoulder and they waited another hour before a doctor emerged from the double doors that cut the waiting room off from the operating rooms. "Mr. Hettinger?"

He rose, gripping Evelyn's hand. "Yes." He couldn't choke anything else out.

"Well, we stopped the hemorrhage. It was a serious rupture."

Trent nodded, feeling as if he was moving in slow motion, staring at the doctor's lips, willing him to say more. "She lost a lot of blood. It's a good thing you found her when you did."

Evelyn grabbed his arm. "Will she be all right?"

"Yes, but we'll need to keep her in the ICU overnight at least. She has to be monitored to make sure her blood pressure doesn't drop again. And we need to use warming blankets. Her body temperature keeps dropping for some reason. It's precarious. But she will survive." He glanced up at Trent. "I believe that her uterus will recover. So you can try again. But not until she's regained a lot of strength. Losing that much blood is going to mean a lot of rest, and careful monitoring even after she goes home."

Trent felt his knees give out, but he kept control of himself, set his jaw and nodded at the doctor. "Can I see her, please?"

"In a few minutes. A nurse will come get you." He glanced at Evelyn. "One visitor at a time, though. Does Miss Rodriguez have a next of kin?"

"Yes. Her mother should be here any minute."

Trent stepped away from them, rubbing his face, feeling as if an army of ants was crawling up and down his spine, parading over his skin. The doctor shot him a look, then was distracted by something on his phone. "I have to go.

She'll be in recovery a while longer. Once she's in the unit, you can see her."

Trent paced for a solid twenty minutes until someone came out and got him. He approached her bed, wary, horrified at himself, battling every demon he'd ever faced to keep from running away and hiding in shame. But he sat in the chair, took her hand, kissed it and whispered in her ear. "I'm here, *bella*. I'm here and I'm never leaving you again."

Her mother appeared at some point, pushing him out of his chair with a string of murmured Spanish. He leaned against the wall, waiting for Melody to open her eyes for hours. He dozed in one of the chairs designed for maximum discomfort out in the waiting room, waking when Josefina prodded his shoulder. "She's awake."

He lurched forward, swiping his tongue over his teeth, so eager to see her that he almost tackled a gaggle of nurses in the hallway.

He ran to her bed. She was staring at the ceiling. He ran a finger down her cheek, tried to turn her face to his. But she wouldn't budge.

"Please leave." Her voice was hoarse.

"I know I was a shit. I was a total, useless ass and I am so, so sorry. Please, Melody. Look at me."

"Go, Trent. You didn't want me when I was pregnant. So you can't have me now, sorry."

She turned her face away from him.

"No. That's not what...I mean. It was a shock and I...I wanted to call you. But..."

"It's all right. I understand. You have your kid. You don't want another. So you broke up with me without even giving me the benefit of a break-up."

He sucked in a ragged breath. "I didn't mean it that way. I don't want to break up. I love you. You know that."

"I knew that," she said, turning to face him again. "But I don't know it anymore. You left me alone. I was okay with that because I...I had..." She put a pale hand on her stomach. "I had something of you that would have been all mine. But now I don't. So you can go."

"You didn't want kids either." He hated himself so much right then he wanted to leap out the window. But the words wouldn't stop pouring out of his mouth. "Don't lie to me about that."

"I didn't want kids, no. But when I had your child, I fucking wanted it. But you didn't and you didn't even have the *cojones* to tell me that to my face. Leave, Trent. I mean it." Her face was red. An alarm went off and he was shoved past again, forced out of the room, relegated to the chairs. He dropped into one, boneless, empty, realizing that she hadn't said a single word that he couldn't refute. He had bolted. He had been scared. He'd been utterly and completely ball-less. And now he'd lost his child, and his woman.

"Oh God," he groaned. "Oh God. Oh God."

Josefina and Evelyn ran up to him, clutching cardboard cups of shitty coffee. "What's wrong? Trent, what is it?"

Josefina threw her cup into the trash and ran for the room, babbling in Spanish and crossing herself like mad. "I don't know. I fucked it up. I fucked everything up." He stood up and glared at her. "I did this. I own this. But she won't see me."

"She'll come around." Evelyn put her hand on his arm but he threw it off.

"No. She won't and she shouldn't. I don't deserve her."

He barely remembered the walk down the hall, the elevator, the ride home. By the time he got there and looked at his phone again, he realized he'd forgotten to meet Taylor at the doctor's office so he could sign for her IUD. "Fuck!" He threw the phone against the wall, shattering it so thoroughly shards went in every possible direction. "Fucking fuck!" His hand fell on something. He picked it up, staring at it without seeing it, then heaved it against the wall too. The vase exploded into a million glass pieces, the flowers—dead as he'd not moved them since Melody had walked out of his life over a month ago — slid down the wall in a brown clump. He put his hands to his face and dropped to his knees in the middle of the floor.

Taylor found him there when she got home, pulled him to his feet and pushed him on to the couch. "Chill, Dad. I'll get you a beer or something."

"No, no, water. Please just some water." She brought it. He drank it so fast he got a headache but the hydration helped him think.

"So, you stood me up but I'm guessing by all this something is really wrong." She gestured to the phone shards, the shattered vase. "What is it?"

He could tell she was nervous by the way she was shifting her jaw around. Not unlike her old man, he thought, reaching out to touch her face. His baby girl, his pride, his treasure — the pain in ass and thorn in his side. All rolled up into a beautiful, near perfect copy of her brittle, acerbic, needy mother.

"It's Melody, honey. I... I did a terrible thing."

She leaned back trying to look nonchalant but kept swinging the leg she had crossed over the other — another of her mother's clear tells. "What did you do?"

"She was pregnant. I... I left her alone. I couldn't handle it. I was scared and a real shithead about it."

Taylor's huge green eyes widened. "Pregnant? You told me you couldn't anymore. You sure she wasn't getting some on the side?"

He dropped his head back with a groan. "I'm sure. I got myself tested. I am apparently still able to do my evolutionary duty, if you get me."

"Jeez, Dad, TMI." She narrowed her eyes at him. "But you knew it was your kid and you dumped her? That's a serious asshole move. Well done."

"I know, I know." He got up and paced, running his hands over his scalp, muttering under his breath.

"So, what happened? I'm gonna have a baby brother that I can't ever see, or what?"

"No." He stopped and pressed his hands against the large window. The cool panes soothed him somewhat. "She had a miscarriage. She almost died. I just came from the hospital."

"Where I assume she kicked your sorry ass out of her room."

He glanced over his shoulder at her. "As a matter of fact, yes, she did."

"Well, good. I think I might like her after all."

He sighed and leaned his forehead against the cool panes. "Fuck me," he muttered.

"Don't worry, Dad. Maybe she'll come around."

"Probably not."

"Well, then I guess you'll have to make some effort. Sounds like you want to."

"I do. But I don't know…"

She grabbed his arm. He turned to face her, marveling all over again at her extreme beauty. Her eyes narrowed and she took his cheeks between her fingers, pinching tight. "Hettingers don't give up."

He shook his head but she pinched harder.

"God damn you, Dad. I'll never respect another word you say to me if you give up on her now. She needs you. Man the fuck up."

She let him go, popping her gum and looking like a surly teenager again. "I need some painkillers," she said, heading for the kitchen. "I'm cramping like a bitch." Rubbing his cheeks, he sat, pondering this day and all it might mean.

"Can I use your phone? Mine's kinda…out of commission." She handed it over, then stuck a heating pad in the microwave. "Thanks, babe." He called Evelyn first.

"Hey. How is she?"

"She's fine. Eating something actually. They're impressed with how she's bounced back."

"Good. Listen, I need your help with something."

"Oh, I don't know…"

"Yes. You do. You're the one who called me in first place."

"Yeah. And if I'm lucky my friend might speak to me again someday."

"She will. And if I play my cards right, she'll be back where she belongs, with me. But you have to advocate for me."

"I have been, you giant shit head. But taking a powder on her after finding out about the pregnancy...." She made a tsk-ing sound. "That's kind of unforgiveable, really."

"I know, I know. But I want...I mean I can make it up to her. I love her. I know she loves me. I have to make this work."

"You are so cute when you're begging."

"Evelyn..."

"Oh all right, fine. But don't think you can just saunter back in to her life. She's gonna make you work for it."

"I'm not averse to hard work. Especially if I know what the end game is." He clenched his fist on his thigh. "I fucked it up but I will make it right. So help me. I will get her back."

"Is Aunt Kayla coming over?" Taylor dropped into the other end of the couch, clutching the heating pad to her stomach. He tossed her the phone. She caught it without looking.

"Do me a favor and text her. I need all the female brain power I can muster right now. Then we'll order out—Chinese I think."

She tapped out a message. That night, he laid out a plan of action. A full-on romance effort that would bring most women to their knees in days.

"I think you'll be at this for at least a month, T." Kayla sipped a soda and picked through the fried rice for chicken.

"I say six weeks," Taylor said, taking a bite of the lo mein.

"I heard he paid off her credit card without telling her," Kayla said, bumping Taylor's shoulder.

"Jeez, Dad, that's kind of stalker-ish. Who do you think you are? Some kind of sugar daddy?" She winked at her aunt who dissolved in peals of laughter.

"No," he said, grabbing the container of lo mein from her

and digging in. He felt good, for the first time in weeks. He had a plan. And it would work. It had to. There was no other viable option.

"I gotta go," Kayla said, standing and stretching. "Early diner shift tomorrow." She kissed the top of Taylor's head then gave Trent a tight hug. "You're all right, baby brother. For a jackass."

He smiled and kissed her cheek. "You all right still? Sure you don't want me to — ?"

"Nope. I'm good. I'm safe. I'm clean. You don't have to take care of me." She winked. "Go take care of Melody. If she decides to take you back, maybe you'll be redeemed."

"I'm gonna give it the old college try," he said. "And she will take me back. Trust me. She won't know what hit her, poor dear." He flexed his biceps and kissed it. Taylor groaned and threw a fortune cookie at him.

"Such confidence." Kayla chucked him under the chin. He mimed falling backward as if she'd slugged him one. "Keep me posted, T. I'll be rooting for you." He walked her to the sliding metal door out to the hallway with the elevator, his arm around her shoulder. "I love you," she said, pecking him on the cheek then ducking out the door.

"All right, all right. Time for bed." He swept the cartons into a garbage bag and switched off the TV that Taylor had just turned on. "I need rest."

He brushed his teeth and put on a pair of soft pants. For the first time in weeks he honestly thought he'd be able to sleep. But it eluded him after about an hour of fitful dozing on the couch. So he did his usual, wandering into Taylor's bedroom and watching her a while, then drinking some tea and staring out into the street lights below, counting the minutes until the morning and he could begin his campaign to win Melody back.

Chapter Twenty-Two

"Dear Lord, that man." I watched while the delivery kid staggered under the weight of the flowers. "Over there, with the rest." I pointed to the amazing display of floral incentives already gracing my desk, Evelyn's desk, Amy's desk, pretty much every flat surface in Fitzgerald Brewing Company.

After spending three nights in the hospital, chafing to get out of there, they'd sent me home. My mother had driven me, still muttering darkly in Spanish as I'd leaned my head against the window, never more grateful for the sun on my face. Trent's full court press had begun the second I'd opened my door to find the place spotlessly clean, my fridge stocked and mounds of my favorite flowers filling the entire room with beauty and fragrance.

My mother had launched straight in with a string of expletives. She'd actually managed to toss two of the bouquets into the trash before I'd stopped her, laughing, but suddenly so tired I could hardly see straight. "Enough, already, Mama."

"He's a terrible man. Just terrible. You did the right thing not letting him near you."

"Ah, Mama. Give it a rest."

We'd spoken in Spanish which made my head hurt. English had been pressed upon me by both my parents. They'd insisted on it, convinced the only way I'd ever make anything of myself would be as an Anglo. I spoke Spanish at home, of course, but the way I had of thinking—in two languages simultaneously—always wore me out. "I'm tired. I need to go to bed."

"Oh my darling, I'm sorry." She'd bustled around, distracted as I'd planned while I touched a petal of the lilies, taking a deep breath of them. I slept for hours that week. And when I wasn't sleeping I was eating. Trent had food delivered daily, including thick, juicy steaks which I devoured like a starving person. A nurse came every day that week to take my blood pressure, pulse and test my iron. By Friday I was sick of the whole thing and ready to go back to work.

But the onslaught continued there. Flowers every other day. Rich Belgian truffles a few times a week. Bottles of horrifically expensive red wine which I didn't dare drink. Boxes stuffed with tissue paper and some of the most beautiful lingerie I'd ever seen.

For two Tuesdays in a row he'd sent over a muscular, good-looking guy with a massage table. He set it up in Evelyn's office and the two of us were treated to deep tissue therapy and a serious case of the giggles, considering her increasingly unwieldy body and the extreme hotness of the man digging his knuckles into our flesh.

I got tickets to the ballet, which I loved and shared with Evelyn. We also went to the opera and saw a traveling version of a Broadway musical. And not once did he call or demand that I see him. I always sent a text with a photo of whatever it was he'd chosen to bribe me with that day. He always replied with the same five words — *You're welcome. I love you.*

By the third week of treats, goodies, outings and massages, I was wondering how he might up the ante. Because I knew he would. What I didn't know was how I would ultimately respond to it all.

"So, you have to help me with this wedding," Evelyn said, rubbing the firm drum of her belly. "It's all I can do to get to work every day, no thanks to you."

"No thanks to Mister Gifty, best I can tell." I chose a truffle from the week's stash and popped it into my mouth, relishing the rich, melty chocolate and getting a sweet, familiar shivery feeling as I pictured him, ordering up all this nonsense.

"Ugh, seriously. You are going to help me, right?"

"Of course. But I'm curious. How will you marry them both? Not sure I can find an officiant for that."

She stuck her tongue out at me. "You know damn good and well I'm marrying Austin. Ross is…just a bonus." She blushed, then fanned her face with a piece of paper.

"I hate you sometimes." I patted her belly. I'd gotten over being unable to look at her, at the way she was blossoming into her pregnancy. "But mostly I love you. Here." I put a truffle in her mouth. "Let's talk details."

She chewed, swallowed and put her chin in her hand. "I can't think straight about anything right now."

"Fine. So I assume you want to have it at St. Vincent's. How many attendants?"

She smiled at me. "Just one. You. And Brock, of course." She named Austin's twin brother. "I'd like to keep it small, maybe seventy or so people. If we go much beyond that, we've got to open it up to over two hundred."

"Yeah, let's avoid that."

Someone knocked on her office door. When it opened, I saw another delivery kid. But this time, instead of an obnoxious bouquet, or box of chocolates, or wine, or tickets to yet another event that I'd always said I wanted to attend but never wanted to spend the money on, he held a large, rectangular box. I tipped him, took the box and set it on the work table. It was a deep red color with the name of an expensive dress shop on it. I'd gotten one like it once before.

Evelyn joined me, rubbing the small of her back and eating another truffle. I ran my fingers over the surface, feeling the raised lettering. So, the time had come. He'd given me four weeks. And now I had to make a decision. I opened the box, peeled back the tissue paper and saw the dress. It was black this time, strapless, with a beaded bodice and a flowing, diaphanous skirt. I held it against me while Evelyn whistled. The shoes were like a dream—a dozen razor-thin black ribbons up the instep, ending with a thick ankle strap studded with what looked like diamonds. The heels were so high I thought I'd get a nosebleed if I wore them.

"Damn, sister. You've got this man wrapped up." She held up the deep red rose that lay next to the shoes and handed it me. "Somebody's got a serious date night."

I sighed and put everything back in the box. "I can't."

"Yes, you can."

"No, Evelyn. I won't. He…he just left me, remember?"

I put the lid on the box, resting my palms on the lid and taking a deep breath. There wasn't a single thing in this universe that I wanted more. But I wasn't ready. My friend put her hands on mine and stared at me. "All right, I'm sick of this shit. You…" She pointed over my shoulder. "Get in here. And you." She poked my shoulder. "You pull your self-righteous head out of your ass. I'm sick of you both." She shoved the box across the table at me. "I love you, Melody, but so help me you have got to be the most pig-headed woman on the planet. That man adores you. Yeah, he fucked up, big time. But Jesus please-us he's going broke trying to prove that he's sorry."

I sensed him behind me. I straightened, and crossed my arms. "Why don't you tell me how you really feel?"

"Oh honey, I just did. Do your worst, Hettinger. It's go time." She walked toward the door. Trent emerged from the gloom as I turned to watch her go. "Don't blow it, Melody. He may be big and ugly but he's yours." She gave him a little shove, then disappeared down the metal steps.

"Thanks," he said to her retreating back but keeping his intense, blue-green gaze on me.

He pulled up two chairs, set them facing each other and sat in one, patting the seat to indicate what I should do. I hesitated, knowing that if I did this, there was no going back. I sat. He took both my hands.

"Melody Rodriguez, I love you. I've never loved anyone the way I love you." He kissed both my palms, then each of my knuckles. "Please forgive me."

I sighed. "Seriously, that's all you've got?"

He raised an eyebrow, opened his mouth then snapped it shut. "You're kidding."

"Maybe." I allowed him a small smile. I put my finger on his lips when he lurched forward for a kiss. "Nope. Not yet." I rose, pulling him with me. "Take me to dinner tomorrow night. And we'll talk, I promise."

"Melody, I..."

I shook my head, backing away from him. I hurt all over I wanted his arms around me so badly. But I had to know for sure. Which meant I had to wait a bit longer.

"Pick me up at seven. You choose the place. Someplace nice though, no dive bars."

He nodded, kissed my hand, then backed away. "Your wish...my command."

I shuddered and grabbed a chair to keep from keeling over in the wake of that particular memory. "I know, *guapo*." His eyes lit up when I used his pet name. "Go on now, get your beauty sleep. I'll see you tomorrow night."

Chapter Twenty-Three

Trent sat in his car, his leg jittering up and down, his pulse racing like a teenager's. His campaign had been spot on and it had, indeed, taken longer than a month. Taylor was going to win that bet after all. He rubbed his head, his lips, checked his tie and shot his cuffs.

"Enough. Get out and go get your woman." The timbre of his voice shocked him. He actually sounded strong, which was the opposite of how he'd felt, ever since seeing Melody in that hospital bed.

When she opened the door, he was rocked back on his heels by the sight of her. She wore a short black skirt and a cream blouse, open to reveal her cleavage. Her neck was bare of adornment. Which was one thing he planned to change tonight. His mouth watered at the sight of her hair, tumbling around her shoulders, framing her newly fleshed-out cheeks. "Looking good tonight, *angelita*." He held out his hand.

She took it with a smile. "Not too shabby yourself, *guapo*."

He grinned at her, tucked her hand in his elbow and walked her to the Jeep. He handed her up, his hands already feeling her smooth flesh, her curves and contours, the silky threads of her hair.

She snapped her fingers in front of his face. "Come back from fantasy land, Trent. I'm hungry."

He shut her door and ran to his side, unbuttoning his suit jacket before climbing behind the wheel. He had that hopeful feeling again. The same one he'd been resisting for weeks. This time, he let it suffuse his brain, coat his nerves and take a slight edge off the anxiety he'd been carrying around like a heavy stone.

* * * *

He'd chosen The Grand, one of the old-school, white-linen-tablecloth style restaurants. He'd asked for a table with some privacy and the staff had delivered on their promise of the perfect option, guiding them to a smallish table near the front corner. The place was full, but that specific table sat empty, which accounted for the unhappy looks the groups of people hanging around in the foyer had given him as they were whisked into the room.

The waiter pulled out Melody's chair and set the large white cloth napkin in her lap, filled water, opened wine he'd ordered ahead of time, poured then retreated without a word. Not that it would have mattered. If he'd chattered away, welcoming them, spouting specials or anything else, Trent would not have heard a word.

He couldn't take his eyes of her. She thanked at the guy pouring water, thanked him again when he let her sniff and taste the wine. When the waiter finally faded, she turned her dark brown gaze to his, her full, lightly lipsticked lips turned up in a small smile. He opened his mouth to speak. Then shut it.

"I got nothin' right now. You look amazing, though." He held up his wine. She shook her head and clinked hers to it. As they sipped, they kept their eyes locked. He set his wine down. She kept hers in her hand.

"This is delicious. French?"

"Yeah. Figured we needed to switch countries for a while. It's a Bordeaux of some sort."

He knew exactly what it was because he'd ordered it specifically, knowing her preference for richness and a rounded mouthfeel.

"False modesty doesn't suit you." She put her glass down. A tiny line appeared between her eyes. Something new, he noted, since the miscarriage. "So I have to tell you what my mother's been calling you lately."

"Oh boy. Can I take a pass?" But she was smiling again, which encouraged him.

"Nope. She calls you *una cabra*."

He tilted his head, flipping through his mental translation list. "I'm a goat?"

"*Si, guapo*. It means that you're crazy, cuckoo, you know?" She swirled her finger around her ear. "I'm pretty sure she means it as a mild insult to me, though." She ran her fingertip around the rim of the wineglass. "*Su novio está como una cabra*." She sighed and picked up the glass, staring into its deep burgundy depths. "Trust me, it's way better than some of the other things she called you...at first."

"I can only imagine." He kept still, watching her, trying to make his mind formulate words to emerge from his mouth.

The waiter appeared with a silver dish of fragrant soft bread and a dish of butter. She looked up, expectantly. But the guy merely gave a slight bow and faded again. "I don't have a menu," she said, uncovering the bread.

"You don't need one. I took care of ordering already."

She sighed and pursed her lips. "I know I should like that. That I should feel, I don't know, better because you ordered my dinner. But I don't." She pulled a bit of the bread and put it in her mouth.

He sighed and fiddled with his utensils. "I told you before, Melody. It's part of me. It's just something that I do."

"I know." She chewed and swallowed. He watched her throat, unable to find words again. "It's all right. I'm just being honest with you."

"Okay." He sipped his wine, wiped his lips and put his hands on the table to keep them from shaking too much.

"My favorite name she had for you was *el hombre fuerta*."

"The strong man, eh?" He made himself pick up bread and eat it.

She raised a dark eyebrow. "You're good."

"I pick up languages fast. Always have. And I had some motivation for this one."

She flushed and dropped the bread back in the dish. He sat back, mirroring her. This dinner was not going the way he'd planned. Not at all.

"So, why strong man? I thought she hated my Anglo guts."

"Oh, she doesn't hate you. She's mad at you still but she called you *el hombre fuerta* because of…well…your sperms. You know."

Unable to stop himself, he grinned. She frowned, but not for long. She shook her head, which sent her soft hair tumbling around her face. He reached across the table and tucked it behind her ear, letting his fingertip trail along her jaw to her lips. "Did you know? I mean…about the sperms thing?"

"Obviously not. Otherwise I wouldn't have gone with condoms, or something else for you."

She blinked fast at that.

"Just being honest with you," he said.

She sighed. "I know, *guapo*. I know. I'm…sorry that I'm being such a…stubborn bitch."

It was his turn to blink.

"That's what Mama calls me — *la perra toca*."

A silence descended between them that Trent let settle before he spoke. "You have nothing to be sorry for. I abandoned you. I was selfish. I ran. Like a weak, useless kid."

She glanced up at him through her long, black eyelashes in a way that made his heart race. "I was no better, Trent. Once I realized that Mama had told you I should have come to you, talked to you, worked out what to do *with* you." She fiddled with her spoon. The wait staff kept their distance. Trent made a mental note to hire their managers to do some training at one of the restaurants he owned. These guys were good.

"Well, yeah. That would have been nice." He reached over and grabbed her hand, needing the connection with her so badly it hurt his chest. "But I understood, on one

215

level. One of the things about being…the way that I am…" He waved at the table, taking in the pre-ordered wine and the lack of menus. "That control thing I need means I make myself understand whatever woman I'm with. Especially after Sheila, I mean."

She frowned and pulled her hand away. "No, stop, don't misunderstand me on purpose. That is your super power, you know."

Her lips turned up slightly then she hid them with a sip of wine.

"I get you, Melody. I know what you like — in wine, food, conversation." He lowered his voice. "And in private. Most especially in private."

Her nostrils flared and a tinge of red hit her cheeks.

"But that makes what I did even worse. I knew you'd be conflicted. I didn't think you'd automatically decide to have the…the baby." He stumbled over the word. "I knew you needed me — I understood that you'd want to talk about it — but I bolted anyway. I will never forgive myself for that."

She put her palm on his hand which was still lying on the table between them. He shook his head and sat back, crossing his arms, needing some space to gather his thoughts. The waiter appeared within that window and set down small plates that held artfully mounded spinach, feta cheese and dried cherries.

She glared at him, then seemed to crumple into her seat. "I was selfish. I wanted you to come to me and I wasn't willing to go to you." Tears made her eyes shine.

"No crying, *bella*," he said, leaning forward again. "I mean, I don't expect that we won't ever argue."

She sniffled and chuckled, touching the corner of her napkin to her eyes.

He took her hand again, the hopefulness now filling him fully. He was going to salvage this. He was. For all his big talk with Taylor, Kayla and Evelyn, he hadn't been nearly as confident as he sounded.

"But if you'll have me back, I…I would be *so* happy."

She didn't pull her hand away this time. He had to force himself not to stare at the deep cleft between her full breasts as she leaned forward and put her fingers to his lips. "I love it when you get all tongue-tied. So happy? Really, *guapo*. Not your usual level of witty repartee." She kissed his knuckles, then turned his hand over and kissed the middle of his palm. The sensation was unlike anything he'd ever felt. Even if it were his favorite move, he decided that he must have a weirdly placed erogenous zone in the smack middle of his palm. He shifted in his seat, when the zipper of his dress pants bit into his sudden erection.

"I want to make you happy. You don't have to be the one always bestowing the happy."

She put his hand alongside her face and leaned into his palm, eyes closed.

"Your very presence in my life makes me happy, *bella*. And I'm learning how to temper my need to fix everything for you, I swear it."

She opened her eyes, but kept his hand pressed to her face. He traced her lips with his thumb, which did not alleviate any of the pressure below his belt. "No more hacking my computer, then?"

He grinned. "No more. But I did fix your credit rating, so…you're welcome."

Her smile widened as she let go of his hand. He kept it where it was for a few seconds, loving the feel of her skin. Her eyes seemed to sparkle brighter as she licked her lips. "You're impossible."

"Guilty as charged."

"I've been reading about your city block project. Sounds like a real success."

He sucked in a breath, unwilling to turn the conversation to anything that didn't involve him and her and them, preferably naked within the next few minutes. She picked up her fork and speared a dark spinach leaf. "Tell me about it."

He swallowed hard.

"I want us to be able to talk about anything. I want this to be not just about sex. I want to...be with you, Trent. As an equal. Not as some poor little Latina charity case that gives great blow jobs and lets you drop hot wax on her, you know?"

Her words, spoken so conversationally, hit him hard. He frowned, formulating his answer.

She took another bite, then put her fork down. "I love you, Trent. And that scares me because sometimes I don't know what you really think of me. I mean, I'm grateful that you freed me from my past. Which you did, you know. I do feel safe and happy with you. But this whole pregnancy thing..." She sighed, then kept talking. "It's like you want me to be some kind of creation of yours. You tell me how to wear my hair, you send me clothes, you...you...pay my god damned credit cards when I told you I'd handle those." She paused. "I am not yours to mold into something you want me to be. And sometimes...I think that's all you want to do and once you're done with me, you'll get...I don't know...bored."

"I respect the hell out of you, Melody. I can't believe you don't know that." This was the first thing that burst from his mouth, even though he was reeling from what she said on so many levels he couldn't begin to parse any of it.

She looked away from him, biting her lower lip which brought his dick back to painful attention.

Is *this just about sex?* He pondered that concept for exactly two seconds.

"I *don't* just love you because of how you make me feel on the outside, although that is pretty god damned amazing. I love you because of your smart mouth, your quick wit, your sense of humor, your ability to turn a hot mess like the Fitz Pub into a seriously successful business. Shit, I'd hire you in a minute to run one of my restaurants."

She frowned at him. "That would never work."

"I know. It's why I'm leaving you with Evelyn and Austin

where you belong during the day." He leaned forward on his elbows, needing her to really, truly hear him for a change. "I would marry you, right now, if you wanted it. And I think you know what saying something like that means to me. I told you everything about me. I gave you everything I had. And if you honestly think that I'm just in this for the fucking then I don't know if we should talk anymore."

Fury made his vision blur and his ears ring. She stared at him, her jaw set.

"It's not like you don't have a rep, you know. Plenty of women have stories about you. About your...abilities." Her eyes flickered down his chest. "They call you Mr. Romance. That you love the build-up, the gifts, the super sexy dates. Then, you just walk away, once you've fucked them a few times."

He made a noise, so shocked by this he was frozen in his seat and unable to speak.

"I'm just being honest," she said, again, as if this made up for her accusing him of only wanting to fuck her, or whatever the hell she'd been talking about.

"Yeah. Me too."

She took his hand. He pulled it away, unable to stand her touch at that moment. "Maybe part of this is your problem. You keep me at a distance, it's like you're watching me, waiting for me to prove that I just want you for sex, or I just want to fix you and make you into...what did you call it? Something that fit my idea of what you should be?" He rose, needing to move, to pace, to think. "And for your information, I may have been on a few dates and fucked a few women before you but if you honestly think that I sat, blindfolded in front of any of them and spilled my damn guts like I did with you, then you're truly delusional." He closed his eyes. Rage was filling his head, swirling around and muttering at him, urging him to say things he'd never be able to take back.

"Trent, sit down. There's no need to make a scene."

He sat, still glaring at her. "You know what Evelyn said? When she let me in the office yesterday to see you? About getting your head out of your ass? Well, that's my response to you right now. I don't know how else to prove to you that you are different. You aren't a sex play toy, or a project, or anything but the woman I love. The woman I want to marry. But you're pushing me out again, walling me off, making me feel like a fucking interloper. You're a closed-off bitch, sometimes." He touched her face. "I just don't know if I can keep fighting this with you. I'm tired of trying to prove my feelings to you. I know I fucked up but if you can't ever forgive me when you know damn well that I'll never be able to forgive myself..." He shook his head, pressed his fingers to his lips, then put them against hers. "I don't know if this will work."

He rose. She remained seated, staring down at her salad. He saw a tear fall to her lap. But he walked away. He had no energy left for this. If she honestly believed that about him, he didn't have a chance at a real relationship with her — the kind of relationship he craved deep in his soul. He sat in the Jeep, staring at the restaurant, wishing she'd appear at the door. But he hadn't been kidding when he'd claimed to know her, to understand her.

She'd said her piece.

He'd said his.

The end.

He jammed the truck in drive and peeled out into the street. His dick was still rock hard. He touched his zipper, his brain fuzzing over.

Hey, dude, maybe you dodged another Sheila-shaped bullet back there. She'll never trust you. So...fuck her. And speaking of fucking...why not go do that to someone who won't accuse you of anything but making her come so hard she screams. You're dressed for a party. Go have one.

He smiled, picked up his phone and made a quick right onto the freeway.

Chapter Twenty-Four

"Well, I really blew it this time," I said as the ride share drove me through the windswept streets.

"Come over," Evelyn said. "I've got wine and I can watch you drink it."

"No, I'm going home. I need to think."

"He'll come back," she insisted.

"No, I don't think so. I said some things that were pretty shitty."

"He'll be back. I guarantee it."

Tears nearly blinded me but I let them flow. I was on a side street, nearing my apartment complex. "It's all right. Thanks for all your help though. I'll be fine." My voice broke.

"Oh, Melody," my friend said. "Want me to call him?"

"No, no, it's fine. Gonna go. Bye." I got out of the car, sobbing like the stupid bitch I was. "God damn, shit, fuck, hell," I spat into the air. "What is wrong with you? Did you really think he'd just…just…just let you say all that and not react?"

But I had needed to say it. I needed him to know my fears about him. About how all the rumors about him that would swirl around me like blown leaves affected me. About how much his abandonment of me had hurt. Even though I really did forgive him for it.

"Then why did you say those horrible things? Jesus!" I wandered around the darkened lawn between buildings, needing the air and space, not the confined box of my apartment. Finally, I was so cold my teeth chattered, so I ran down the steps and threw open my door. The space, which had looked like something I was about to put behind me after tonight's date, was back to its dreary, single-working-girl vibe.

"Fuck!" I shrieked and threw my purse against the wall. "Fucking asshole! I hate you!"

I dropped to the floor where I stood, screaming, cursing, crying like an insane person. Gripping my arms, I rocked back and forth, recalling the horror of my life before Trent. The lonely hours, the boring jobs, the pretending that I had all I wanted.

Sobbing and shivering, I crawled to the sliding glass door, needing fresh air. I opened it a crack and sat, sucking in the cold oxygen, curled in a ball on the floor. All I could see was his face and his eyes, so compelling and beautiful, and so very hurt by me and what I'd said. I glanced around the room, picturing him there, in the chair with his blindfold and confessions. He had trusted me. And I'd tossed that in his face like so much shit.

"You're a closed-off bitch." The words rolled around in my head, taunting me, reminding me that I had very likely just ruined something that could be — would be — perfect.

I sat, shivering the air, but wanting it at the same time, staring into the dark for an hour, maybe more. By the time I got up, stiff and sore, my head pounding from crying and regret, it was nearly ten-thirty. I drank some water, pondered and rejected food and stared at my phone screen, wishing he'd reach out and knowing that I'd nailed that coffin good and shut.

I slid to the floor again and sat in the kitchen cross-legged, chin in my hand, ticking through ways I might get him back. It was my turn to make the gesture. But as long as I sat there and tried to conjure one, a solution wouldn't present itself.

I got up and shed my clothes — chosen carefully to highlight the things he loved about my body — on my way to the bathroom. I turned on the shower water, stared at it a while then wrenched it back off with a curse. I stood in my bra and panties, staring at myself in the mirror. I put a hand on my stomach, where I'd held his child for a brief time, for all the wrong reasons. I blinked at myself, realizing this. I'd not had the abortion for a lot of reasons, but one of them had been, plain and simple, to prove something to him. But I didn't have to prove anything to him.

I flinched at this reality.

Nice work, Melody. Seriously, well done. The world's most perfect man told you tonight more than once that he wanted to marry you and you called him a Svengali-esque playboy?

"Oh Jesus," I moaned out loud, hand to my lips. I ran for my phone, skipping the text and going straight for a call. It rang and rang, and when his deep, delicious recorded voice hit my ears I cursed, and dialed again. After the sixth time, I left a message.

"I'm sorry, Trent. I didn't mean it. I was awful. I love you. Please…call me back."

I stared at the phone, my heart sinking. I pulled the blanket over my near naked body and curled into a ball, clutching the phone in both my hands, praying like I'd never prayed before.

The doorbell rang in my dreams first. I was in the middle of the floor, naked, blindfolded, softly bound at my wrists. But I wasn't afraid. I was happy, so happy that I was laughing. Then the doorbell rang once, then again. I stopped laughing and turned to the door, confused by the interruption.

I opened my eyes with a gasp when the doorbell changed to pounding and yelling. I dragged the blanket around me and peered out the peep hole. Pulse racing, I opened the door. Trent stood in the dim hallway, crisp dress shirt wrinkled, tie pulled low, cufflinks undone and the sleeves rolled up. He had both hands on the doorjamb, propping himself up.

"I tried," he said as he stared at the floor. "I tried so hard."

I wanted to touch him, to pull him to me, but something held me back. My inner cold bitch would not release me to act the way I wanted to act. I stared at him, frozen to the spot.

He sucked in a breath and blew it out, bathing my face in whiskey fumes. "I wanted to forget you. I tried. I was going to...to...do what I needed to do. I was going to fuck some random, blindfolded woman's ever loving brains out. And forget all about you." He looked up and the expression on his face did two things to me at once—fear trickled into my mind, while a warm rush of sweet, Trent-induced lust filled my chest. "I needed to purge you," he spat at me. "I have to be rid of you. I can't do this anymore."

I touched his chest. He flinched, removed his hands from the wall and rose to his full height. The heat of his skin through the wrinkly shirt ramped up my longing for him.

"This isn't just about sex," he insisted, taking a step forward straight into my personal space.

"I know," I said, standing my ground. Our bodies were centimeters apart. He loomed over me, but I wasn't afraid. I was loved.

I touched his face. He didn't flinch but he did close his eyes.

I was loved. I was treasured. I was damn lucky that he'd come to me, and I was not about to blow it this time.

I started unbuttoning his shirt. "I know it's not just about sex, *mi amor*," I said. "I know all of this. I'm sorry." I slid the shirt off his arms. He kept his eyes closed as I kissed his chest, going up on my tiptoes to kiss the long line of his neck. "I'm sorry, *mi amor*," I kept saying. "I love you...*me haces feliz...te adoro...te necesito...eres el amor de mi vida...*" The Spanish was so much more vivid and alive in my mouth as I tasted him, falling straight back into the warm, wonderful world he'd shown me.

He didn't move as I crouched down and helped him out of his shoes, then unzipped his trousers and shoved them to the floor, breathless with eagerness to get at him, to prove to him...no not to prove...just to love.

I smiled as I gripped his thick shaft, swiping my finger across the fluid and putting it to my lips. "*Quiero que estés dentro de mi,*" I said. He shivered all over. "*Quiero, mi amor.*" I put my other hand against his rough cheek. "Open your eyes. Look at me."

When he did, I nearly fainted from a combination of desire, fear, and a wild swirl of abject happiness. When I accepted that I could be this happy, that I was allowed to let go of the tight grip I kept on myself in the face of a life full of nothing but shittiness, I felt the tears form. He touched my face. "No more crying, *bella,*" he whispered. "No more."

I nodded, and when he swept me into his arms and carried me to the bed, I laughed out loud, like I had been doing in my dream.

"So, I'm funny now?" He fake-glared at me. I giggled, unable to stop myself, and pressed my tear-stained face to his neck.

"No, *guapo,* you're perfect."

"Huh, well, that's more like it, *bizcocho.*"

I pulled away from his skin. "Did you just call me a sponge cake?"

"Yep," he said, tossing me onto the bed so hard I bounced. "*Mi sol…mi teroso…mi bizcocho…*" He stared down at me, hand on his erection, licking his lips as he called me his sun, his treasure, his sweet and delicious treat. "So beautiful," he whispered, slipping my panties down and off and unhooking my bra. "So perfect." He hovered over me, kissed me lightly, teasing me. "So mine." He stared into my eyes. I nodded and lifted my arms over my head.

"*As lo que quieras, mi amor,*" I whispered, nipping at his full lower lip. "Do whatever you want to me, my love. I trust you. I want you to…oh my God!" My back arched when he bit down on my nipple and tickled his fingers down my torso. I tried to put my arms around him but he held my wrists in place.

"No," he said. "I'm touching. And the rules still apply. No coming. Not until I let you." He licked the edges of my lips, dipping his tongue into my mouth just enough to leave me panting before he licked his way down my neck and found my eager, peaking nipple again.

"*Ai, papi,*" I sighed.

He groaned and pressed his fingers inside me, going deep and right for my sweet spot, as he liked to call it. I writhed and moaned, feeling the orgasm approaching me, unable to stop it. He pulled his fingers out just in time, and sucked them, as he stared down at me.

"You taste so good, *bella*. Like the sweetest cream and honey."

I flushed and shifted so my legs were wider. I needed him inside me. I wanted it so badly I was about to scream. Every inch of my skin wanted him.

"I love you," he whispered. "So much." I nodded, keeping my hands off, knowing the rules and loving him for maintaining this control over us both. He kissed the corners of my mouth, my jaw, my earlobe. When he rolled off me and stood, he left me breathless and needy, on the urge of both an orgasm and a crying fit.

He reached down and pulled something from his trouser pocket, then flopped back down beside me and dropped the silvery, heavy chain onto my belly. I propped up on my elbows and looked at it, more relieved to see a silly hunk of expensive jewelry than I ever thought I might be. He tugged it up, circled it around both of my nipples, kissed me then sat, pulling me with him. After fastening it, he held me close from behind. "Thank you," he said.

I pulled away and pushed him down on the bed, loving the heavy weight of the locket against my neck. "Don't thank me yet, *enamorado*. Maybe, after this." I bit each of his nipples, loving his distinct, sweaty, manly taste in my mouth. "*Mi tigre,*" I muttered as I kissed my way down his flat belly, until my chin bumped into his dick. He hissed when I tickled around the edge of his head with my tongue, sucking the pre-cum and drinking it down like ambrosia. He threaded his fingers in my hair and pulled, just enough to make me gasp in pleasure.

"Please," he said. "Please…"

I smiled up at him, then did exactly what he wanted. I knew my man. And I knew that all I had to do was close my eyes and take him. He groaned and shot hot liquid into my throat, then pulled me up fast. "More," he growled, digging his fingertips into my thighs as I hovered over him, denying us both the connection we craved. "I need to be inside you, *bella*."

"Wait, wait," I said, staring down into his face. "We need a condom or something."

He grinned, gripped my hips and angled his. We both exhaled as he slid slowly into my body. "I don't care anymore," he whispered, cradling my face with one hand as he rolled his hips, giving me all the connection I required. "I want to play with fire...with you."

"May I...Sir?" I was coming already but knew he loved to hear me ask. "Oh...Jesus...yes!" I sighed and leaned back, loving him so much I wanted to cry. I ground down and felt him touch me deep inside as I cried into the dark room and he filled me, his back arched, his jaw clenched with the effort as he repeated my name over.

We slowed, our breathing calmed as I lay on his chest, drifting, happy — no, more like ecstatic. I kissed his sweaty chest, then sat up all the way.

He opened his eyes and smiled up at me. "Shit, woman. You are...amazing."

"This may not be all about sex, *guapo*, but I sure do like that part."

He chuckled. I rose off him and headed for the bathroom. After staring at the bright diamond embedded in my locket for a few minutes, I returned and sat by him, stroking his scalp, his face, his shoulder his neck. I couldn't believe my luck.

"*Gracias, amigo*," I whispered, thanking God. Trent opened one eye when my stomach grumbled.

"Go check outside the door," he said, rolling onto his belly. "I'll be out in a minute. I want to just lie here in the afterglow a little longer."

Curious, I pulled on a silk robe — one of the many lingerie gifts he'd bestowed on me — and opened the door a crack. I looked down and saw two large brown paper bags. With a huge smile I warmed up the steaks, potatoes and Brussels sprouts, put them on a plate and carried it to my bed. Trent was on his back, propped on my pillows, hands behind his head.

I tried not to reveal how gorgeous he was to me just then. But it felt like a losing battle. I sat next to him and held up a sprout. He took it with a sigh of pleasure. I cut the steak and fed us both, trading bites and bits of conversation about Evelyn and Austin's upcoming wedding. I knew full well what this seemingly innocuous action meant to a man like him.

He smiled, grabbed the fork when a few bites remained and fed them to me. "Do we sleep here? Or my place?"

I crawled in next to him and draped my arm and leg over his body. "I don't care. As long as I'm with you."

He kissed my hair, heaved a sigh, and we both fell asleep in minutes.

* * * *

I woke slowly, languorously stretching and feeling that strange happiness fill me from head to toe. I rolled and found the other side of my bed empty.

When I wandered in to the kitchen I found the coffee pot full, a deep red apple and an equally red rose on the counter, with a note propped against them.

Bella, he'd written. *I had an early meeting so had to sneak out although leaving your warm bed was harder than I thought it would be. I want to revisit something with you, if you would. Look outside the door again. The car will pick you up at nine tonight. No need to reply. Let's save all our talking and anything else that might arise, for tonight — including a serious discussion about playing with fire.*

Te quiero con todo mi corazón.

I opened the door and picked up the large dress box, carried it inside and called Evelyn.

"Be jealous of me, *chica*. I got my man back."

"Of course you did, Jesus, I told you so. And yeah, I'm jealous."

"Good, 'cause I'm jealous of you too, bitch. Two men for the price of one? Such riches..."

She snorted. "I don't know. They're like a double whammy of super annoying right now."

"All set for the weekend though, right?" I knew we were. We'd planned the thing to the last possible detail, even in short notice.

"Yeah." She sighed. "I'm worried about Ross."

"Oh?" I bit the apple and opened the box, running my hand along the beaded black silk bodice.

"Yes. He's so distant right now. Like he's here, but not here."

"He doesn't strike me as a man who'd want to share...I mean for more than a few rolls in the hay. Which I'm sure is way fun."

"It is. But...yeah. I get you. I don't think either of them are taking this well and I have no idea what to do about it."

I picked up the dream shoes again, smiling so wide I thought my face my split in half. "So...got one *those* dates tonight."

"Cool. He brought the dress and stuff back?"

"Yep."

"Damn...go after that, girl. And do *not* let it go this time."

"I don't plan to. Of course, there is still the horrible teenager problem. He's going to be stuck between us. I know she'll make it tough."

"Eh, that's her job. To make her parents' life hell for a while. She'll grow out of it. Don't let her change your mind about what you want."

"Oh, I don't plan to. Not this time. I'll talk to you

tomorrow."

She chuckled. "Yeah maybe, if you *can* talk, or walk."

I giggled. "Yes. Indeed. Bye, *mi amiga*."

"Farewell, future Mrs. Hettinger."

I whistled my way into the shower, contemplating how much I liked the sound of that.

Lightstruck

Excerpt

Chapter One

On her wedding day, Evelyn spent the requisite number of hours primping and sweating the details. One detail in particular.

"Are you sure… I mean, this is kind of…shit."

"Relax. It's all good."

She glanced at Melody. Evelyn had never had a ton of women friends. In fact, she'd always claimed she preferred men to women when it came to socializing. Easier, less fraught, minimal drama.

Once again, Evelyn congratulated herself for hiring Melody to be in charge of the formerly floundering Fitz Pub. The woman oozed confidence and the sort of inner peace Evelyn thought the stuff of cheesy Internet memes. She was unafraid of her own inner emotional life and that balanced Evelyn in a way she never realized she needed.

And now, she really needed all of that. And some more. Considering she was about to walk down the aisle with a man she'd spent so much energy rejecting as a legitimate possibility for herself, it felt more than a little surreal. Not to mention the rather alarming surprise she had planned for him.

She smiled at the memory of him—of her Austin—and how joyously they'd reunited.

He was already house hunting for a bigger place, where Ross could have his own space, even though Ross had protested that it wouldn't look right. She'd half-agreed with him, until a few mornings ago, when Ross had come up from behind her as she studied her changing body in a full-length mirror, turning side to side, front to back. With a smile, he'd put both of his hands under the slight curve of her belly before sliding them up, inevitably, to her boobs, which were also changing, growing heavier, her nipples darkening. She'd sensed his erection pressing against her ass, and had been about to turn and accommodate him, when she'd sensed something wet hit her shoulder.

Knowing that any sort of emotional acknowledgement was harder than pulling his own teeth, she'd smiled and let Ross cradle the baby—their baby—growing inside her in his hands, as tears had rolled down his cheeks in silence. She hadn't said anything. There'd been no need.

As she regarded herself now in the mirror, her smile faded and she put a hand on the shelf of her stomach, wondering just how much this little wrinkle would alter their dynamic. Austin claimed not to care at all that Ross had fathered the child. If anything, he thought it the most ideal beginning to their lives as a family.

But still…the two men—her two men—were straight-up alpha males and many times she wondered how it could possibly work. How could she love them both? And if she did, what in the world was she doing, marrying one of them?

For the thousandth time, Evelyn thanked God for his

mercy in returning Austin to her, and for letting her keep Ross in the process. Such an excess of riches might've scared some women but Evelyn was determined not to let superstitious nonsense color her future.

"Sweet Jesu, woman. Relax." Melody sipped from her glass of dark porter. The smell tempted, but Evelyn waved it away. She'd moved past the mild nausea stage pretty quickly and had tipped over into something new and different and very, very sexy. It was as if she were ripe, full of promise and hornier than a sailor on shore leave. "You're gonna mess up your makeup, chica. Cut the waterworks already."

But Melody's own gaze was watery as she patted Evelyn's cheekbones with a tissue.

"Honestly I don't even understand why you have any right to feel upset about a damn thing. Marrying one. Getting two? Fuck me six ways to Sunday... Oh, right, you already do that, you silly cow."

"Shut up, puta. You're not helping." Evelyn grinned at her friend.

Melody rolled her eyes and muttered a long string of Spanish words she couldn't make out.

"Oh, hell." She stared at herself in the big mirror in the bride's room of the church. "He's gonna kill me."

"Very possibly, yes," Melody said.

Evelyn turned away from the mirror. The tone of Melody's voice was odd. Strained in a way she'd never heard.

Melody had not required an abortion after all. She'd had a messy, scary miscarriage that had landed her in the hospital for a week. A week that Trent had spent lurking around, trying to get her to see him only to be rejected over and over — loudly, usually accompanied by thrown objects. Evelyn had stayed with her around the clock, knowing Melody would have done the same for her. She'd tried hard to convince her friend to at least talk to Trent. The poor man had been out of his ever-loving mind with panicked worry over her. But Melody wouldn't even allow her to speak his name after a while.

A knock on the door interrupted her train of thought.

"Hey, ladies, can I...?" A newly familiar face appeared in the doorway. Evelyn sucked in a breath. Melody took several steps back. "Sorry," Brock said, retreating as if sensing the stress his appearance had caused.

"No, no, I'm sorry," Evelyn said, motioning for him to step inside. "Come on in."

Brock Fitzgerald entered the room, filling it with the force of his personality and extreme good looks. He had his twin's bone structure, but his take on the Fitzgerald genes manifested into a more model-like arrangement of his features, slightly fairer of skin and hair, more chiseled of facial features, with eyes the oddest shade of hazel she'd ever seen. Since the moment she'd seen his email, she'd spent some time getting to know him—or at least as much as he would allow.

She'd agreed to hire him after he'd reappeared, reaching out to her, asking for help, but she'd wanted to surprise Austin. When she'd agreed to marry him, and had set a date, she'd also decided on her own that Brock would escort her down the aisle.

Ross had been more than a little dubious but went along with it, once he met Austin's long-missing twin and had found him worthy—if on probation for causing Austin so much unnecessary grief.

"Dear God, you are exquisite," Brock said, putting his hands on her shoulders and smiling at her into the mirror. "My brother is one lucky son of a bitch." He took her hands and gave them a squeeze.

Evelyn sucked in a breath and tried to convince herself that this—any of this—was a good idea.

Tried, and failed.

"Knock knock."

Evelyn jerked her hands out of Brock's grip.

"Hey, hon, I need to talk to you about something," Austin said through the door.

"Don't let him in here," she whispered to Melody. "I mean it."

Brock stood, tucking his hands in his tuxedo pockets, squaring his shoulders and facing the door. "Let him in, Evie," he said.

She glared at him, as panic ran up and down her spine. Melody stood, arms crossed over her chest, her eyes on the half open door.

"Evie?" Austin said as he stuck his head into the room. "Who the hell calls you tha—oh."

"Austin," Brock said with a wide smile. "I wanted to surprise you."

Evelyn clutched the skirt of her wedding dress, anxiety at foisting this on him twanging all her nerve endings.

Austin stepped into the bride's room, his face slack, his eyes dark with something resembling anger. He had an envelope gripped in one hand with handwriting on it. "Brock...you're...here? Now?"

"Austin, I..." Evelyn said, moving toward him.

He held up a hand, keeping his gaze on his long-lost brother. When he spoke, his voice was flat, devoid of emotion, and terrifying. "I'm sorry, but it was my understanding that you were, I don't know, dead or something like it. Which would explain your non-communication with me, your fucking twin brother, for the last, what, six years?" Austin's face flamed an alarming shade of red.

When Evelyn tried to move closer to him, Melody grabbed her arm.

Brock seemed to deflate at his brother's words. Then he squared his shoulders and lifted his chin in the face of Austin's fury. "Yeah, well...I'm not dead. I was gone for a while, but I guess, I needed space."

"Space," Austin repeated, his jaw clenched. "You needed space. You needed...fucking..." He blew out a breath. "Does our mother know you've decided to pull a Lazarus? What about Caroline? You sneaking back into that poor girl's life again?"

"Yeah, Mom knows." The two men glared at each other across the room. "And what I do or don't do with Caroline is none of your fucking b—"

"Excuse me? This is my day, gentlemen," Evelyn interrupted, stamping her foot, her heart pounding so hard it deafened her. "Cut the crap. You"—she pointed at Austin—"get out of here and back into the chapel. Unless you've changed your mind, of course." She rested a shaking hand on her stomach. The baby inside her—a girl, she already knew but had told neither Ross or Austin—gave a quick flutter, a new trick this week, as if sensing her mother's stress and reminding her to be aware of her blood pressure.

Austin seemed to snap out of a trance and turned to face her, blinking fast. It broke her heart, how undone he looked. She steeled herself and motioned over his shoulder, indicating the direction he should go. He sucked in a long breath and held out the envelope with a shaking hand.

"He's gone," he said.

Evelyn stumbled backward. Melody caught her by the elbow and shot a barrage of Spanish curse words in Austin's direction before helping her down into a chair. She pulled out the note, read the sparse lines and closed her eyes.

"What is it?" Melody demanded, trying to pry the paper out of Evelyn's cold fingers.

Austin crouched by Evelyn's chair and put his hand on her leg. "Ross left."

"Left?" Melody spat out. "*Jesu*, you three are worse than the worst *Telenovela*." She kept muttering as she handed Evelyn a cool glass of water.

"Are you going to be okay?" Austin's soft query made tears fill her eyes again. She nodded, took Melody's proffered hanky, swiped her tears away and got to her feet. This was no big surprise. And something she'd simply have to deal with later. Austin blew her a kiss then slipped out of the door.

"You," she said, focusing her glare on Brock who stood

nearby, looking sheepish. "You have a lot to answer for so be ready. I love that man," she said, pointing to the empty space once occupied by Austin. "All I want is for him to be happy." She took a long breath. "So help me, Brock Fitzgerald, you are gonna help me achieve that today. Got it?"

He nodded and cocked his elbow at her as the sounds of flower girl music swirled around them, indicating that the bride's music was next. She hesitated, her long-ingrained resistance to this very moment reasserting itself with a vengeance.

"Come on, Evie." He wagged his eyebrows at her.

She frowned, felt herself hyperventilating, sensed Melody at her side, providing support with her presence.

"Let's do this thing, future sister-in-law." Brock grabbed her arm and dragged her forward. He winked then pressed his lips to her damp cheek.

Interesting times ahead. She tucked her hand into the crook of Brock's elbow.

"Relax," he insisted, as he led her into the hallway and the harp music switched to something that made her pulse race faster.

"I can't," she said.

"Yes, you can. And you will. Just focus on Austin, Evie. That's all you need to do. Tell you what. I'll do it too, okay? I think we both need to focus on making his day today."

She took a long breath, and did exactly that. "Promise me one thing," she said, before taking her first step down the aisle toward her future husband. "Don't ever leave again."

He sighed.

"I mean it, Brock. He needs you just as much as he needs me." She gripped his arm. Their eyes met.

"Okay," he said. "I promise."

"Okay," she said. "Then take me to him, why don't you?"

More books from
Totally Bound Publishing

Book one in the Brewing Passion series

One hot entrepreneur plus a driven saleswoman and sultry brewer – simmered in the craft beer world for a unique, sexy reading experience!

Book seven in the Secrets of Stone series

Can we keep our bond intact? Do we have the courage to find out?

Domination, obsession, possession — where the all-powerful Frost comes toe to toe with Juliet Sinclair, a submissive to no one, until her first touch of Frost.

Sydney was being coerced into marrying a man she didn't love. Then Caleb crashed into her life and one little white lie turned her universe upside down.

About the Author

Liz Crowe

Amazon best-selling author, mom of three, Realtor, beer blogger, brewery marketing expert, and soccer fan, Liz Crowe is a Kentucky native and graduate of the University of Louisville currently living in Ann Arbor. She has decades of experience in sales and fund raising, plus an eight-year stint as a three-continent, ex-pat trailing spouse.

With stories set in the not-so-common worlds of breweries, on the soccer pitch, in successful real estate offices and at times in exotic locales like Istanbul, Turkey, her books are unique and told with a fresh voice. The Liz Crowe backlist has something for any reader seeking complex storylines with humor and complete casts of characters that will delight, frustrate and linger in the imagination long after the book is finished.

Don't ever ask her for anything "like a Budweiser" or risk bodily injury.

"Liz Crowe writes intense true-to-life stories that make you feel. Whether it's anxiety, love, fear, hate, bliss, or loss woven into her plot lines, you will feel it deep down to your very soul." ~ Audrey Carlan, #1 New York Times Bestselling Author

"Liz Crowe is one of those rare authors who knows how to take the emotions of her characters and make them real for her readers, binding you to the story." ~ International Best Selling Author Desiree Holt

Liz Crowe loves to hear from readers. You can find contact information, website details and an author profile page at https://www.totallybound.com/

TOTALLY
BOUND

Home of Erotic Romance